CLARITY

Gabbie S. Duran

Other books by Gabbie S. Duran

Unspoken Memories
Unspoken Promises
Unspoken Endings
With Me

To anyone who has
ever felt like Taylor,
never give up on trust.

PROLOGUE

"COME ON TAYLOR, let's go somewhere more interesting," Josh whispers into my ear, already urging me away. I follow, thankful we are finally leaving. I've felt uncomfortable from the moment we arrived. As we walk away, I take one last glance over my shoulder, my eyes immediately catching the flames of the fire, wishing it farewell. For the past hour, the odor from the smoke has been unsettling my stomach, or it could just be the alcohol. Either way, I'd rather be anywhere but here. If it hadn't been for Josh's persistence I accompany him tonight, I'd most likely be at home alone.

Leading me farther into the line of trees surrounding us, his hold around my waist tightens as he tugs me to follow along. The alcohol I've been drinking for the past hour has finally caught up to me and my walking is more of a stumble. Had it not been for his tight grip, I'd most likely be face down on the ground by now. The laughter and shouts of everyone we've left behind begin to slowly fade as we walk farther into the forest. I begin to grow apprehensive of leaving them behind the deeper we travel into the woods.

"Josh, are you sure you know where we're going? Wasn't the car back that way?" I slur, looking over my shoulder in search of his car before stumbling over a branch and losing my balance. The alcohol is definitely impairing everything, including my speech.

He stops in an open spot, and before I get a chance to ask why, his lips slam down onto mine as he urges me down to the ground. My alcohol infused mind has my head spinning, barely allowing me to register the reason why.

"Josh, what are you doing?" I muster through our kiss while trying to push his heavy body off me. Ignoring me, his hands aggressively grasp at my breast through the fabric of my dress.

"Josh," I sternly repeat against his mouth, hoping he'll stop, but he doesn't budge or answer. Instead, he starts to run his hands inside my dress. The heat of his palms gliding against my ribcage is distracting, rousing a sensation I'm unfamiliar with.

Suddenly, the absence of his hands has me believing he has come to his senses and has finally heard my plea, but I'm deceived when I hear the rattling of a zipper. I'm startled back to reality with the sound, comprehending his intentions as to why he's brought me to such a remote location.

I may never have had sex before, but I know enough to realize what he expects, and it's not what I want in return.

"Josh, stop. Get off me, please," I repeat, trying once more to push him off me.

I'm rendered speechless by his mouth. This time it's not

tender but forceful as his tongue moves inside my mouth. I'm now panicking, my pleas vibrating into his mouth as I shove at his chest. My urgent attempt to push him off is useless since Josh is so large. He's your typical jock and keeps in shape, one of the reasons why I found him so attractive.

The weight of his body keeps me trapped underneath him and my panic increases tenfold. The sound of my underwear ripping goes unheard due to my urgent whimpers pulsating in my ears. I let out an agonizing scream as he slams inside of me, no gentleness in his actions, pure purpose to get what he's after—sex, and nothing less, his thrusting fueled by determination.

"Stop," I whimper one last time with the only breath I have left. He ignores my continuous pleas. Tears cascade down my cheeks as the pain intensifies. My will to struggle has diminished, the fight leaving me completely the moment he entered me and tore the walls of my virginity. What's the use of fighting anymore? He's taken what I've kept protected of myself, leaving no choice but to lie pinned to the ground, hoping it will be over soon, praying the pain will fade if I lie limp and willing. But most of all, I pray the earth will open beneath me and engulf me, taking me completely from this world.

As the painful torture continues, one of my prayers is answered when he tosses his head back, letting out a piercing grunt as his rocking comes to a stop. His breathing is labored and drifting against my skin as he remains above me, leaving me feeling disgusted and ashamed of myself while I lie trapped underneath his wary form.

Slowly, he removes his weight, leaving me sprawled out on the ground.

"You going to get up?" The sound of Josh's voice pulls me from the tragic haze I sent my mind to. The sound of his zipper is once again heard, causing me to empty the contents of my stomach. Josh's laughter is heard above me, humiliating me, triggering more tears.

With nothing left but bile, I wipe my mouth with the back of my hand and I will myself to stand, ignoring the protesting ache between my legs.

"Come on, Taylor, I should get you home," Josh unenthusiastically says while patting off his jeans. The thought that he has no concern for what has occurred adds to the disgust churning inside of me.

I feel a stickiness dripping down my legs and the realization of what it most likely is causes my stomach to turn once more.

Josh reaches for my hand, triggering me to swat it away, not wanting him to touch me anymore. Another chuckle echoes in the darkness before the crunching of his footsteps notifies me he's walking away. Having no choice but to follow, my steps are enraged and unhurried all the way back to his car.

The entire thirty-minute ride home I spend next to Josh in silence, my body aching from being taken on the forest floor. When we eventually pull up to the trailer park where I reside, he parks directly in front of my trailer. As I'm about to open the car door to exit, he grabs onto my arm and I immediately tense from his touch.

"Taylor, it wasn't fair that you were holding out on me for so long," he states, forcing me to turn and glare daggers at him. "It's not a big deal, Taylor. It was just sex."

"Screw you, Josh," I growl at him through clenched teeth.

The hand on my arm tightens slightly, frightening me. "The way I see it, Taylor, you're lucky I even fucked you. Do you really think you can do any better? You're a nobody," he remarks, glancing around at our surroundings. "You should be happy I even looked your way," he scowls in my face before releasing my arm.

Without hesitating, I exit his car and slam the door behind me, needing to put distance between the two of us.

Entering the trailer I share with my mom, I find her sitting at the tiny table inside with a bottle of liquor in her hand. Rushing past her, I catch a glimpse of her drunken stupor on my way to my room. Her reason will most likely be she had another crappy day at the diner where she works. It's been a constant excuse every night since I was a child.

Reaching my room, I enclose myself in the solitude of my space. Sitting on the edge of the bed, I draw my legs up against my chest, straining with all my might not to cry as I recall the horrific memory of the night. I've already wasted enough tears.

My mother's footsteps can be heard as she makes her way towards my bedroom, stumbling into the wall along the way, reminding me of how I was not so long ago—another reminder of why I should feel ashamed. The door opens and her arched eyebrows are high as she stares at me.

"What's up with you?" she slurs, looking me up and down, her eyes stopping at my legs.

"Did you finally get some?" she asks, a wide grin spreading across her face, pissing me off that she can't even act like a real mother when I need one.

"Get the fuck out and leave me alone," I snap at her since she's the only one here that I can take my anger out on.

She shrugs her shoulders before saying, "Hopefully you'll end up pregnant. It'd be one good thing for you. Easy money."

I didn't think anyone could disgust me more than Josh had tonight, but I'm proven wrong.

"Get. The. Fuck. Out!"

This time my angry outburst works and she turns to walk

away, slamming the door behind her. The tears finally fall as I ponder both their hurtful words as they keep repeating over and over in my mind. The stabbing pain of the realization that Josh may be right about me always being a nobody brew in my head.

Up until the day he acknowledged me, nobody cared who I was. The day he asked me to help tutor him for science was the day I began to exist in the social world of our high school. Before that, I pretty much kept to myself, not really fitting in anywhere. I didn't have a stable family. The only thing I had was enough brains to get me through my classes without failing. Now with school over, I'm back to where I started: a nobody in the small town where I grew up.

I have a worthless mother, no family, or friends. I don't even have money. But that doesn't mean I'm stuck in this town forever. No, the minute I can get out of here, I will, and I'm never looking back.

ONE

Mornings are not for me

Taylor

I HATE MORNINGS. Despise them. A morning person I am not. It's why my roommate is currently shouting through the bathroom door.

"Taylor, hurry up or we're going to be late!" Katie screams, invading my last two minutes of nirvana. My forehead rests against the cold tile of the shower as I try to savor the steaming water running down my back for a couple more minutes. It doesn't last long, though, as she's already banging on the door a minute later.

"Calm your tits, woman!" I throw back at her.

Releasing an exasperated breath, I silently curse because

7

it's Monday. Why do the weekends have to be so damn short?

You're probably thinking I despise Mondays because of work, as most people do, but it's far from the true reason. I actually love my job, but I repeat, I'm not a morning person. It usually takes a minimum of twenty ounces of caffeine to jump-start my mind, and even then, I'm still an unpleasant person. Add Mondays to the equation and you best keep a good distance if you don't want your head chewed off. Somehow, after three years of living together, Katie still hasn't learned, but it's because she's just as fearless of facing the dragon as I am. Give us a challenge and we take it head on, which is why she's my best friend.

We met in college five years ago when we argued over a question posed by the instructor. She declared both our answers to have valid points and were correct, but to this day I believe she was merely preventing world war three in her class. Eventually, the same instructor paired us up for a "hands on lab" that forced us to work as a team, one that hasn't been separated since. Once we became acquainted with one another, we discovered how similar our personalities were—the only thing we had in common.

Katie was raised with a loving mother and father, opposed to my never knowing who my father was and rarely seeing my mother. She lived in the same house with a white picket fence her entire life in a beautiful suburb of Chicago. I know because I've seen it. I, on the other hand, was raised in a trailer home that I swear was held up by the grace of God, and the only fence surrounding the trailer park was made of chain link, a far cry from the perfect dream I always wished for.

"Taylor, if you don't get out of there and get dressed in five minutes I swear to God I'm leaving you and you'll have to hoof it to work this time," she irritably yells through the door.

Already done drying my body, I roll my eyes and wrap myself in a towel before opening the door to stare right into hazel eyes belonging to Katie. She's petite with her five foot three frame compared to my five foot seven frame, but don't let the lack of height deceive you. She's a firecracker underneath.

"You know, for someone who gets laid enough for the both of us, you sure don't act like it," I scowl, brushing past her while ignoring the eye roll she's most likely giving me.

Reaching my dresser, I pull out a pair of matching under-wear and bra to put on then grab a set of scrubs from my closet next. An advantage to working as a physical therapist is that I don't have to invest in my wardrobe, saving me a ton of money, which goes right back to my student loans I'm pretty sure I'm going to be paying off for the rest of my life at the rate that I'm going.

I can feel the blaze of Katie's glare as I dress. She's upset because we're running five minutes behind. Katie is OCD when it comes to time. She would rather be early than on time. To her, being on time isn't acceptable, so since we're running late today, I know she's fuming. I've learned over time to ignore her. It may be the only solution other than declaring war against her, which would not guarantee any survivors.

Turning around, I find her glowering at me with an arched brow.

"There. Are you happy now? We can go," I say, walking past her and into the living room to grab my purse and keys.

"You know one of these days you're going to be late and it's going to bite you in the ass, and I'm not going to hesitate to tell you *'I told you so,'*" she reprimands on the way to the door.

"I look forward to it," I retort.

Minutes later, we're climbing into her car and on our way to work. Between the two of us, Katie will always be the chauffeur. She's the one with the car and license. I don't have either one. The last thing I want is to add the stress of a car payment I would not be able to afford, so what's the point of getting a license?

I was unlike Katie, who has had a car since the day she received her license. I learned to depend on public transportation from an early age. Luckily, I'm privileged enough Katie and I work together, so I am able to carpool with her to and from work.

We did our residency together and were able to prove how well we worked as a team, so they decided to keep us both full-time after graduating.

Thirty minutes after leaving our apartment, we pull up to our employment building and I quickly exit the car, desperate for my liquid fuel. Katie despises coffee and the smell of it, so if I want to get my fix, I have to head to the local coffee shop or make do with what we have at work. Depending on who made it, it can be tolerable on most days, which is why my first destination is always the break room after reaching our floor.

Waving goodbye, we split in different directions.

Katie somehow always has a patient scheduled upon arriving. How she can tolerate dealing with people the moment she walks in still leaves me puzzled. Not me. I need at least an hour for the caffeine to kick in before I can face anyone. Otherwise, they will receive some form of silent treatment during the duration of their appointment.

"Hey there, girl. How was your weekend?" Sarah's bubbly voice says behind me as I'm pouring my coffee, taking a sip before I answer. "Oh, just the usual. Caught up on my sleep." Which is exactly what I did.

Sarah is also my co-worker—the only other person who I can call my friend. Katie and I are more experienced than her by two years, but she performs her job just as well, earning our respect early on.

"I don't know why you keep yourself cooped up inside all the time. Katie and I had a blast this weekend. You should've joined us."

"I had just as much fun sleeping."

Chuckling at my remark, she pours her own coffee while my mind drifts back to the particular details of Katie's recap of her weekend. She'd been MIA the entire time with some random guy she hooked up with.

"You really need to get out more," Sarah scolds.

Sarah's cousin had her birthday party at a local club this past weekend, and of course party girl Katie jumped all over that. I, on the other hand, stayed home. Partying is not in my nature. I'm not that kind of girl. I'd rather stay home with my TV and bed, catching up on my crazy reality shows, as unrealistic as they are. If it weren't for Katie's random check-in texts, as ordered, I wouldn't have known she was alive.

Holding my hand up, I attempt to ward off a future lecture from Sarah. "Trust me, from the stories I heard from Katie, you two had enough fun for the three of us," I answer before exiting the break room and heading straight for the office I share with Katie. I ignore the snicker heard behind me from Sarah.

Reaching the small sanctuary of my office, I start the day with my usual morning routine: reviewing my charts for the patient's I'll be seeing throughout the day. Unfortunately, I haven't accomplished brushing off Sarah since she's now hovering at my doorway. She's still speaking, but at this point, I pay no mind as she demands I be in attendance for her bachelorette party this upcoming weekend. I've been evading the subject since the day she announced her engagement and started planning the thing. It's bad enough I'm forced to go to her wedding, why does she have to torture me with a party to celebrate her getting tied down?

"Taylor, have you heard a word of what I've said?" Sarah irritably snaps at me. Feeling guilty that I started to tune her out halfway through the discussion, I give her a forced smile. "If you think you're getting out of this one, you're not. Even if I have to drag you by your teeth, I will. You are not missing my bachelorette party. This is probably the only chance I'm going to get you to have some fun. Besides my wedding, of course," she adds, smiling as her eyes close. She's probably daydreaming about her wedding again, making me roll my eyes at her. When she opens them, they are glaring at me in threat.

Slumping back into my chair, I know when it comes to Sarah and Katie ganging up on me, I won't win. I'm going to end up going no matter how much pleading I do.

"Where are you having it, anyway?" I ask, a little curious since I will have to endure the thing.

"It's at the new club Trevor is promoting, remember? *Eclipse?*" she says, very excited. I've heard about the club. Her fiancé, Trevor, being a marketing director, was handling all the promotional aspects of the club and it was quickly getting a great deal of hype. He did his job well, so *Eclipse* was now the number one place to party in town. At least, it's what I've heard. I wasn't stepping on anyone's toes to get in.

"Sarah, are you sure you really want me there?" I practically plead, hoping she'll feel some sort of sympathy for me. "You know I don't like that kind of scene. I'm already going to the wedding. Can't you be happy with that?"

"Oh, no you don't. Don't try to pull that bullshit on me. You're going. End of story," she orders with a wag of her finger, leaving me to scowl at her. Maybe some sort of miracle will happen between now and Saturday that will prevent me from going.

Is that too much to hope for?

Who am I kidding? I would have to be lying in a hospital on my deathbed in order to avoid having to go. At this point, I'm considering stepping in front of a bus to make it happen. Now that I think about it, it doesn't sound like too bad of an idea. It would get me out of going to the wedding as well.

Laughing at my own thoughts, I take another sip of coffee and rummage through my files. This is one week I hope passes very slowly . . . The slower the better.

Nick

The blaring sound of my phone ringing awakens me from my slumber. I'm already cursing whoever is calling to hell. Pulling my pillow over my head to shut out the noise, it works for the couple of seconds it takes for the ringing to stop. Grateful, I'm already falling back to sleep before the ringing begins all over again. Groaning, I ignore it until it starts up again, forcing me to actually answer it so it can shut up.

"What!" I growl into the phone as I answer.

"What are you doing still sleeping?" The voice of my manager speaks back to me through the phone, already irritating me.

"What do you want, Mendoza?"

"I called to remind you of your appointment today. Knowing you, you've already forgotten."

Grumbling to myself, I reply, "I'm not going."

"You bet your ass you're going," he clips into the phone.

"You know I don't need any fucking therapy."

His chuckling isn't amusing to me. "You make it sound like we're sending you to some shrink."

"It might as well be."

"Get your ass out of bed and get to that appointment, or else you're sitting out the rest of the season. And that isn't a warning this time," he orders before the line goes dead.

Running my hand down my face as I silently curse into the darkness of my room, I feel a hand start to run along my chest, startling me. Catching it with my own, my mind tries its best to remember last night. I must have been too far gone if I can't remember even getting home. My thought is distracted when a slim leg starts to rub against my groin.

"You ready for another round?" the girl lying next to me seductively purrs, making me smile. I have the entire day ahead of me. What better way to spend it than with what is next to me?

TWO

I hate Mondays

Taylor

WITH THE COFFEE finally starting to kick in, I wake my computer from its sleep mode to double-check my schedule. I remember my boss mentioning he was assigning me a new patient this week, but I have yet to discover who it is. It's most likely an urgent VIP since it's a last minute add-on. Somehow, I always end up with those.

I didn't intend to specialize in sports medicine when I chose my profession, especially since you'll never find me watching sports. But during my residency, I found it was the specialty where the patients didn't expect me to be personal. They were here for one reason: to recover and get back to doing what they love, which was playing. They didn't want to talk about their personal life, or ask about mine. It was the perfect job for me. Get them in, get them fixed, and get them out. Simple and done . . . No questions asked.

Among my coworkers, I'm known as the least friendly person to associate with, especially since I keep to myself. It's how I prefer it. I do my job well, so well I'm one of the top sports physical therapists in demand. My lack of social skills is overlooked as long as the job is done correctly, the first time.

My mind returns to my schedule, taking in my usual patients for the week. With the exception of the one new patient at the end of today, I was set. The sooner I get this day started and over with, the sooner I can get home.

My day goes as normal. No major difficulties until three o'clock approaches. It's the expected time for the new patient and he has yet to arrive. Glancing at the clock, I realize he's already late. Irritably huffing, I take the time to research his file to distract myself.

It shouldn't surprise me he's late considering who he is. He's a short stop for the Chicago White Soxs. This explains his VIP status. Because he's a starting, and regular player at that, they were looking to get him back on the playing field as soon as possible. It was most likely his manager who requested he get in ASAP. I already know I may have a challenge ahead of me considering his lack of concern to arrive on time.

Further researching his injury, I soon discover this it his second injury in the last year. First time was a simple sprain; this time around, it was fractured, explaining why he was now required to take therapy.

The sound of footsteps in the room breaks my concentration, causing me to lift my head in that direction. From the cocky persona of the gentleman who is the cause of the footsteps, it informs me this must be my patient.

Still wearing his aviator glasses, he looks in my direction, his steps unhurried, as if he's purposely taking his time to reach me. I watch from the spot in which I'm sitting on a stability ball in the corner of the room. Eventually reaching the location where I'm sitting, he stands directly in front of me, forcing me to tilt my head up to look at him. He's tall, physically fit, and the tight tee he's wearing emphasizes the chiseled muscles of his chest.

Lifting his hand, he removes his glasses. My breath hitches as he greets me with the brightest blue eyes I've ever seen. Add his 'didn't bother brushing, sandy blond hair' and half-smile and I'm completely flustered. The once half smile is now turned down, irritating me further.

Lowering my head to look back down at his file to distract myself, I begin speaking. "Mr. Hunter, I assume?"

"Nick," he corrects. Confusedly snapping my head back up to look at him, his brow is now arched. "It's Nick. Mr. Hunter is my father."

Disregarding his retort, I continue. "You can take a seat on the exam table," I order, pointing at the bed beside me. He questionably looks in its direction, resuming his position directly in front of me. The only movement he gives me is the crossing of his arms over his chest. Challenging me.

I've learned one important aspect from my first day on my job: never show my patients any weakness, whether it be physical or mental, and right now he is expecting me to show mental weakness by allowing him to defy me.

Now I'm the one quirking my brow at him as I point my pen once more towards the bed. "The longer you stand there, the longer it's going to take for us to get started." Severing eye contact with him, I return to reviewing his chart.

"Look, I don't really need to be here, so why don't I just save us both the time? Just sign whatever little paper you need to so I can get back out onto the field," his deep voice says above me in an exasperated tone.

If he thinks he's irritated, he doesn't know the half of how I feel about his arrogance. Snapping my head back up with narrowed eyes, I say, "If you don't want to be here fine, I don't care, leave," then wave my hand toward the door. "But if you think I'm going to jeopardize my job for you by signing your release back to the field, then you're wrong. So it's your decision, Mr. Hunter. Either you sit your ass on that table, or leave. Either way, I don't give a crap. It's your career, not mine," I say, pointing at the table again with my pen for what will be the final time.

My response surprises him as he slightly snaps his head back. Seconds go by as we both glare at one another, but it's me who wins in the end when he steps over to my side and climbs up onto the exam table. The crunching of the exam table paper as he seats himself overtakes the awkward silence between us.

Although the exercise ball I'm sitting on still keeps me below him, I can't bring myself to stand just yet. At times like this, it helps with my anxiety when I lightly bounce on it, calming the frustration that has built in me. Now, it's helping to keep calm my urge to strangle this man.

"Your chart states your cast was removed last week. Are you experiencing any discomfort when you walk or during any other physical activities?" I ask.

Now looking back up to him for his answer, his lips are once more up to one side. "No pain when I walk, but I don't think I really need my ankle for any of the other physical activities that are important to me," he states with his voice dropping seductively low.

"By other physical activities you mean running, or exercising?" I inquire, not quite catching the intention of his statement.

He leans down towards me, mere inches from my face as he answers, "I guess you can consider sex an exercise since it does involve sweating. But no, no pain from the ankle there."

Is he fucking serious?

"Mr. Hunter, what goes on in your personal life is none of my business and I'd rather we kept it that way. So I'm going to ask again, have you experienced any discomfort with your ankle?" I ask, attempting to emphasize the importance of the question as I try to get the appointment back under control.

I must have made my intention clear because his face grows somber. Shaking his head to indicate no, I make a note in his chart then remember what he was wearing when he arrived.

"Did you receive the paperwork which should have been mailed to you upon the scheduling of your appointment?" I ask, knowing it's procedure to send patients the paperwork explaining the dress requirements for the appointment. It explains how the patient is to wear loose, comfortable clothing to ensure their movements are unhindered during the exercises involving their injured muscles. We don't want any restrictions from clothing getting in the way.

He nods his head in agreement. "Yeah, I received it, but I didn't bother reading it. I've already told you I don't need to be here, so why are you wasting my time?" he insists.

Appearing bored with the subject, he leans back on the table, bearing his weight on his extended arms. "If *you* insist on continuing with this whole charade, then just roll up my pants and do your thing."

He's correct. The clothing he has on won't cause any restrictions with the exercises he's required to perform since it's for his ankle. I *will* be able to work with what he's dressed in, but if every other patient follows orders, why shouldn't he be expected to do the same? His defiance of following simple instructions and arrogant manner warns me I'm not going to get anywhere with him today.

Standing, I snap his chart closed. "Fine with me. When you do decide to read the paperwork, you can call to reschedule your next appointment. Have a great week, Mr. Hunter," I reply without looking back, leaving him sitting on the table, pissed he didn't take his appointment seriously and wasting my time.

Nick

Watching the saucy little female marching away renders me speechless. I'd expected to have to pull out my charms to convince her to sign the paperwork, but I *wasn't* expecting to be rejected in the end. It's never happened before. No one has ever said no when I've worked my charms on them.

Knowing I need my paperwork signed to return to the field, I come to my senses and climb off the bed to follow her. Reaching the door in which she disappeared through, there are only two options as to where she could have gone; one towards the direction I'd come in, and the other through a set of double doors marked *"Employees Only."*

I choose the latter.

Heading through the double doors, I'm already a couple of steps inside and turning the corner when a security guard stops me.

"I'm sorry, sir. No patients are allowed back here," he orders, firmly holding out his arm to deny me any further access. Taking me in, his eyes go wide in recognition. "Are you Nick Hunter?"

Excellent. A fan. "Yes, nice to meet you," I greet, holding

my hand out to him. Excitedly, he shakes it. "You didn't happen to see a girl come in right before me? Brunette, about this height," I state, holding my hand up to my shoulder. His once glowering frown returns and I may just be screwed. "I seem to have upset her and want to apologize. You know, you can never leave a lady feeling mad or else you'll be in the dog house when you get home."

His eyes go wide, stunned by my statement, before a hint of laughter spreads across them. "No, can't be having that," he jokes. "She's down the hall. First door around the corner," he explains as he points ahead of us. "Good luck. She's a little firecracker when she's pissed," he adds with a mocking grin.

I'm about to walk away when he asks, "Are you getting back onto the field soon?"

"I'm working on it. It's up to my little firecracker," I reply with a wink. Giving me a nod of understanding, I leave him to make my way to my destination.

Within seconds, I reach the doorway and see her sitting at her desk. Her hands are digging into her hair as she lets out an aggravated growl.

"Am I that frustrating?" I ask, stepping into the office and leaning against the wall.

My question startles her. Her wide eyes questionably stare back at me once her head snaps up. She stares at me with confusion then looks past me, as if searching for someone.

"What is it you need, Mr. Hunter?" she asks calmly, but from the tight appearance on her face, I know she's far from calm as she folds her arms across her chest and stares back at me with irritation. I'm beginning to wonder if it's the only expression she carries. Now I know what the guard meant by *"a little firecracker."*

"You really shouldn't be standing like that. It will only

cause more stress to your ankle and it won't help with your recovery time," she states, pointing her chin down at my feet. Looking down, I see I'm bearing most of my weight on my injured ankle, making me stand up straight.

"To answer your earlier question, Mr. Hunter, yes, you're frustrating me."

Normally I would despise anyone calling me by my last name, but the way it rolls off her tongue makes me begin to reconsider that feeling.

"If you'd just sign the paperwork, I'd be off your hands and you wouldn't have to put up with me anymore," I suggest.

With an angry scowl on her face, she repeats the command. "No. I already told you. Either do the therapy sessions or you don't get clearance. End of story," she throws back at me.

Oh, yeah. She's a little firecracker. "I don't know why you're being so difficult." I uncontrollably growl back at her.

My temper has gotten the better of me, causing my voice to rise. I am not accustomed to being refused anything. Her eyes have returned to the size of saucers, but this time with a hint of fear as they frantically dart past me. Glancing over my shoulder, wondering if the person she was searching for has arrived, I find the hall still empty. Confused, I look back to her. Her right hand is on the phone, as if ready to call someone. Then it occurs to me, I'm the one startling her and she's most likely searching for someone to rescue her.

"I'm sorry for getting upset, but you're being difficult," I explain, hoping to calm her. Her once rigid body relaxes and it is then that I know my apology has worked, at least temporarily.

"If you would have taken the appointment more seriously, Mr. Hunter, you would have been one session closer to recovery. But since you didn't, then you're back to square one. It's your decision whether you want to do this or not," she lectures as she pinches the bridge of her nose, closing her eyes and taking a deep breath.

The conversation feels as if it's going around in circles. It's obvious she isn't going to budge. I'm ready to admit defeat and beg she give me another chance—something I *never* thought I'd have to do with a girl—but it's not required when she states, "I have an open appointment for this Wednesday at 9 A.M. If you want it, I'll put you on the schedule. It will give you enough time to go home, read over your paperwork, and decide whether you want to take your therapy serious. If you show up, great, if not, then we both know you won't be returning to the field anytime soon. You decide," she clips out before standing. "Have a great day, Mr. Hunter," she orders through clenched teeth, brushing past me and out the door.

My mouth is slightly open as I gawk at her.

She dismissed me.

Me.

I'm usually the one dismissing the girls when I'm done with them. How in the hell did it happen to me? Still standing in her office, I take a moment to consider her offer. The time is not what I would have chosen for myself, but since she has clearly walked away without giving me a chance to respond, I'm left with no choice.

This girl better be worth it if I have to get up so damn early in the morning.

Taylor

I hightail it as fast as I can then step into the ladies' room, hoping he isn't following me. I would have thought he'd be happy when I left him behind in the exam room, but I was clearly mistaken. How the hell did he get back here, anyway? There are signs forbidding patients to do so. You'd have to be incompetent to not see them. Where the hell was the security guard?

Reaching the ladies' room, I lock it behind me and lean against the door, trying to calm myself. It works, eventually, after a few minutes. Taking deep breaths, my aggravation dwindles and I'm able to bring my erratic heartbeat under control.

Taking one final breath before I unlock the door, I brace myself in case someone is on the other side; thankfully, there isn't. With the coast clear, I make my way back to my office, hopeful he isn't still waiting for me. I'm relieved when I find it empty.

Sitting back down behind my desk, Katie walks in, taking her spot behind her own with a look of excitement on her face. "Taylor, you'll never believe who was here." I already know whom she's referring to, forcing me to internally roll my eyes. "Nick Hunter!" she excitingly exclaims. "Oh. My. God," she sighs, fanning herself. "He was so hot, too. What do you suppose he was doing back here?"

"He's one of my patients. He must have followed me back here," I answer while organizing the mess I've made. I'd thrown his file across my desk, scattering all the others I had resting upon it.

Wide-eyed and stunned, Katie looks back at me. "What? I can't believe you didn't tell me you were seeing Nick Hunter today," she barks at me, obviously disappointed I didn't inform her. I'd forgotten how much of a fan she was of the White Sox. She was born and raised on them. She could probably have given me every detail about Nick Hunter without me having to ask.

"It's not a big deal, Katie. You know we see professional athletes all the time. I don't understand what makes him so special," I say, wondering what the whole fascination with athletes is all about.

Her eyes grow wider, as if I've just grown a second head. "Are you kidding me? He's like the most eligible bachelor in the sports world! And you get to touch him . . . freely . . . without having to ask," she says, waving her hand around to emphasize her point before her eyes go all dreamy. With that look, I can only imagine the way she would touch him, especially in the most private of places.

"You know what, he didn't really like me so why don't you take him? I could transfer everything over to you," I say, hoping she'll take the bait so I don't have to deal with his ignorant ass if he returns. Her eyes light up with excitement, but just as quickly she shakes her head.

"I know what you're trying to do, and it isn't going to work. No, if I take him on as a patient, I won't have a chance at dating him, and I'm not ruining that chance. You'll just have to give me details on exactly what he likes, so start taking notes," she orders.

Dammit.

She *had* to remember how we're forbidden to have relationships with our patients.

"He's probably being difficult and now you don't want to deal with him," she proclaims.

"I can handle him," I grumble, trying to convince myself more than her.

"Good. Just don't manhandle him. That's my job," she says with a wink.

Rolling my eyes then turning them back to my computer, my thoughts unwillingly return to *Nick*. He may be good looking, but lucky for Katie she doesn't have to worry about me being any sort of competition. I'm not seeking a relationship, especially with a jock. I've learned my lesson. Today was proof that they're all the same. They're only after what benefits them.

I'm pretty sure when it comes to Nick Hunter, I'm going to have to build up the ice in my veins to get him to obey, because he's already showing signs he wants a battle, and I was ready to give him one.

THREE

Wednesday's are not any better

Taylor

TUESDAY NORMALLY COMES and goes, but when I awake on Wednesday morning and open my eyes, I'm already dreading the day to come. There's no doubt in my mind today will be a struggle. At least it may be if Nick shows up. I have to remind myself that after Monday's fiasco I've decided to give him the benefit of the doubt. For the first time in my life I've done my research on a patient, and from what information I gathered on Nick Hunter, he's dedicated to the game. He has been since the first time he stepped up to the plate, so I wouldn't expect anything less from him when it comes to his therapy if he wants to return to the field.

Katie hasn't ceased hounding me, constantly suggesting questions for me to ask Nick. After a couple of hours I couldn't take anymore and irritably snapped at her. It wasn't intentional. I was at my limit with her ogling Nick. She was upset with me for the remainder of the day, but by the time we got home, she had gotten over it. I'd repeated exactly what he'd said during his initial appointment, yet it only fueled her quest. She saw him as an easy score. One she wouldn't have to work hard to get. Rolling my eyes at her response, I just walked away, completely giving up.

Looking over at the clock and noticing the time, I force myself to finally get up and ready before I have my own personal drill sergeant yelling at me. Dragging my sleepy body over to the shower, I hope the cold water will finish waking me up. I get in and find it helps do the trick, to an extent. I still need my caffeine. Today feels like another Monday, but only because I don't feel like going to work. Maybe if I called in sick it'll force Katie to take over Nick's therapy session and she can grill him herself. Sighing to myself, I know I can't. I wouldn't do that to my other patients.

An hour later, we arrive at work and Katie goes straight to our office while I make a beeline for my much-needed coffee. On the way back, I stop at the vending machine to pick up some chocolate, already knowing it's going to be one of those days. When I have a bad day, chocolate always seems to perk me up. God knows it's better than drinking.

Reaching my desk, I hide my stash in my drawer and start downing my coffee before I head over to my first patient of the day. It's a girl in high school who I've been seeing for the last month after she sustained an injury to her arm playing volleyball. Before her injury, she was really good and was already being scouted by colleges. She wants to be fully recovered before summer camp comes up, so she was determined to get better. She came to every appointment and gave me 100% without any questions asked. It made me wish a certain person felt the same determination towards their recovery.

The appointment goes well, as usual, and with today's progress, I inform her she'd probably only need a couple more sessions and would be set for clearance. With her leaving excited, it brings a smile to my face until I look over at the clock and notice the time. Her progress made me so excited that I had lost track of time, pushing her session a bit late into the next time slot. It was 9:18 A.M. by the time she walked out of the door. Clearly, someone was late. Giving Nick the benefit of the doubt, I wait fifteen more minutes before I finally grow tired of waiting and return to my office.

At this point, I'm pissed, but not surprised he blew me off. What was I expecting from someone like him? I knew from the beginning he wouldn't care. However, I'd ignored my inner reluctance and given him the benefit of the doubt. Reaching my desk, and knowing I now have the next half hour to myself, I start preparing the paperwork I need to mail out to help distract myself. I'm licking the envelope closed when I hear a deep voice from my doorway.

"I could give you something else to lick when you're done with that," Nick says, making me jump in my seat and knock my knee on my desk, giving me a major Charlie horse.

Grimacing, I rub at my kneecap to help relieve the stinging tingle in my leg then snap my head up to face Nick. He has a huge smirk on his face as he stares at me with his head tilted, looking pretty smug with himself. I want so badly to slap that look off his face.

He stands there with his hands in the pockets of a pair of black basketball shorts and White Sox t-shirt. "You're not supposed to be back here," I bark at him, still holding the grudge over my injury against him. He thinks he can just parade himself around the building? Where the hell is security when you need them?

Shrugging his shoulder at me, he casually answers, "You weren't in the room where we're supposed to meet."

"If you would've shown up on time like you were supposed to, you would have found me there. Since you're—" I look over at my clock on the wall for the time and notice it's now 9:52 A.M., "—fifty-two minutes late, Mr. Hunter, I took it as notice that you didn't care about your career. With that being the case, I'll inform your manager," I throw at him.

His face grows irritated instantly and his jaw tightens up. I can practically see him grinding his teeth under the skin of his cheek. I've finally gotten to him and I don't know whether to be ecstatic about it or worried with the look he's giving me.

"I'll repeat, you're not supposed to be back here. So if you would please leave, I'd really appreciate it," I say as I reach for the phone, ready to page security, but for some reason I can't force myself to do it and my hand hovers motionless over the receiver.

"What's so wrong with me being back here?"

"You're a patient, and patients are not allowed back here for security reasons."

I'm pissed. With any other patient, I would have already called security on them for violating the rules, but with Nick I find myself breaking them. Nick is about to respond when Katie walks into our office. The moment she spots Nick at the door, she grows excited, immediately starting a conversation with him, batting her lashes as she vies for his attention. Great, she's only encouraging his behavior. Within a couple of minutes I get a page over the intercom announcing my next appointment.

Standing then exiting the office, I leave Katie to ogle over Nick, rolling my eyes on the way out. I guess I should feel relieved about not having to deal with him, but I don't. For some reason I'm irritated he's back there, probably already getting Katie's number and setting up his next easy score, as Katie has put it.

I look around searching for security and I don't see them anywhere. I'm going to have to have a stern talk with him for not doing his job and allowing the patients to just roam around freely. What the hell are we paying him for?

Regardless, at least Nick Hunter is no longer my priority. My next two patients are. I'll just deal with Nick when the time comes, which will most likely be never again since he's proven he doesn't care about his career after all.

The next two hours go smoothly, ending my morning and allowing me to escape for lunch. Today I need out; I need to get some fresh air, especially so the fresh air can get a specific someone out of my head who has managed to weasel his way in. Explaining to Katie that I didn't feel well enough to go out for lunch with her and Sarah, she leaves without me and I'm relieved I won't have to hear whether or not she was able to get a date with Nick. Grabbing a sandwich from the local deli, I make my way to the building's outdoor picnic area. It's usually empty of people and I like it that way. What I need right now is some peace and quiet . . . My alone time.

Nick

Looking at the clock it's almost 12:30 and I know she should already be taking lunch. It's odd that I still don't know this girl's name. In my mind I've been referring to her as my little firecracker, although she's far from being mine. Up until now it hasn't once occurred to me to ask somebody for her name. I could've asked her friend, but the girl never gave me a chance. From the moment she spotted me, she was all over me like a cat in heat, desperate to get laid. It was clear as day on her face. Normally, I would be all over girls like her. They're easy targets, no questions asked, but my mind was somewhere else. For some reason Little Ms. Firecracker seems far from easy and I find myself curious as to why. For the last two days she's been on my mind. Her spitfire attitude has had me constantly thinking of her. Not even the girl I slept with last night could help clear my mind of her. It was driving me fucking insane.

My only problem was this girl was going to be a challenge. I knew it the moment I walked into that room and our eyes met. Hers didn't light up as I'd expected them to do. At first my purpose was to escape her by convincing her to sign off on my paperwork, but the harder she put up a fight the more curious I was to know more about her. Does she have a boyfriend to put up with her saucy attitude? If she did, how the fuck does he tame the beast in her? It's something I'm determined to find out.

Growing frustrated when I don't find her, I continue roaming the halls searching, knowing she hadn't left with her co-workers for lunch. I'm about to give up on ever finding her when I spot her eating alone in an outdoor break area. Making my way outdoors to join her, I take a seat next to her and her body immediately tenses when she senses me at her side.

"What do you want, Nick?"

The sound of her saying my *actual* name is amusing since she's been so reluctant to use it when I've asked. "So out here it's Nick, but in there it's the stuck up Mr. Hunter?" I sarcastically throw at her, trying my best not to laugh at her stunned gaze.

"In there, I'm your physical therapist. Since you've interrupted my lunch break, I can call you whatever I want," she

32

clips out, looking as if she'd prefer to curse me instead. I can no longer contain my laughter as I throw my head back and let it out. It obviously doesn't amuse her since she's now glaring at me.

Clearing my throat, I try a different tactic. "I just wanted to apologize about this morning. I was late because . . ." I pause to think of an excuse. "I'm not really a morning person, and well, 9 A.M. is really pushing it with me," I say, hoping she believes it.

It's half the truth. I did get up on time, but after waking up with the same girl from the other night, and then trying to get her out of my apartment, I was late. Damn girl wouldn't get the point and fucking leave. Two nights with her and she was already thinking we were in a committed relationship.

It's clear from her arched brow that she isn't buying my excuse. "I'm not a morning person either, but it's called responsibility, and if you choose not to have any then don't bother wasting my time," she states, already trying to stand. I reach out for her arm and she just as quickly yanks it back, causing her to lose her balance. Rapidly standing to catch her, my arm wraps around her waist, pulling her up against my chest.

Her blinking eyes look up at me with shock, not knowing what to do. Taking advantage of having her in my arms, I breathe her in, and the first thing I notice is there isn't an overwhelming scent of perfume radiating off her as there normally would be from a girl. The void of scent is alluring. Her cheeks are slightly blushed, making me smile. My reaction causes her to start frantically looking around, as if searching for someone.

Glancing around, I find we're still alone. "Looking for someone?"

She pushes herself away from my chest and unwillingly I relinquish my hold of her, missing the feeling of her in my arms.

"No, but I have to get back to work," she mumbles while gathering up the remains of her lunch. "Look, Mr. Hunter," she adds, back to her professional self, "since you don't plan on taking your therapy serious with me, I'll put in a request to have another therapist work with you. Maybe you'll have better luck getting that clearance from someone else. Have a great day," she says sharply, already making her way to the doors leading into the building.

Swiftly catching up to her before she can enter the building, I block her retreat. "I meant what I said earlier. I'm really sorry. I'll be on time next week, I promise," I practically plead.

She sighs, but her eyes never leave mine. Her almost sympathetic look gives me hope. "Fine, but one minute late and the deal is off," she answers, sidestepping me and yanking open the door.

This time I let her leave, but my eyes follow her down the hallway. Right before she turns the corner, she takes one last quick glance over her shoulder. The thought that she couldn't resist looking back at me keeps me smiling. She finally disappears and it's at that moment I realize I still haven't learned her name. It doesn't matter now. I always have next week. Until then, Little Ms. Firecracker fits her perfectly fine.

FOUR

It's a small world

Taylor

I COULDN'T BRING myself to step in front of a bus to avoid having to go to Sarah's bachelorette party, so here I am, forcing myself to get ready to attend it.

Katie, being the shopaholic that she is, dragged me along with her a couple of days ago when she went shopping for a new dress for tonight. She was so excited about it she looked like a child in a candy store, as always. I, on the other hand, hate shopping. I would rather have my teeth pulled without anesthesia than wander through store after store for clothes.

I'm a simple kind of girl. A pair of jeans, a simple tee, and Chucks is what I'm happiest in—one of the reasons why I love my job. I don't have to spend money on work attire; it's already provided. Simple scrubs are all I have to wear to work every day, meaning I never have to go shopping for business clothing to impress anyone.

The only reason why I'm wearing a dress tonight is because I'm being forced to; otherwise, I would have shown up in jeans and a hoodie. Most clubs are dark anyway, what difference does it make what I'm wearing?

Since .my idea of dressing down was vetoed automatically by both Sarah and Katie the moment I suggested it, I'm now wearing a tight black mini-dress, which shows more skin than I wish to expose. Somehow, it manages to emphasize what little I do have in curves. The moment Katie spotted it, she said it was perfect for me, but I'm still trying to see the "me" in it, besides the reflection staring back at me from the mirror.

"You look like you're about to walk straight into a torture chamber," Katie comments from my doorway while I'm trying to zip up my dress. The darn thing is winning as I struggle with the zipper.

"Here let me help you," she offers.

The sound of a zipper still sends chills through my blood, an unwelcome reminder of Josh. "Now let's get your hair and make-up done, or else we're going to be late," she urges gently, shoving me out of my room.

Heeding her command, I follow her into the bathroom. Better Katie than I when it comes to styling my hair. She knows how to work magic on the simplest person, which would be me. After impatiently sitting, grinding my teeth not to complain about the fuss and prepping she's performing, she eventually finishes. The moment I take in my reflection it's hard to recognize myself. Katie has done a stunning job of highlighting my eyes so they pop, as my hair falls down my shoulders in a wave of amazing loose curls.

Placing her hands on my shoulders, she stares at my reflection. "If we don't find you a guy to get you laid tonight, then I'm definitely losing my touch," she comments.

Her remark makes me grimace. "I'm not looking for a one night stand tonight, so don't feel disappointed since I'm telling you right now it's not happening," I reprimand as I return to my room in search of my heels—another selection by Katie.

Following closely behind, she leans on the doorframe as she crosses her arms over her chest while watching me attempt to stumble into my heels. "I don't know why you're against having fun."

Sighing, I clarify to her, "I'm not trying to avoid having fun. I'm just not looking for a fast screw like everyone else in the world."

"You can't let your past determine your future, Taylor. Not every guy is *him*."

Her lecture takes me back to all the times I've tried having a relationship, only to discover it was difficult to do with me always comparing them to Josh and his actions. My trust issues wouldn't allow anyone to hold me, let alone kiss me, which quickly had them running in the other direction. Eventually it was easier to not date than to wallow in self-pity from disappointment.

Seeing the offended look on Katie's face, I quickly correct myself. "I'm sorry, Katie. It might work for you, and I have nothing against it if that's what you choose, but we both know it's not going to work for me so let's not fight about it, okay?"

Nodding her head in agreement before turning to walk away, she looks disappointed, most likely from my comment. I have a bad habit of always speaking my mind, which usually ends up getting me in trouble.

Katie goes off to work on herself, finishing much faster than she did on me, of course. Soon we're exiting our apartment and taking a taxi ride downtown. We haven't quite arrived yet and my stomach is gradually beginning to knot with dread over the night's possible outcome.

We arrive and the bass of the music pumping from inside the building seeps into the taxi before we even get out, intensifying my nerves. Katie loops her arm with mine and has to practically drag me to the entrance. With a line already formed around the block as we approach the entrance, we get plenty of nasty glares when we completely bypass it straight to the front door. Katie informs the bouncer that we're on the guest list by giving him our names and handing him our IDs; verifying the information, he lets us in.

As we enter the club, darkness engulfs us completely with only the flash of the strobe lights to lead our way. It takes a few minutes for my eyes to adjust to the darkness to locate Sarah. From the sway of her dancing and the delighted beam in her eyes, she's clearly drunk. I would know, the demeanor is forever engraved in my mind.

She reaches us within seconds and the alcohol is emanating from her mouth as she speaks. "Hey, you guys finally made it!" she shouts, trying to yell over the pounding of the music.

Sarah's sister, who is now trying to hold up her drunken body as Sarah loses her balance, looks over in our direction. "We got here an hour ago and she was impatient. We started right away," she sympathetically says as she looks back at Sarah, who is now trying to catch the straw in her cup with her tongue.

When Sarah realizes what her sister has said about her, her mouth drops open. Offended by the statement, she tries to shove at her sister, but fails as she loses her balance, forcing Katie to catch her.

"Hey, it's my night to party," she scolds. "It's not my fault you guys didn't get here sooner," she says, directing the comment at Katie and me.

She looks down at Katie's hands, which are now attempting to balance her. "Why is your hand without a drink? Let's get you a drink," she shouts at Katie as she looks around the club, probably trying to find a waitress to fulfill her order.

Her fast movements cause her to slosh her fruity looking drink all over the floor, adding to the stickiness we're standing in. It's evident she needs water instead of alcohol at this point, but I'm frightful of what she'll do to me if I tell her so.

Instead, her sister proceeds to pull her towards a short staircase leading to a raised area off to the side of the dance floor, giving Katie and I a quick tilt of her chin to follow. Making our way to a table, my eyes take in everything sitting upon it: bottles of vodka, tequila, and juice; everything but water, unless you count the ice cubes sitting in the bucket. I wasn't going to wait for them to melt to quench the thirst I arrived with.

Searching around for a waitress, I don't spot one right away, so I inform Katie I'm headed to the bar for my water. Giving me a nod, she acknowledges my comment. I make my way through the crowd of dancers, politely shoving my way through before finding the only open spot in a corner to patiently wait. As I stand there waiting to catch the attention of the bartender, I feel a hand on my ass, and I instantly react by slapping the hand away before turning to face a guy who looks completely wasted.

"Hey baby, you don't have to play hard to get," he says as he steps closer.

Trying really hard to put distance between this jerk and myself, I lean back as far as I can, hitting the wall. His persistent smile goes up to one side as he reaches out his arm to grab me. Pushing it away, I warn him, "Don't touch me."

He looks frustrated. For a moment I believe he's about to turn and leave, but I find I'm mistaken when he tries once more.

"Come on," he cajoles, leaning forward, trapping me between his body and the wall.

"Get off me!" I yell as I try to shove him off.

It does no good as he laughs at me.

I'm about ready to deck this guy with my fist when I feel him being pulled away from me. Stunned, I realize someone is now between me and the drunken jerk. His back is towards me, obstructing my view of his face.

"She's obviously not interested, so I suggest you back off unless you want me to kick your ass," I hear the stranger growl to the drunken man. It only takes me a couple of seconds to register who the voice belongs to.

Leaning my head to the side to take in the view in front of him, I see the guy already holding his hands up in surrender as he backs away and leaves. The guy takes one quick look over his shoulder before he disappears into the crowd of dancers, leaving me there alone with Nick, who turns to face me with a look of concern.

He gently rests his hands on my hips as he looks down into my face. "Are you okay?" he asks, his anxious tone calming me. I nod my head, unable to answer him just yet. From where I'm standing, I can see behind Nick. Katie is rushing towards me shouting my name. "Taylor!"

She quickly reaches me and engulfs me in a hug. "I'm so sorry. I saw everything. I tried getting here as fast as I could." She tightens her embrace to comfort me.

"I'm fine," I mumble into her hair.

Releasing me, we both turn to face my hero, her eyes going wide when she takes him in. "Nick, I didn't know you'd be here," she purrs up to him, reaching in to hug him next. He half-heartily returns her hug. Seeing them embraced stirs an unfamiliar emotion inside of me, fueling a hatred and envy I hadn't known existed within me.

Nick sees my narrowed eyes glaring at both of them as he pulls from her arms. "So it's Taylor? You never did tell me," he remarks with a sexy half smile. His eyes are hooded as they graze up and down my body, staring directly into my eyes once he finishes his perusal.

Leaning down, his mouth reaches my ears and I can feel his warm breath gliding across my skin. "The name doesn't suit you. You're much sexier than a typical *Taylor*," he claims. I can't help but blush from the husky tone he delivered the comment with. The room may be warm, but there are shivers running down my spine as my cheeks turn a bright shade of crimson. I'm thankful we're surrounded by the darkness of the room. It disguises how much his attention is affecting me. His knight in shining armor persona is working to his advantage at the moment.

Katie yanks at his arm, drawing his attention back to her. "Do you want to go back to our table?" she asks, her lashes batting as she extends the invitation.

Nick glances in my direction as he answers. "Sure, why not?"

Katie's eyes light up and her smile widens in triumph as she loops her arm into Nick's and begins to tug him away. "You coming, Taylor?" she shouts over her shoulder as she drags Nick behind her.

I'm internally fuming as I watch them disappear, my mind still trying to process what had suddenly transpired. Not wanting to risk another confrontation, I am left with no other choice but to follow, my wayward emotions rising with every step as I trail behind them towards the VIP area.

Reaching the entrance, Nick pauses and waits until I reach it before he proceeds to enter. The thought of his action has my heart fluttering, until Katie tugs him over to the only couch available to seat the two of them alone and immediately beginning to work her flirtatious charms on him. The sight of Nick responding with a smile fills me with disgust as I take my seat on another couch. It then dawns on me that I never did get my water. I force myself to push my irritation aside and start to check my emails on my phone, using it as a distraction. It's bad enough I don't want to be here, but to have to endure watching everyone drool over Nick, since he's the only male surrounded by a flock of drunken females, is irritating.

"What's wrong?" Nick shouts from the other end of our section. I ignore it, not once thinking he's speaking to me.

"Taylor!" I hear Katie shout right after him.

My head irritably snaps up at her to find Nick's casual form leaning back with his arm thrown over the back of the couch. He is staring at me with a question in his eyes as he too waits for my answer.

"Katie, you know I don't want to be here," I say. The roll of her eyes reveals she isn't satisfied with my response.

"Have a drink. You'll be having fun in no time," she claims, already shoving the drink in my hand. Pushing it back at her, I refuse to take it. "Why are you being a party pooper?" she asks then frowns with a childish pout.

"Yeah, Taylor, why are you such a party pooper?" Nick mockingly asks, fueling my anger. I can easily handle Katie's shit because I expect it from her, but I refuse to put up with Nick.

Standing up, I look for Sarah, finding her on the dance floor with a group of girls. Without notice, I make my way down to them, feeling the need to remove myself from the source of my frustration. Approaching her, she happily smiles at me while leaning in for a hug. I use the opportunity to say to her, "I'm going to head home." She's taken aback, staring back at me with a frown.

"Why?"

"I'm sorry, Sarah. I tried, but I just don't feel comfortable here." I glance back in the direction of where Nick and Katie are sitting and find them making their way down to the dance floor, hand in hand. "Who's that guy?"

"Nobody," I croak out, attempting to mask my wounded emotions I'm feeling within. Looking back at Sarah, I realize my broken-hearted appearance must have given me away. A frown is still marring her face, but this time it's full of sympathy.

"Oh, Taylor," she says as her eyes look in their direction.

Shaking my head in denial, I say, "It's no big deal, Sarah. I'm just going to leave." Turning to depart, I push my way through the crowd of dancers. As I near the exit, I'm brought to a halt and turn to face Katie.

"Where are you going?"

Nick walks over to us, stopping to stand behind Katie. "I'm leaving," I tell them, aiming my answer more at Nick than Katie.

"But we just got here, Tay," she whines. Nick's deep voice speaks up. "I can give you a ride home if you want."

"No, thank you," I throw back at him then quickly look at Katie. "You stay and have a good time. You know this isn't my kind of scene."

The hand wrapped around my arm is lightly tugging at me as she comments, "Just come back to the table and have a drink.

Before you know it, you'll be drunk and you'll start having fun," she encourages, grabbing Nick with her other hand then tries to drag the both of us back to the table.

She's finally crossed the line with her comment. Yanking my arm from hers, I make a beeline for the entrance of the club. I don't care what she thinks at this point, I just want to leave. Behind me I can hear her yelling my name, but I ignore her, needing to escape. I don't need this shit. This is what I get for coming? It's not worth it, or my time.

The minute I make it outside, the cold night air hits my face and I welcome it as I take in a deep breath, trying to calm myself.

"Hey, slow down," Nick yells behind me, encouraging me to quicken my steps. Some of the bystanders outside recognize him and instantly start to swarm him, allowing me to put distance between us. I try flagging down a taxi, to no avail. It's a busy night so I don't have any luck right away, but I don't give up. There has to be at least one that is going to stop in front of the club to drop someone off, so I keep trying.

A couple of minutes later, with no luck, I feel Nick walk up next to me. "Taylor, what are you doing?" he asks, confused. I probably look more like a hooker trying to get my next John with the dress I'm wearing, but that's also not my fault, either. I blame Katie for that.

"What does it look like I'm doing? I'm trying to get a taxi to take me home," I sarcastically respond, like he's the dumbass, which I'm sure he's probably thinking I am at this point.

Frustrated with my results, I give up on the taxi idea and start walking down the sidewalk towards the L. It's still kind of early and I'd be able to get home that way. Nick's hand wraps around my arm, stopping me in my tracks. Angrily, I turn to face him for trying to stop me.

His pleading eyes are bearing down into mine. "I just want to make sure you get home okay and I don't trust public transportation to do it. Let me give you a ride home," he states. "Please?" This time he pleads.

Standing there eyeing him up, I'm debating whether I can trust him. "I promise to keep my hands to myself if it makes you feel better," he conveys, his head tilting in his signature pose I now associate with him. He's taunting me, but it's amusing at the same time.

I hope I won't regret what I'm about to do. "Okay," I reply, knowing I'm taking the biggest risk I've taken in the last six years, but I would rather get a ride home in a car than take the L, or a taxi, by myself.

He doesn't hesitate to release my arm and take my hand as he leads us to his car. I'm not used to wearing heels so I struggle to keep up with his brisk steps. I soon stumble, forcing Nick to catch me before I land on the ground.

"You okay?"

"You were walking a little too fast for me."

Resuming our steps, he apologizes. "I'm sorry." Slowing his pace to match my own, he keeps me tucked at his side. I know I should pull away, but his embrace makes me feel safe. I can smell the tantalizing scent of his cologne with him so close at my side, and it slowly arouses my senses.

After a couple of blocks, we reach a private parking garage, entering it through a secured door that leads straight up some stairs. There are only half a dozen, but he takes the first two steps in one, yanking me with him, making me stumble again. I practically twist my ankle on the way up from him dragging me to keep his pace. If he keeps this up, I'm going to be the one giving myself physical therapy for the same type of injury he has.

"I'm sorry. I'm used to taking stairs two at a time," he says, helping me stand up straight.

"That's bad for you, especially with your ankle in the condition that it's in. You're going to end up fracturing it again since it's still very sensitive."

"It feels fine to me."

"Whatever," I sarcastically reply. "Who am I to tell you how to treat it?"

From the corner of my eye I see his lips curve up. "The last time I checked you were still my physical therapist, so technically you have every right to lecture me," he answers. His admission makes me smile in return as we walk side by side.

Before long we reach a caged off, private section of the garage containing an array of expensive cars. Of course, I wouldn't expect anything less of Nick Hunter. Entering a code into the lock, he leads us to a shiny black car in a corner then straight to the passenger side to open the door for me. His action surprises me.

"It's very rare when men still act like gentlemen and open car doors for girls," I comment, smiling at his gesture.

"I only do it when she's worth it."

His response leaves me shocked as I step into the car and he shuts the door behind me, making me wonder what he meant by the comment. When he climbs into the car, I stare at him, still curious about his remark. Catching me gawking at him, I blush from being caught.

With a smirk he starts up the car, asking me for my address to enter it into his GPS. Within minutes we're driving out of the building towards my apartment.

"I take it by the way you acted back at the club, it wasn't your idea to go?" His question brings me back to the reality of the night.

"No, I don't usually go out."

"Why not?"

It's a simple question, but the tone he used gives me the impression that he's teasing me for something I should normally do. "Like I said, it's not my kind of thing."

"So, you have a boyfriend?"

"I appreciate the ride, but had I known this was going to be the perfect opportunity to question me about my personal life, I would have taken the taxi instead."

"Are you always this uptight?" I'm not surprised by his remark. It's actually a common assertion I get from people.

"Yes," I unwillingly admit. "No to your earlier question, I don't have a boyfriend. Most think I'm too *uptight*," I mock, repeating his comment. I expect another comeback from my response, but instead I'm surprised when he laughs.

"Little Ms. Firecracker," he mumbles.

Shifting my gaze in his direction, I find him completely focused on the road ahead of him, a smirk remaining on his lips as my eyes linger on his face a little longer than needed. When I catch his eyes glancing at me, his lips widen and I turn my head to look out of the passenger side window, now blushing from head to toe.

The remaining twenty-minute drive to my apartment is made in an awkward silence, except for the occasional command from the navigation system. When he puts the car into park I automatically reach for the door handle. "Thanks for the ride. I really appreciate it," I politely tell him, already opening the door to step out of the car.

Nick climbs out from his side of the car then rushes over to my side. "I'll walk you up," he strains out.

His face looks pinched, as if in pain. Looking down at his ankle, I find him slowly rotating it.

I gasp. "What happened?"

Grimacing, he replies, "I stepped on it wrong as I rushed out of the car."

"Don't move it like that! You're going to stress it more!" I shout, dropping down on one knee and grabbing for his ankle to lift it in my hands. I place it on my bended knee. "Taylor, get up off the ground," Nick commands before he tries lifting me up by my arm.

I ignore him and begin to massage the muscles in his ankle. Within seconds I no longer feel Nick protesting to pull his ankle away. When I feel completely satisfied he should be feeling better, I place his foot back on the ground and this time allow Nick to help me up.

"You didn't have to do that. You've probably gotten all dirty."

Looking up at him with confusion, I remember what I'm wearing. It hadn't occurred to me. My actions were second nature and something I would have normally done at work.

"Can you walk on it?" I worriedly ask, giving him a minute to test the pressure while bearing weight on it. He nods, but from the look on his face I know he isn't telling me the truth. Rolling my eyes, I lead him to my apartment, mentally praying I won't regret bringing him in.

When we reach my door I open it, allowing him inside and ordering him to take a seat on the couch while I head to the kitchen to retrieve an ice pack from the freezer. Returning to him, I grab a throw pillow and place it under his ankle on the coffee table. Nick winces as I place the ice pack on his jean-covered ankle, making me smirk at his reaction.

Men can be such babies sometimes.

Satisfied for the moment, I leave him and go to the bathroom to retrieve two ibuprofens from the medicine cabinet and return to him with a glass of water.

"Here, take these. They're anti-inflammatories. And leave the ice on for at least twenty minutes," I order, handing him both the water and the pills. He looks back at me with skepticism, but I shove the pills into his hand and sternly order him to take the pills with a glare. I watch him swallow the pills, feeling satisfied.

Taking a seat on the other end of the couch, I make sure to keep a generous gap between us. The pain from wearing the heels tonight finally catches up to me so I remove my shoes. Closing my eyes, I tilt my head back and let out a satisfied moan while massaging the ball of my foot. I hadn't noticed how badly my feet were hurting until now.

"You know, you look really sexy right now," Nick huskily says. My eyes shoot open from his comment and I stare back at him as he watches me. His words make me stand up from the couch, needing to put much more distance between us.

My heart is racing and I'm beginning to grow worried knowing I'm alone with Nick. I don't like it. Heading over to the wall, I stand against it with my arms crossed defensively over my chest, hoping my reaction will not cause alarm. The last thing I want Nick realizing is how terrified I feel being alone with him.

When I look at him, his disappointed face is studying me. "Did I say something wrong, Taylor? I was just trying to compliment you."

Shaking my head at him, I try to explain. "I don't need your compliments, Nick. I'm not interested, so don't bother wasting your breath or time on me," I reply with despair clear in my voice, already turning my head to look out the window to avoid his scrutinizing eyes. A silence overtakes the room before I hear him sigh. He stands up and heads in my direction. Seeing his determination only makes me panic. It's more from being alone in a room with him and not knowing what his intentions are than anything else.

I automatically start to retreat into the kitchen, hoping to keep the distance between us. With the counter separating us, he seems perplexed by my reaction. His lips turn down into a frown as his brow furrows.

"I think I should just head out. Thanks for the pain killers," he voices, leaving the bag of ice on the counter. My eyes follow him to the front door. "I'll see you later," he says without a backwards glance as he leaves the apartment.

The pain swells in my chest from the hurt of watching him walk away, like a knife stabbing at my heart, knowing it's entirely my fault. My lack of trust caused me to react the way I did and I hate that I keep letting it do this to me.

I'm left standing alone in my kitchen, hating how no matter how badly I want to trust again, I won't allow myself to do so. If I don't change, I never will be able to.

I end up going to bed, depressed and disappointed with myself about what happened, eventually crying myself to sleep. I wake up late the next morning as I usually do on the weekends, but instead of getting up like a normal person, I lie in bed staring up at the ceiling. I know I shouldn't feel guilty about what happened. Telling Nick I wasn't interested was an automatic reaction. It's what I tell every guy that attempts any type of relationship with me. But this time, it actually hurt when I saw the rejection on his face. I had stood there in the kitchen for a while, wishing I'd gone after him, but knew deep down inside I couldn't.

Not because I didn't want to, but because he was my patient.

Katie did eventually come in to check on me, but just to

scold me for leaving the club the way I did. I simply ignored her, knowing if I let her vent she would eventually leave me alone. Although I wanted to tell her about what happened, the last thing I want to hear from her is another lecture about needing to start trusting again, so I didn't say a word.

Eventually, my lack of response to her argument cued her into the fact that something was wrong. She knows when I get in this bad mood, it's just best to leave me be. There's nothing that will cheer me up or get me out of bed. So instead, she left me alone for the rest of the day, allowing me to wallow by myself without another word. I keep repeating the sequence of events that happened last night over and over in my head. No matter how many times I try to tell myself that it's for my own good that things ended the way they did, it still hurts knowing it did.

FIVE

One step forward

Nick

I'D SPENT THE rest of the weekend going over everything that occurred on Saturday night and I'm still confused. My mind keeps telling me to let Taylor be, but somehow her vulnerability was intriguing. With every new piece of information I've discovered about Taylor, I'm tempted to keep peeling off the layers she's desperately keeping around herself. Today I was going to attempt to peel another one off, and the only way to do that was to get on her good side.

"You're on time, Mr. Hunter. I can honestly say that I'm surprised."

"I promised I'd be on time, didn't I?" I comment before

hopping up onto the exam table. Taking Taylor in, I wonder who knew a pair of scrubs could look so damn sexy? Or maybe it was just the girl wearing them.

It's clear my remark has offended her by her dejected expression she is wearing when she reaches for my ankle and begins to examine it. Throwing myself back onto the table to try to distract myself from the feel of her silky smooth hands gliding up and down my ankle is the only thing I can do to keep my dick from growing hard.

"How is it feeling today?" she asks, still massaging my ankle. "Did you have any major swelling or discoloration with the ankle after you left?"

"Left when?" I question up to the ceiling. I can feel the tension in her hands. Lifting my head up to look at her, I find her nervously glancing to the side before her eyes find mine. She's apprehensively biting her lip and it occurs to me she means Saturday evening.

"No."

Her hands relax and return to their massaging. Still biting her lip, it takes more determination than I'd expected to not grow hard as my mind wanders to remembering what she was wearing Saturday evening when I left her.

The next hour is a struggle as the minutes tick by, but thankfully her small demands are my distractions. Taylor is all business when it comes to my therapy session. No matter how long my eyes watch her, she is entirely focused on my ankle. Towards the end of the appointment she demonstrates the exercises I'm expected to practice at home on a nightly basis. The only thing I can do is nod my head, wondering what it would take for me to convince her to come over to my place on a nightly basis and do them for me.

"Mr. Hunter?" she lightly snaps, breaking my thoughts.

"Any questions?" she asks, finally making eye contact with me.

"I was thinking if maybe I should come in twice a week instead of one to help speed up my recovery."

Her narrowed eyes worry me. "I agree. The Wednesday morning spot is still open and you're welcome to take it," she informs me with an arched brow, as if testing me.

Fuck. Why does it have to be a morning appointment? Considering it's my only option at this time to get more time with her, I agree to it. With a small salute goodbye, I exit the therapy room. I'd told myself I wouldn't push my luck by interrogating Taylor at this appointment, and I'm sticking to my plan. One layer at a time is how I'm going to get her to open up. My one layer today was getting more time with her.

Entering the club, I'm already thinking this may not have been a good idea. Normally the pounding of the music is welcome, but tonight I'm just not feeling it. Eyeing my friend in the VIP area, he's already waving me over. Pushing my way past the crowd leading towards the secluded area, I check out several girls who are clearly eyeing me as I walk by. Usually I'd tease them by responding and act as if I'm interested, knowing it may help get me laid later in the night. But tonight, taking one of them home is far from my mind.

Reaching the private booth where my friend Jeremy is waiting for me, he greets me with our usual handshake. "Hey, man, didn't think you'd make it tonight."

"Yeah, I almost wasn't going to."

I'd turned down the offer of going out tonight knowing I had my appointment with Taylor in the morning, but with much coaxing from one of my closest friends, I had caved.

"Here, you look like you could use a drink," he states, shoving a double into my hand. Without hesitating I throw it back, allowing the alcohol to course down my throat. Looking at the bottle of Patron sitting on the table, I may regret doing that. Jeremy takes the glass from me and is already handing me another.

"I'm good," I comment, trying to gently shove the glass away, but he's persistent. "Quit being a pussy. It's not like you have practice in the morning."

He does have a point. Taking the glass from him, I down it just as fast as the earlier one. With a satisfied smile, he replies, "That a boy."

"Speaking of practice, how are things going?" I shout over the music as we sit on the couch provided for us.

Shrugging his shoulders, he says, "It's going. The replacement they got for you is worthless. Doesn't know how to throw for shit." The statement makes me laugh since Jeremy is the first baseman and it's usually him I'm throwing the ball to.

"You'll figure him out sooner or later," I joke.

He snorts. "I don't want to figure him out. What I *need* is for you to get your ass back on that field."

"Yeah, well, I'm working on it," I grumble.

Jeremy is about to continue speaking, but is interrupted when Tracie, the girl who I'd kicked out the other morning, stands in front of me with a satisfied smirk on her lips. Arching my brow up with confusion, I wonder what the hell she wants. Before I get the chance to ask, she takes a seat on my other side, her hand slowly creeping up my leg. The alcohol is evidently already taking effect since her simple touch has already given me a hard on. Her hand reaches my dick, gently gripping it.

"Someone is happy to see me," she hums in my ear. Sighing, I know it's more a result of the tequila I'd swallowed than her. "Behave, Tracie," I clip out as I shove her hand away, not wanting to encourage her.

She pouts like a child, but the gleam in her eyes tells me she's far from giving up. My mind is slowly starting to grow hazy, making me regret skipping dinner.

Looking over to the dance floor to distract myself, all I can do is hope the next hour goes by as quickly as possible. It's all I'm giving myself before I leave. The last thing I want is to encourage Tracie into thinking she's coming home with me.

Taylor

Wednesday morning comes and to my surprise, he doesn't show up. I'm left sitting on my ball, pissed that he's wasting my time. I have to remember it's not my job on the line, but his. So why should I care? With any other patient I would have just brushed it off, not giving a shit, but for some reason Nick has gotten under my skin and it's pissing me off.

Finally giving up on waiting, I head back to my desk at 9:30, deciding to take advantage of the time and catch up on my paperwork. As I enter my office I hear the phone on my desk ringing and decide to let it go straight to voicemail. I'm so pissed right now, I wouldn't want to take it out on the person on the other end of that phone call, especially if it's a patient or parent. They shouldn't have to feel my wrath.

Taking a seat, I wait for the flashing light to indicate a voicemail, if they leave one. When I see the little light on the phone flashing, I pick up the receiver and punch in my code to retrieve the message. What I do not expect is to hear Nick's voice on the other end.

"Hey, Taylor, I'm really sorry about missing my appointment this morning, but I woke up with the flu and I didn't want to get you sick," he says, sounding pathetic as he speaks in a hushed tone. "I'm sorry, but I'll be there on Monday."

I'm left wide-eyed with surprise and staring at the wall ahead of me as I hold the receiver in my hand. I now regret not picking up the phone and giving the person on the other end my wrath. Especially since it was the person who caused it. I'm beyond pissed that he had the audacity to wait until the middle of the appointment to call me. He probably thought I'd still be waiting for him in the therapy room like a desperate puppy.

Slamming the receiver down on its cradle with a little too much force, I let out a frustrated growl. This fucking asshole insisted that he come in this morning, but then tries to use the excuse that he has the flu. He has some damn nerve to think that I'd actually believe his pathetic excuse. It was clear in his voice that he was out drinking last night and he has a fucking hangover. He's just too chicken shit to admit it. I've had enough experience with this shit to know the telltale signs. I'm surprised he was even able to get up to call me; that pisses me off even more. If he was able to call me then he was obviously able to crawl in here if he wanted to.

Resting my elbows onto the desk, I drop my head into my hands and grab my hair. I take a fist full in each hand, allowing the burning of my scalp to mask the anger boiling up inside of me. I just want to scream at the top of my lungs, but knowing that I can't at this moment, I restrain myself from doing so, and just sit there with my eyes tightly closed for a couple of minutes to calm myself. I stand up to head to the vending machine to grab some chocolate. I already have a feeling it's going to be one of those days . . . again.

After finishing my chocolate, I make a rash decision to put in a request to have Nick transferred to another sports physical therapist. I'm not putting up with his bullshit anymore. You've screwed with me one to many times, Nick Hunter.

Not that he even cares for one bit that he did, but I do.

Once the request is put in, I'm left feeling a little satisfied, yet disappointed in myself for easily giving up. How I've managed to let myself get so involved with this one patient is beyond me. Normally this would never happen. I really must be losing my mind.

My only answer is chocolate. Chocolate will never disappoint me, which is the reason why I'm going to take the remainder of Nick's appointment to satisfy myself. Maybe it will help cool my temper before my next appointment. Yet, I wouldn't have to do so if it weren't for Nick being such an asshole.

Nick

Just like the other day, the ringing of my phone awakens me from my slumber. Why can't people just let me sleep? But then I remember I'd called and left Taylor a message and it may be her calling me back to reschedule.

Grabbing the phone, I quickly answer it.

"Nick?"

I know I'm still hung-over, but the voice on the other end is definitely not Taylor's. "Yes," I hesitantly answer.

"Hi, it's Katie from Chicago Sports General. I was calling to inform you that you've been reassigned and I'm now your current sports physical therapist. I just wanted to notify you so you won't be alarmed at your next appointment."

Confused, I ask, "Wait, my new what?" Rapidly sitting up, my stomach contents threaten to rise.

"Your new therapist," she repeats.

"What happened to Taylor?"

The other end of the line goes silent for a moment before

I hear a sigh.

"Taylor put in the request this morning to have you reassigned to a different sports therapist." My hand fiercely grips the phone as I force myself to not scream into it. "Nick?" The girl worriedly questions from the other end.

"Yeah, I'm still here," I grimly reply.

"Do you prefer to keep your appointments in the afternoon?"

"Yes, afternoons are better," I answer since it's clearly evident I can't keep my morning ones to save my life.

"Great. I'll see you Monday afternoon," she cheerfully replies before we end the call.

Throwing the phone across the room, it hits the wall, shattering as it makes contact. Next, my head lands on my pillow as I wonder how the fuck I let this happen. Grumbling to myself, I realize I know exactly how this happened: my stupidity. I knew the moment I woke up next to Tracie in my bed that I'd fucked up last night by drinking too much. My drunken stupor had gotten the best of me and I had brought her back to my apartment. Thankfully, she'd been the one to wake me in the morning or else I would have slept the entire morning away. Her voice begging for another round instantly woke me up. The hangover I was nursing kept me from leaving my bed or performing any other activity for that matter, further pissing Tracie off and sending her stomping from my apartment. Her tantrum was the least of my problems at the moment. My only concern was how upset Taylor was going to be at me for not showing up on time when I finally realized what time it was—twenty minutes after nine by the time my eyes popped open. With dread, my fingers dialed Taylor's office, but the call went straight to voicemail, which is why I'd tried to sound as apologetic as I felt.

I knew my little firecracker would be mad, but I never

thought she'd go as far as having me reassigned to another therapist. If she thought for one moment that I was going to allow that to happen, then she was clearly mistaken. There was no way in hell she was getting rid of me that easily.

Taylor

The day goes by normally. The rest of my morning patients come and go. Lunch is over and done with and I'm happy with the day as it passes through into the afternoon without any problems. As my workday draws to a close, I sit in my office reviewing the files for the next day, preparing myself for the rest of the week. Suddenly, I see Nick walk into my office, stopping to stand just inside the doorway, furiously looking at me.

Looking past him into the hallway, I wait for the security guards to quickly swarm him, but am disappointed when all I hear is silence. I'm going to make sure someone gets his ass fired if this keeps happening.

Glaring at him, I say, "What do you want, Nick? I've already told you you're not allowed back here."

Cocking his head, he stares at me a moment as if considering his answer. "I got a very interesting phone call from my new therapist this morning," he conveys, using his fingers to make air quotations to emphasize the words *new therapist*. "Apparently, someone put in a request for it. Would you happen to know who did? Because I'm pretty sure I didn't," he says, eyes glaring back at me.

Obviously, he's pissed about what I did, but at this point I don't care anymore. He threw away any chance of me caring about his feelings the moment he decided to not show up.

"You brought it upon yourself," I casually answer.

He seems taken aback by my response.

"I called you. Did you not get the message?" he throws back at me.

"It doesn't matter. We had a deal. You broke it," I reply, powerfully attempting to control my temper. He's angered me to a point that my blood is boiling, as it usually does when he mocks me. It makes me want to strangle him. "I refuse to work with someone who isn't willing to give me one hundred percent of their dedication to their recovery. And since you don't seem to take yours seriously, I think it's best you work with someone else you can easily *fuck over,*" I growl at him through clenched teeth.

Bravely, he steps further into the office and shuts the door behind him. "I had the flu, Taylor, what part of that is refusing to give you one hundred percent? Would you have preferred for me to be in here puking my brains out on your floor?" he barks back at me, his echoes vibrating in the room.

Refusing to allow him to intimidate me, I slowly rise from my chair. "Don't lie to me! I know you were hungover! I refuse to put the reputation of my work on the line so you can pick and choose when you decide to show up!" I snarl at him, my voice rising with each word.

His jaw tightens as he takes a step further in my direction. "Oh, so I get it. If I fuck up, you look bad," he declares. "I bet you've never fucked up before, have you, Taylor? You're worried because you might have actually found someone who will jeopardize your reputation. Am I right?"

I'm still trying to keep my temper under control, my hands curling to grip the edge of my desk, allowing me to physically take my anger out on something besides Nick. "No, I've never had anyone fuck up before because I've never given anyone the chance. You're lucky your ass got transferred to another therapist or else you'd be begging your manager to give you another chance!" I exclaim. His eyes are wide as I continue. "Now I'd appreciate it if you'd leave, because you don't have any other reason to be here!" I shout at him, my hands growing numb as my grasp tightens.

His mouth opens to argue back, but he is rendered speechless when Katie enters. "What the hell is going on in here? We can hear the shouting all the way down the hallway and it's starting to worry the patients."

Looking past her, I take in the security guard now standing in the doorway. Oh, now he decides to show up. He takes a moment to assess the situation before turning to usher away my co-workers who have gathered at my door before shutting it.

Mortified at how out of control I've gotten with Nick, I slowly slump back down into my chair. Closing my eyes to take a breath, I once again attempt to temper my rage. I've never raised my voice to a patient and I can't believe I'm doing it now.

Snapping my eyes open, I look directly at Katie. "I'm sorry, Nick was just leaving. I promise no more shouting," I tell her as I stand to try to leave the room. Nick uses his body to block my escape, making me glare up at him to try to ward off his move, failing as he scowls down at me. "Like hell it's over. I don't want somebody else."

My heart starts to beat erratically. My body tenses as my breathing comes to a complete stop, my rage now slowly rising from his refusal.

Katie steps between us, her body facing Nick. "It's obvious that you and Taylor have issues with each other, so maybe it's a good thing you were transferred," she calmly states.

"I already told you, I don't need to be transferred!" he argues back.

"Well, too bad because it's done. Either you take it or leave it. It's your decision. I gave you the benefit of the doubt and you screwed me over!" I say around Katie, shoving my finger into his chest.

Catching my wrist with his hand in a gentle grip, we lock eyes, both stubbornly refusing to break eye contact. Surprisingly, the feeling of his hand wrapped around my wrist calms me, his simple touch somehow managing to send a shiver down my spine. He sighs as his shoulders drop in defeat. "Fine," he growls through his teeth, "but this isn't the last you're going to see of me, Taylor. I don't give up so easily," Nick says, gently dropping my hand.

The comment leaves me both puzzled and speechless as he turns to walk out the door. From the corner of my eye, I can see Katie standing there with her mouth gaping open, looking just as perplexed over the situation before she rushes over to shut the door behind him.

Glaring straight at me, she asks, "Care to tell me what's going on?"

"Nothing," I clip out, still irritable. I'm starting to tremble now that Nick has left the room. My heart is still rapidly beating and I take a deep breath to calm it. My mind is still trying to comprehend what happened as my anger gradually begins to fade. Forcing my leaded feet to move back over to my desk, I find the comfort of my chair. My hands go straight for my head, taking a fist full of hair in each.

"Apparently it's more than nothing." I ignore her comment as my shivering begins to subside and tears slowly build up, forcing me to blink to push them away.

Tilting her head, as if considering something, she asks, "What exactly did happen after you both left the club?"

"Nothing happened," I mumble, but her expression doesn't falter an inch. "You know me better than that, Katie," I add, somehow feeling the need to defend myself, lowering my elbows onto my desk to grab at my hair as before.

"Then why did I get a lecture from Sarah for fawning all over Nick at the club? Had I known you had something going on between you and Nick, I would have backed off," she says then sighs.

Letting go of my hair, I look straight at her. "I already told you there isn't anything going on between us. I just got tired of him playing games and showing up when he wanted to. You'll find out soon enough when he starts pulling the same crap on you," I clarify, waving my hand and breaking eye contact with her. "Anyway, I'm not even his type," I mutter.

"And what type would that be, exactly?"

Rolling my eyes, I know she's pulling this conversation out longer than needed. "You know exactly what I'm talking about," I say, eyeing her up and down, realizing she's anyone's perfect type. "Someone like you."

"Taylor," she sympathetically drags out my name. "You're just as beautiful, but in the girl next door type of way. You just refuse to see it. And since when do you start arguing with the patients?" she asks, as if attempting to change the subject. "Normally you wouldn't care if a patient didn't show up."

She's right. Nick isn't the first patient who has attempted to pull this stunt, but for some reason though Nick has gotten under my skin, and it's annoying me.

"That's beside the point. Didn't you want to get your hands all over him?" I ask, grabbing for the first chart I see on my desk, pretending to review it.

She still stands in front of my desk, her brow arched as if she's unconvinced. "You can lie to yourself all you want, Taylor, but it's written all over your face," she scorns before turning to walk out of the office, leaving me gaping at her.

A minute passes as I wallow alone in silence. Tossing the

chart onto my desk, my head leans back onto the chair and my eyes close as I wonder how I managed to get myself in this situation with Nick Hunter. The man is clearly a danger to my sanity. Thankfully, he's Katie's problem now and I won't be seeing anymore of Nick Hunter anytime in the future, regardless of his threats.

SIX

One step back

Taylor

SURPRISINGLY THE NEXT couple of weeks go by smoothly and I actually manage to keep Nick from creeping into my mind more often than I'd expected. He was still slightly weaseling his way into my thoughts every now and then when Katie spoke of his progress. According to her, he was obedient and on track to returning to the field soon. Her praise only made me resent him. It's evident he was better at following orders when it came to his appointments with Katie than he was with me. That *pissed* me off. Why couldn't he have just done that with me from the beginning instead of giving me a fight? I kept telling myself it shouldn't matter, but it felt like a rusted knife stabbing at my emotions. I'd finally resorted to snapping at her to change the subject when she'd mention him, insisting I didn't want to hear about it.

It worked.

At least I'd thought so.

One day Katie and half the staff called in sick due to them catching the summer flu that was making its way around the building. It left Sarah and I to handle five employees' worth of clients, *on a Monday.* If I didn't already hate Mondays, this would have been reason enough.

We were lucky, though. We both didn't have too many patients on the books this day. Many patients were convinced to reschedule, and the ones that couldn't we divided amongst each other. It left us working through our breaks, but our focus was making it through the day.

I'd left Nick up to Sarah to reschedule, but apparently he was one of the few who insisted on coming in so I designated Sarah to take him for his therapy session. She didn't argue, feeling privileged enough to touch him. Rolling my eyes at her, I left her to go work with him. At the end of the day while sitting at my desk with the only break I'd have for the day, I'm in the process of returning important phone calls when Sarah walks in looking troubled.

"What's wrong?" I ask, already having a feeling it involves Nick.

"Um, I don't know how to say this, but we need to swap positions at the moment," she says, biting her lower lip, looking worried.

Drawing my eyebrows down at her, I ask "Why?"

"I seem to have a little problem with Nick Hunter. He was expecting to work with you since Katie was sick. But when he saw me he refused to cooperate," she rambles.

Sarah's a big pushover with strangers and apparently Nick was taking advantage of it. Standing up and taking a deep breath, I make my way over to the therapy room with Sarah following close behind me. When we enter, Nick is sitting on the exam table with a smug look on his face as he eyes me. He's clearly happy to see I've reacted to his bait. "Well, Ms. Taylor, it's a pleasure to see you again," he says, clearly happy with himself.

Stopping directly in front of him with my hands on my hips, I say, "Since you're badgering my co-worker here, I can't say the same. What seems to be the problem, Nick?"

"You're here now, so I don't see the problem anymore," he smugly replies.

"I'm only here to tell you to stop giving Sarah your shitty attitude and let her do her job. If not, you know where the door is and you can reschedule when Katie is feeling better," I snarl at him.

He leans forward and the hint of cologne I recognize from the night he drove me home has my heart picking up speed.

"But it's really you I want touching my body today."

His husky whisper mixed with his warm breath caressing my ear forces me to shut my eyes as the shiver runs throughout my veins. My heart starts rapidly beating and my breath is taken completely from my lungs. I'm using every ounce of willpower to keep myself from collapsing as my knees weaken.

I'm angry with myself for allowing his seductive tone to overtake my emotions, but I'd be lying if I said I didn't miss his voice. Especially since it's not screaming back at me. Slowly my eyes open again to find his blue eyes gazing at me, his mouth mere inches from my own. If my heart weren't already racing, it'd be now. His lips gradually curl up to the side as he waits for my response.

Yanking my head back to put distance between us, I shake it to clear the fog that has overtaken my mind. "I'm not falling for your crap, Nick. I don't know who you're trying to compare me to, but I'm not one of the many bimbos who throw themselves at you," I growl at him just above a whisper for only him to hear.

He's taken aback by my response. It gives me the chance to turn and walk out of the room. Whether he stays or goes, I don't care anymore. It's his problem not mine and I'm sure as hell not going to stress over it.

The closer I get to my office, I remember how Nick had followed me there before and I'm pretty sure he'd be brave enough to do it again. So instead, I go to the one place that I know I can escape to without the fear of him following me: the bathroom. It worked before. It's not the best hiding place, but it will have to do, even if I don't have to go. Once my emotions are under control, I slowly creep the door open, making sure the hallway is empty before I make my way back to my office.

Thankfully, it's empty when I return. Sitting in my chair, I find a Post-it note sitting directly in the middle of my desk. Picking it up to read it, the scrawling across it has my earlier emotions returning full force.

No one will ever
compare to you,
Taylor
                    Nick

I can't control the smile spreading across my face, or the

warm fuzzy feeling that erupts throughout my body. Placing the note inside the pocket of my scrubs, I wrap my hand tightly around it, not wanting to sever contact with it just yet. After a minute, I pull myself together and force myself to get back to work.

This Monday may not have been so bad after all.

Nick

I never intended to upset Taylor. My goal was to spend time with her. It was my first thought when Sarah called and tried to reschedule my appointment. I immediately knew after she explained it was only her and Taylor that it was possible Taylor might take over my appointment. The plan apparently backfired on me. Hopefully, the note I left her will help smooth things over. For the past two weeks, I endured my appointments like a good boy, but I'd used them as time to question Katie about Taylor. If I wasn't able to peel the layers myself, then I'd do it through the next best person. Evidently, I'd gotten much more as well after discovering Katie was her roommate. Katie still hasn't revealed how she's come to be the little firecracker that Taylor is, but it had to be something deep from the way she keeps emphasizing Taylor just needs time to trust. It was the reason why she was pushing me away.

If I thought Taylor was a firecracker, Katie was just as much an equal, which I discovered during our first appointment. She came marching into the therapy room looking like she was out for vengeance. The sweet, flirtatious girl I'd first met was no longer there. She was now replaced with a girl who was ready to fight. My mind wanders back to the memory of that first session

"What is really going on with you and Taylor?" She imme-

diately demanded to know.

Confused by her question, I simply answer, "Nothing."

Slanting her head, she looks at me doubtfully "That's what she said, but I don't believe either one of you."

"What did she say?" I cheerfully ask, my curiosity getting the better of me.

Instead of answering my question, her eyes narrow.

"I don't know what it is about you, but for the first time Taylor has let someone get to her, so it means something." That made me perk up, but just as quickly she attacked again. "I'm warning you, Nick. You mess with her, you're messing with me, and I'm not one to mess with. Do you understand?" she scorns with an ugly twist of her mouth.

Holding my hands up in surrender, I say, "Understood. I would never do anything to hurt her."

She still looks unsure of my answer, but quickly lowers her head and points at my ankle. "Good. Now get your foot up on that table so I can do my job. In the meantime, we're going to figure out just how serious you are about Taylor." Doing as she orders, I easily become stunned from her comment. "Don't look at me that way. I'm not stupid. I've caught you eyeing her, so I know there's more than the both of you are telling me and I intend to find out."

Her comment makes me laugh.

"But I mean it. You break her heart and I'll break your ankle again."

My ringing phone brings me back to the present. Looking down at the screen, I see it's my mother calling and the thought of speaking with her has me silently cursing.

"Hello, Mother," I answer, knowing the next twenty minutes will be a lecturing hell. No matter how much I try to avoid my parents, it's inevitable, especially with my mother.

SEVEN

Demons

Taylor

THE DAY ENDS without any further problems, although we had a circus of a day. We managed to pull through and the next day is much the same routine. It isn't until the end of Tuesday when I'm on the L that the events of two non-stop days catch up with me. By the time I walk into the door of my apartment, I feel exhausted. Katie is in the kitchen cooking dinner, already appearing to be her cheerful, bubbly self.

"Hey there, I'm cooking spaghetti tonight so I hope you're hungry," she states before pounding the spoon on the pot and placing it on the counter. The sound alone makes me wince from the headache I've been keeping at bay on the walk home. I was also sweating the entire time, as if I'd just completed a marathon. The thought of eating has my stomach twisting in knots.

"I'm sorry, Katie. I'm tired. I think I'm going to just go lie down for a bit." Giving her an apologetic smile, I make a beeline for my room. Shedding my coat, my scrubs come off next and I throw myself on my bed. All I want to do is sleep. It seems only a couple of minutes later have passed when I hear Katie lecturing me.

"Are you ever going to get up?" she asks from my doorway. Rolling over to face her, I'm barely able to crack my eyelids to make out her silhouette. My mouth feels dry and my stomach is turning in every direction.

"I'm sorry, Katie. I'm still not hungry," I mumble.

The effort alone is making me want to throw up. I'm completely soaked all over, feeling as if I just exited the shower.

"Taylor, it's morning. You slept straight through the night," she informs me, her voice sounding as if it's echoing in the room. The cool touch of her hand is felt against my forehead, and it's welcoming. "Shit, Tay. You're burning up."

Groaning, I attempt to sit up but it only makes me dizzy and I'm forced to close my eyes to keep the room from spinning. The movement threatens my stomach contents to rise up my throat, making me gag. Katie is quick to bring over my trash bin seconds before I begin to vomit. When there is nothing left to throw up, my head lands back on the pillow in a hard thud, feeling as if a hammer has pounded on it.

"I was lucky enough to not have a fever, so that must suck for you." Katie's remark makes me groan in pain. Her retreating footsteps can be heard through the darkness behind my closed lids. A few minutes later she returns and hands me some pills. Opening my eyes, I find her holding out a glass of water.

"I'll make sure to let our boss know it's your turn to stay

home," she voices before pulling the covers up over my shoulders and disappearing. The sound of the front door can be heard opening and closing soon after, notifying me she's left.

With Katie gone, the apartment is draped in silence and I'm able to drift off into sleep again. Time passes in a peaceful bliss, but I awaken when the touch of something cool wipes at my face and neck. The coolness of the cloth is refreshing on my burning forehead. With every effort I can muster, my eyes open to a slit and sitting next to me is a silhouette of a body. The scent reminds me of Nick, but I'm sure I must be dreaming. I have to be.

Awakening again, this time with the urge to pee, I push my weakened body from the bed, struggling to stand up.

"Hey, you're finally up." The deep voice causes me to snap my head up and look in its direction. Walking towards me is Nick carrying a tray containing a bowl and other contents I can't clearly make out at the moment.

"What are you doing here?" I rasp out. My throat feels dry and scratchy. "How did you even get in?"

"Katie gave me her key," he casually answers, placing the tray down on my side table before standing and sliding his hands into the pockets of his jeans. He's so tall; I have to crane my neck to look up at him, giving me a crick in my neck.

"Why?"

"She told me you had the flu now and I convinced her it'd be a good idea for me to check on you in case you got worse."

Knowing Katie wouldn't just give in so easily to his request, I skeptically look at him. "I know you're lying," I throw back at him.

He chuckles. "I may have also told her you could be here having a seizure from the fever and she wouldn't even know it." A grin spreads across his face, evidently satisfied with himself.

"That one pretty much did it for her."

Katie would have been a sucker for that proclamation.

With the heaviness of my bladder making itself known once again, I attempt to stand one more time, but my weak legs have me nearly stumbling to the floor. If it weren't for Nick's quick reflexes, I would be lying sprawled across the floor.

"You really shouldn't be getting up out of bed," he says to me, sounding upset that I even attempted to get up.

My miserable attempt to shove him away fails since my arms are so weak. The action takes the only energy I have left, leaving me slumping against his chest.

"I need to go pee," I confess, sounding pathetic when I say it.

I yelp in surprise when he picks me up and walks us down the hall towards my bathroom. I'm too delusional from the spinning still in my head to be able to enjoy the touch of our bodies. Inside the bathroom, he gently places me in the middle of the room then steps back to casually look at me.

"I've got it from here," I inform him, grabbing onto the sink for support. In the reflection of the mirror, I catch the uncertainty in his eyes. I patiently wait for him to comprehend my unwillingness to move until he leaves. When he gets the point, he gradually retreats from the bathroom, closing the door behind him. Finding my reflection in the mirror, I'm mortified when I see I'm still only wearing my bra and underwear. I'd completely forgotten I had disrobed.

Ugh . . . Great, now I have to live with the thought of knowing Nick has seen me half naked. My urge to pee has me quickly pushing the thought aside to take care of business. Washing my hands and face when done, I brush my teeth next. God only knows what my breaths smells like after this morning's retching. Wrapping myself up in a towel, I muster the strength I will need to return to my room before I open the door.

I wasn't expecting to find Nick waiting for me in the hall-way. He's standing against the wall looking impatient with his arms crossed over his chest. "Took you long enough. I was about to go in after you in another minute," he chastises.

Glaring at him for his comment, I try to take my first step out of the bathroom, but Nick is already stepping forward to pick me back up.

"Nick, I can walk," I argue, but he ignores my protest and continues back to the room, gently lowering me onto my bed. The soft feel of clean sheets brushes against my skin, unlike the ones I had awakened in. "Did you change my sheets?"

"Yeah, the other ones smelled pretty nasty," he replies, pulling my comforter up to cover me. Feeling my forehead, he grimaces while he asks, "When was the last time you took some medicine?"

"This morning. I think?" Still feeling disoriented, I can't quite remember.

"You should lie back down and I'll go search for the med-icine."

"I feel as if I've been sleeping for days."

He chuckles at my response. "That's normal. Just lie down and I'll be right back," he urges, gently shoving my shoulder back down towards the bed. The stubbornness inside of me doesn't want to lie down as I try to sit back up.

"Stay down, Taylor." This time I'm forcefully pushed back with a reprimand.

A memory resurfaces and I panic.

The image of Josh forcing me to the ground flashes through my mind. His appearance is clear, as if it's currently happening. As before, I try shoving him away with as much strength as I can muster, but I fail. I'm weak. My arms don't

CLARITY

have the strength I'm searching for. His words to stop fighting are screaming in my head. The grip on my shoulders continues to force me down, pushing me to keep fighting as I scream at the top of my lungs, praying someone will save me.

My fists are pummeling his chest. My head is thrashing back and forth with every scream. My legs have managed to kick him, giving me the chance to scramble away. It doesn't matter where; my only aim is to escape. My will to fight keeps me moving, regardless of where I'm going. I fall, landing with a thump against the ground, leaving me confused. Wasn't I already on the ground?

"Taylor!"

The deep tone of a man's voice snaps me back into action, but for some reason I'm unable to move. My chance of escape is rendered hopeless as a pair of strong arms wrap around my waist. In my mind, Josh has caught me and he's going to continue what he'd intended from the beginning.

"Get off me, Josh! Get. Off. Me!" My hysterical pleas to stop are pathetic to him as his grip tightens. I'm trapped with nowhere to go. As much as I want it to end quickly, I want him off of me. Now.

"Taylor—Taylor, please calm down, baby."

Is he actually pleading his request?

I'm usually the one begging.

Then it occurs to me, he's never held me in his arms. He's never pleaded. The deep voice rumbling next to my ear doesn't sound like him, either. This voice is calming, yet sounds so familiar and makes me fight to leave the darkness. I fight with all my might to reach for it. My fight is now to push the awful image of Josh away. The nightmare surrounding me starts to fade away and I register it's Nick's voice pulling me away. It's his voice demanding I leave the nightmare. He's still holding me

77

tightly as I slowly start to calm down.

"You're okay, I'm right here. It's only me, Nick."

"Nick?"

I can feel him rubbing his hand on my back in an effort to comfort me as he says into my ear, "It's okay, baby. It's okay." His voice is laced heavy with concern. The sound of his voice keeps pulling me back, removing me completely from the darkness that's my nightmare.

With my eyes now completely open, I see I'm not in the dark forest anymore, but in my bedroom, and I can still hear Nick murmuring into my ear to calm down. Just hearing his voice and knowing that I'm safe, I know he's right and I breakdown crying. My tears turn into uncontrollable sobs as he keeps me wrapped in his arms. My fist automatically grabs onto his shirt, refusing to allow him to pull away. Nick's voice has managed to pull me from the darkness of my nightmare.

I don't know how long I sit in Nick's arms crying, but he never once complains, leaving me gratified for the comfort. Eventually my emotions calm enough to look up into his eyes, which are curiously looking down at me.

"Hey there, you okay?"

My throat is dry and hoarse from all the screaming, or maybe the crying. I don't know which. Either way, I nod, feeling embarrassed over the entire situation.

"I'm so sorry," I rasp out.

"It's okay," he whispers, his hand smoothing the hair from my face.

His body is warm and the feeling of his breath against my ear has me shivering with delight. Leaning my head against his shoulder, I take advantage of his arms still wrapped around me. With my eyes closed, I savor his unique smell while trying to figure out why it all started.

I've only ever had those episodes in my dreams. Katie has dealt with them in the past, but never once have they occurred with anyone else, especially with a man. I've never once allowed myself in a situation where it might occur.

Feeling ashamed for still being in Nick's arms, I try standing but find I'm still too weak. Lifting me up by the hips as if I weigh nothing, Nick helps me to stand.

"Taylor, what just happened?"

With too many emotions coursing through my mind, his question is like a bucket of cold water to the memory I've just left. I wish I could tell him, but I refuse to accept his pity at this moment. I'm ashamed as it is.

"Are you going to answer me?"

"No," I answer, trying to step around him.

"Why not?"

"Because you don't need to know," I clip out as I glare at him.

Nick stays silent, but by the hurt in his eyes, I know I've offended him.

"Trust me, Nick. You don't want to know," I reply, managing to step away to the other side of the bed. "I'm so sorry for messing up the bed," I utter, trying to tidy up as much as possible to distract him.

His chuckle behind me makes me turn to face him. "It's fine. I would've preferred we mess it up another way." The comment has me growing furious, especially so soon after my episode.

"That's all you ever think of, isn't it?" I snap at him.

"Taylor, I'm sorry." His agonized tone makes me turn away. "It's just a bad habit I have." I hear his apologetic plea from across the room where he's still standing by the bed.

Already at my dresser retrieving a shirt to put on, I yank it on before taking my anger out on the drawer as I slam it shut.

"It's not your problem, it's mine. I have to learn how to deal with it," I forcefully say while trying to blink away the tears forming in my eyes. "I think it's best if you leave, Nick."

"Taylor, I don't want to leave you alone."

"Just leave!"

Silence surrounds us both for the next couple of minutes.

"I'm really sorry about what I said, Taylor," I hear him say from the doorway, his footsteps soon following his words.

Hearing the click of the front door, I finally break down and cry again, the painful memory of what I've done shattering my entire soul. Using the only ounce of energy I have left, I walk to the bed and throw myself onto the mattress, allowing the tears to fall as I lay in misery over what I have done.

EIGHT

Regrets

Taylor

I'M STILL CRYING when Katie knocks on the door. Remembering Nick borrowed her key, I get up to let her in, still crying as I open the door. Katie takes in my tear-streaked face and she looks ready to attack.

"What did he do?"

"It was my fault," I respond between sniffles as I shut the door. Her perfectly arched brow goes high, doubtful of my answer. Breaking down, I tell her everything that occurred. By the time I'm done explaining, she's trying to comfort me.

"He probably hates me," I murmur, wiping my nose with the tissue she hands me.

"He doesn't hate you, Taylor. But I wouldn't be surprised if he's confused as hell."

She grabs my hand, coercing me to open it. "What is this?" she asks, trying to take the small Post-it note I've had clutched in my hand since Nick walked out of the door. I'd taken it from my side drawer near my bed after he'd left, wanting to have a piece of him near after I'd so crudely pushed him to leave. Reading it, her eyes go wide before finding mine. "When did he give you this?"

"Monday, right before he left. We had another *disagreement* during his appointment and I'd escaped to the bathroom to hide knowing he'd go straight to my office afterwards. I found it when I got back."

A smile spreads across her lips.

"What?" I question the smirk on her face.

"I knew it!" she exclaims, looking smug with herself. "You like him."

"It's not what you think, Katie." Her eyes narrow at me with an unsatisfied scowl. "You know damn well nothing can come out of this. He was my patient."

"*Was,*" she clarifies. "He's my patient now, which means you're welcome to date him."

Shaking my head in denial, I say, "We've already gone over this. I'm not his type and he'd only resent me when I don't put out."

Rolling her eyes at my proclamation, she asks, "Who said you have to put out?"

I look at her with arched brows. "You can honestly tell me he won't expect me to have sex with him?"

"Nobody said you had to put out right away. Guys like to earn it sometimes," she voices with a wag of her brows. I glare at her for her persistency. "Taylor, give the guy a chance.

What's the worst that can happen?"

I want to say by giving him a chance he'll most likely do as Josh did—break me in more ways than one: my heart, my soul, my spirit. But to tell her all those reasons would be to admit that Nick is the first person who makes me believe it can happen again.

"I don't know, Katie," I croak out.

"You won't know unless you try," she argues.

My audible sigh has her smiling. I remain silent as she rises to walk over to the kitchen, leaving me on the couch still pondering my thoughts. She returns minutes later, handing me a glass of water and holding a glass of wine in her own hand. Tapping her glass to mine, she says, "Here's to falling in love."

"I'm not in love," I defend.

"Not yet."

My glare has returned, however it does nothing to diminish Katie's hopeful smile.

Pondering her remark, the words slowly begin to sink into my mind. It has only been a couple of weeks since I met Nick, yet he's managed to get emotionally closer than I've allowed any other man in the last six years. Even though I'am aware I should be moving forward with my life, it's hard to do when your past refuses to let you live normally.

My heart feels heavy and my eyes are full of unshed tears as I ask, "Can we not mention this again?"

Katie releases a disappointed sigh before she embraces me in a tight hug. "I can't make any promises, but I'm not letting you have any regrets for something that isn't your fault."

Katie has known from the start what happened with Josh. A week after moving in together I had my first nightmare. I'd practically scared the pants off of Katie when she heard me screaming from my room, demanding someone to get off me.

She was about to call 911, believing there was someone attacking me. But when she walked into my room to try to fight off the intruder, she didn't find anyone. She was completely confused until she realized I was simply dreaming, which sort of forced me to tell her.

I usually wake up after a couple of minutes, but every single one still feels as real as the incident. As if it were happening all over again. In the dream, no matter how much I ran or fought him, it still happened all over again. Every agonizing touch repeated from beginning to end.

Since the first night, Katie understood why I had difficulties trusting men. She'd instantly suggested therapy, which only lasted a couple of sessions. The nightmares were bad enough and having to endure the nightmare while I was wide-awake made it worse. While in therapy, the nightmares started occurring more often and it felt useless, so I stopped going. I wanted to forget, not remember, and I found discussing the situation would only do that.

Unfortunately, it was also the reason why Katie didn't bring any of her dates home with her anymore. The first time she did, the noises coming through the wall threw me into a spiral of emotions. I had to leave the apartment, ending up at the local twenty-four hour diner all night, drinking coffee and counting the hours until I could go home. When I walked into the apartment the next morning, Katie was frantic with worry since she didn't find me in bed at 3:00 A.M. After explaining what happened, Katie immediately insisted she wouldn't bring anyone home anymore. I felt awful over her decision and I kept telling her she didn't have to do that. I would eventually learn to deal with it. She didn't change her mind, though. She claimed it helped prevent her from being the bitch and kicking the guy out when she was done with him, it was easier for her. All she had to do now was leave when she chose to. No strings attached.

Katie had suggested I try dating, hoping if I found myself a decent guy I would be able to put the memory behind me. I tried. It ended up turning out to be a total disaster.

In the back of my mind, all I could do was judge them by thinking that all they wanted to do was take me home to bed me. It felt strange to even let them hold my hand. Kissing them was harder. It rarely happened and if they got lucky, it was simply a peck on the cheek. After a couple of tries, I gave up.

Nick makes me wonder if I am ready for a new beginning. He had a way of making me catch my breath, something that had yet to ever occur with any past dates. Was he the one to help me push the memory of Josh away?

It's a question I may be left asking myself if Nick is insulted by my earlier behaviors and chooses to never speak to me again. Only time will give me the answer.

Waking up the next day with the fever gone, I feel as if I've been run over by a train, but I'm able to get up and make an effort to get ready for work, not wanting to miss another day. Remembering how much of an inconvenience it was to Sarah and I when the rest of them were out sick, I didn't want to burden my co-workers with the same problem.

Even with the illness slowing me down, I manage to make it out of the door only three minutes late. Katie is surprisingly not nagging me, leaving me hopeful that today might me a good day.

Halfway through the morning, I enter the office to find Katie on the phone having a casual conversation. "Yeah, she came in today," she says into the receiver. Her response doesn't alarm me quite yet, until I hear her reply. "No, she's not mad at you. I swear." She glances in my direction.

I take a seat at my desk, staring at her with alarm.

"Great, I'll see you on Monday, then," she says before hanging up the phone.

Suspicion is slowly traveling throughout my mind. Somehow my conscience is alerting me to the fact that the person on the other end of the phone may have been Nick.

Leaning back into my chair, I now glare at her. "Who was that?" I ask, trying to keep my voice calm and unsuspicious.

"It was Nick," she casually answers, adding a shrug of her shoulder while shuffling the paperwork in front of her, acting as if she's tidying up her already organized desk.

She's definitely hiding something.

"And why would you need to tell him that I was fine?" I irritably drag out the question.

"He wanted to know if you were mad at him about yesterday." Her face cringes with her response, as if she knows I'm about to blow. Why the heck would he ask Katie? Why couldn't he just call me and ask me himself?

Chicken shit.

Rolling my eyes and shaking my head, I turn to face my computer, needing the distraction. I still feel like crap, so I'll blame my sour attitude on my illness.

"You said last night you weren't mad at him," I hear her say. "He would have asked anyway at his next appointment."

Without looking at her, I ask, "Does he usually ask about me during his appointments?"

From my peripheral vision, I watch her eyes light up. "Of course, every single one."

"In the future I'd appreciate it if you'd keep me out of your conversations," I resentfully let out.

I don't know what I'm more pissed about, the fact that I was stupid enough to fall for either of their traps, or that they're discussing me without my knowledge.

I see her open her mouth to say something, but quickly closes it the moment she's paged over the intercom. It saves me from an argument that I know would have occurred had she continued to pursue the conversation.

Katie stands to depart the office, leaving me relieved that she's gone. It allows me to release the breath I hadn't known I was holding. Now ignoring my computer, my mind returns to my conversation with Katie, realizing she's at it again. She's trying to find another potential candidate for me to date. When is she ever going to understand that not every girl is cut out for happily ever after, especially with someone like Nick? He's clearly pointed out his lifestyle and I was not intending to be another notch on his bedpost. Sighing to myself, I get back to work, pushing all the thoughts from my mind and forcing myself to focus on my job. I have so much to catch up on because of my absence yesterday.

Three hours later, I'm finishing up with another patient and returning to my office when I begin to sneeze. At first, I don't make anything of it, until it continues in a rapid procession. By this point, I look around in search of any blooming flowers; they are the only reason why I would be uncontrollably sneezing. There aren't any bouquets in view so I'm confident my sneezing bout will soon end.

I proceed to my office, knowing I have Benadryl in my desk to help with my allergies, the source of my condition stares back at me. My office looks like the showroom of a local flower shop. There are flowers in every corner and crevice you can place a vase, and in every type of assortment you can think of. My eyes go wide as I suck in a shocked breath. It only makes it worse. Stumbling back to try to escape, I collide with the file cabinet standing in my office. A large bouquet of flowers falls upon me, the pollen of the sunflowers dropping onto my face feeling as if nails are traveling down my lungs, constricting my every breath. Tossing the arrangement vase and all to the floor, it lands with a loud crash as the glass shatters.

I'm still uncontrollably sneezing, shuddering from head to toe with an ache following every sneeze. My stomach is tense, my throat feeling as if sandpaper is grating against the walls of my windpipe with every sneeze I let out.

My office phone starts ringing, and I debate whether I should let it go to voicemail or not. The decision to answer outweighs the need to escape as I remember I'm expecting an important phone call from my boss. Forcing myself to take the steps to my desk, the sneezing subsides for a moment, leaving me to think I'd be able to handle the call. "Hello," I manage to get out in between a sneeze and an intake of breath before I sneeze again. "This is Tay—Tay—Taylor," I barely get out the last of my name before sneezing again into the phone.

I can't even imagine how unprofessional it must have sounded on the other end. However, there's no controlling it and the sneezing starts all over again. By the grace of God, Katie walks into the room, taking the receiver from me. It allows me to grab some tissue from her desk to blow my nose, but instead I sneeze into it. My stomach is cramping to the point that I just drop to my knees, wrapping my arms around my waist, as if it would help relieve the pain. Of course, it doesn't.

I can hear Katie talking into the phone, her voice full of worry. Looking up, she's staring down at me with concerned eyes. "Yeah, she got them, but she's deadly allergic to flowers," she says into the phone, still looking at me as I sneeze over and over again while clutching my stomach. I can't even move because I don't have the strength or balance to get up. The pollen from the flowers is everywhere, and there's no escaping it.

"What the hell were you thinking?" she growls into the phone. I know for sure it's not our boss on the other end of the line by the way she's talking to the person. There's no way she would speak to him like that, at least if she valued her job. "Yes, I mentioned it, you dumbass! During our first visit, remember?" I hear her say in between my sneezing. "Fine, but if you kill her, it's on *your* ass!" she yells before slamming the phone down and rushing over to me.

I'm on the ground on my hands and knees, trying to crawl out of the office because I have no strength left, but I'm desperate to get away from all the flowers. That alone makes me try. Katie helps me stand up then leads me down the hallway in a rush to get as far away from our office as possible. I can barely hear her barking orders at someone to donate all the flowers to the labor and delivery ward at the hospital before she informs them that she's taking me to the allergy department.

My sneezing slowly subsides, but is soon replaced with an uncontrollable itch as we make our way towards the other side of the building.

What feels like hours later, but was really only minutes, we walk into the allergy department. They take one look at me and lead us immediately into a room. One advantage of working in a specialty building is that you have connections everywhere, and today those connections were going to practically save my life. The doctor takes in my labored breathing then orders the nurse to immediately give me an antihistamine injection. Once she does that, within minutes, I'm able to breathe again. As I'm lying on the exam table trying to comprehend what happened, Katie is at my bedside rubbing my arms, trying to calm my nerves. I remember most of the conversation she had on the phone and realize that she knows who sent me the flowers. She was pretty pissed at them for doing so.

"Who sent all those flowers?" I rasp out in between the slow breaths I'm taking. Katie bites her bottom lip and I roll my eyes.

I'm not going to like this answer.

"I'm so sorry, Taylor," she guiltily replies, looking down at her hands that she's nervously wringing. "It was Nick."

Letting out a groan, trying to calm my breathing. I stare at the white ceiling above me, pondering why he would do such a thing.

"Was he trying to kill me?" I unintentionally ask the question aloud.

"No, Tay. He was trying to apologize, but he says he forgot that I mentioned you were allergic to flowers in our conversations." Her body cringes when she answers. I know she's also blaming herself for the flowers, and as cruel as it sounds, I do too. She shouldn't have been discussing my personal life with Nick.

Taking in another deep breath, trying to fill my lungs with pollen free air, I throw my arm over my eyes and try to push away the new nightmare that is going to now haunt my dreams: attack of the blooming flowers!

When the doctor comes in some time later to check on me, she writes me an excuse for work in hopes that they'll let me go home. When I look over to the clock on the wall to take in the time, I see it's practically the end of the day, so I don't see how it would be a problem. When I'm given permission by the allergist to return to my own department, my boss is already expecting me. He immediately came rushing over after another employee had called him to tell him I was dying on my office floor—an overreaction to the situation. Taking one look at the state I'm in, he sends me home. Even though it is only two hours early, I wasn't going to complain. The sooner I get to leave this nightmare that is today, the better, even if it means taking the L home.

Unfortunately, during the walk to the L, I receive many awkward glances from strangers. It was making me wonder just how bad I appeared.

As soon as I step onto the train, I go straight over to a mirrored wall to take in my reflection, instantly regretting doing so. My eyes are slightly puffy and every inch of skin is still faintly covered with blotchy red spots, a reminder of my reaction.

Taking a deep breath, I know I have to allow time for it to eventually go away; I tell myself there's nothing I can do at this point but be patient. Thankfully, I'm alone on my train and hope it remains that way the entire ride home. Within the hour, I'm exiting the L and on my way to my apartment. I've never felt more relieved in my life, until I see Nick sitting in the hallway, leaning against my door. His knees are drawn up with his feet flat on the floor so he can support his extended arms as he stares at the smartphone in his hand. As if he's heard my footsteps, his head jerks in my direction, his eyes immediately growing sympathetic when he takes me in. Just as rapidly, he stands to meet me half-way.

"What are you doing here, Nick?" I ask, already digging into my purse for my keys. Finding them, I'm about to insert the key into the doorknob when Nick stops me, requesting I face him as he speaks.

"I was heading to your office, but Katie told me you were gone when I called to check on you. I came here instead," he explains. "I was worried something really bad might have happened to you when I realized you were allergic to flowers." His apologetic gaze stares back at me before his hand reaches up and caresses my cheek.

"I'm so sorry, Taylor," he tenderly whispers. "I never meant for this to happen. I swear. I completely forgot that Katie told me about the flowers. Lately she's been throwing so many hints at me about you that it started to all blend together."

I remain silent, returning to my resentful reaction as he reminds me they were discussing me without my knowledge.

"Most girls want flowers sent to them when they're upset, but as much as I kept racking my brain trying to remember which flower she mentioned were your favorite, I couldn't recall. So I had the florist send you a little of everything," he says, shamefully sighing. "Now I know why she never mentioned a favorite flower. I really *am* sorry, Taylor. Please tell me how to make it up to you." His pleading eyes are bearing down at me, begging me to forgive him.

"Just don't send me flowers again," I murmur around the lump lodged in my throat.

His eyes light up.

"Promise," he says then pauses, allowing the silence to surround us.

"Is it okay if I stay until Katie gets here? She asked me to make sure you don't have another reaction."

"Is Katie asking, or are you using it as an excuse to stay?" I ask, remembering how manipulative he can be.

Smirking, his hand goes to the back of his neck to massage it. "To be honest, I used her as an excuse. But she did say she'd be home soon and I'd really like to spend some time with you until she gets here," he pleads.

"Fine." I surrender to the guilt he's making me feel in return.

Taking a deep breath before I turn the knob, Nick patiently waits until I allow him entrance before stepping into my apartment. His hands are tucked into the pockets of his jeans as he looks around the room apprehensively.

"Do you want anything to drink?" I warily ask, trying to break the awkwardness between us.

"I'm fine."

With my throat still feeling parched, I make my way over to the kitchen to pour myself a glass of water. Returning to the living room shortly after, Nick is already seated in the middle of the only couch in the room. His eyes find mine, regret still evident in his gaze. It helps calm my anxiety of being alone with him.

My heart starts to beat erratically, my nerves slowly being replaced by a sense of giddiness. The room is draped in silence, making every beat of my heart echo in my ears. My breath hitches when he reaches over and takes my hand with his and gently begins to caress it with his fingertips. A jolt of sparks travel through my blood from his touch.

"Do you need anything? Maybe some allergy medicine?"

Swallowing the lump currently sitting in the center of my throat, I say, "I'm fine. They gave me an antihistamine injection at work, so I think I'm set for the next couple of hours."

My mouth still feels as if it's stuffed full of cotton balls, reminding me of the glass of water sitting in my hand. Taking a gulp, I keep my eyes on Nick.

"I really am sorry about today, Taylor."

"You can stop apologizing, Nick. You didn't do it on purpose," I say before taking another sip of water, not knowing what else to convey to him. Looking down at our joined hands, I'm lost by the sight of our connection. "Since I already know you don't like flowers, what is it you do like?" he asks, breaking my trance.

I consider his question for a moment before answering.

"Chocolate. I like chocolate, and I already know I'm not allergic to it," I laugh out.

"I guess I should have known you'd like chocolate. It's sweet like you." His crooked smile melts my insides as he keeps rubbing his thumb across the back of my hand.

The sensation of his touch is something I'm still unfamiliar with. The tenderness of the act was rare even with Josh, when he *did* hold my hand. The thought of Josh's name sends me spiraling back to his memory.

"Taylor?" Nick's deep voice pulls me from my ghastly daze.

Standing, feeling the need to put some sort of distance between Nick and I, I'm a mere step from the couch when he brings me to a halt. "Did I say something wrong?"

Trying to reassure him, I shake my head no. "It's not you, Nick. I just have issues you don't need to know about," I say, turning away to avoid his gaze.

"I know, Taylor."

The blood drains from my face, terrified Katie told him about Josh. Turning to face him, I search his face for any sort of disgust he might feel towards me. "What exactly *do you* know?" I rasp out, barely able to form the words.

"I know from the way you were screaming the other day it's something serious."

"You have no idea," I reply, dragging out the words.

"Then tell me."

"No." Shaking my head again, I refuse his request.

"Why not?" he pleads. "Maybe I can help."

"You getting what you want isn't going to help. It will only make it worse."

Startled from my remark, he asks, "What exactly is it I want?"

"Don't act stupid. You're just looking for an easy way to get me to have sex with you."

He's taken aback by my words, flinching as if I'd slapped him across the face. "Is that what you think I'm after? Just getting you to have sex with me?"

"Of course you are. The only difference is at least you're trying to earn it, instead of demanding it."

His expression turns from disbelief to anger at my declaration. It's then I know I've disclosed more information than I should have.

"It'll never happen, Nick, so why keep trying?"

"Because you're different, Taylor. I've known it since the first day I met you."

"Yes, I am. I can barely let a guy close enough to kiss me so you're wasting your time," I shamefully admit.

He steps forward, closing the distance between us. My attempts to keep retreating are broken when my back hits the wall. He stands in front of me, his blue eyes staring down into mine. His hands come to rest on my hips, trapping me in place. My breathing becomes shallow as his lips curve up into a half-smile.

"Then I can consider myself lucky if I'm able to do this." His lips slowly meet mine. No longer accustomed to the feeling of being kissed, anxiety spreads inside of me. The feel of his lips lingering on mine are gentle, unrushed. The beat of my heart is racing as my breath hitches, afraid it's all simply a dream. Gradually my eyes close, wanting to savor the feeling of all that is happening at this moment.

Slowly he brings our kiss to an end, causing my eyes to open, worried I've done something wrong. I'm stunned to find him hesitantly staring down at me, his eyes searching for any type of reaction. Before I can question what's wrong, he lowers his head back down again and our mouths are fused once more, my eyes automatically closing as before. His tongue pushes against my lips and I willingly open up to him, my senses spiraling out of control when my tongue meets his. The taste of his mouth is like nothing I've ever experienced before, instantly intoxicating.

His body leans into mine, pushing me further against the wall. The nightmarish feeling of being trapped hits me full force, frightening me. Using all my strength, my hands shove against his chest, my once giddy heartbeat now racing from terror.

"What's wrong?"

"You have to go," I say, unable to catch my breath.

"Why?"

"Please, Nick," I whimper, my frantic mind full of uncontrollable emotions.

Suddenly, Katie walks in the door. Taking in my fearful state, she asks, "Tay, you okay?" She gives Nick a worried look as I nod my head in response.

"Nick was just leaving," I tell her. Looking over to Nick, I narrow my eyes into a slit to emphasize my demand.

"I was?"

"Yes, I think you should go now," I croak out.

His confusion is replaced with sympathy before he steps forward, taking my head between his palms and kissing me on the temple. "I'm leaving to give you time, Taylor, but I'm not giving up," he declares, sounding like a promise.

Stepping away, he leaves the apartment without glancing back. Katie shuts the door behind him before turning to face me.

"Taylor, are you okay?" she repeats.

"I'm fine, Katie," I answer, bringing my fingers up to my still pulsating lips, his words repeating like a broken record.

With a hint of a smile, she turns to walk to her room, leaving me alone with my thoughts. Minutes later, I make my way to my bedroom with Nick's kiss still overtaking my feelings. Reaching for the Post-it note I keep tucked in my bedside table, I tightly clutch it in my hand as I fall asleep pondering what it is about Nick Hunter that has me infatuated with him, hoping the thoughts will keep me from my nightmares of my past.

NINE

Little gestures

Taylor

WHO WOULD HAVE known what a difference a few days could make? The days can come and go, people arrive and depart, and through it all, little gestures to make one think of someone are made.

For the past four days, Nick has kept his presence in my mind. His promise of no more flowers was kept. Instead, in their place, was chocolate. It never occurred to me that he'd overwhelm me with the gesture, but it was sweet in more ways than I could have ever imagined.

It's now Monday afternoon and I have yet to see Nick since my allergic reaction and his absence is alarming. Little gestures can only go so far when my mind is still wondering what his words could have truly meant.

I'm sitting in my office wrapping up the final notes for my patient's charts when I hear a light knock on my office door. When I look up my eyes find Nick smiling back at me. Instantly, my heart halts, but just as rapidly starts beating back to life. An unexplainable giddiness spreads inside of me. For the last four days, both my mind and heart have constantly been thinking of the man standing just mere feet away from me.

"You almost done?" his deep husky voice glides across the room, hitting me full force, leaving me with incoherent thoughts. "Taylor?"

Shaking my head, I attempt to clear the fog it was sitting in. "Uh?"

Taking the steps needed to close the distance between us, he places his hands on the desk and leans across the front of it.

"Miss me?"

If he only knew . . .

His laughter fills the room, as if he's read my thoughts, making me blush. "Thank you for the chocolates, by the way," I say, feeling the need to change the subject. Returning my attention to the files in front of me, I use them as an excuse to break eye contact with him.

"Was it enough?"

Now I'm the one laughing. Opening the largest drawer I have in my desk—which used to house my purse at one point—it is now filled to the brim with every chocolate possibly made in the world. With a wave of my hand to show him the inside, I say, "I think I'm set for the next year, thank you."

"Good."

"Would you like some?"

He tilts his head to answer, his gaze entirely focused on

my lips. "No, thank you, but there's something else I'd prefer."

"I bet you would," I breathlessly reply.

My erratic heartbeat has returned, and I'm having trouble breathing. Turning my attention to my computer, I try to bring myself under control. Glancing back at Nick, I find him leaning against Katie's desk. He's standing with his arms tightly crossed at his chest, showcasing his broad shoulders. My mind ponders what could be underneath his shirt and how it would feel to run my hands across his bare skin.

"You keep looking at me like that and I may have to take back the promise I made to myself." His husky voice breaks me from my trance of erotic thoughts. Before I can ask about said promise, he asks, "What time do you get off?"

Before answering, I force myself to clear my mind. "In another half hour, maybe. Why?"

His lips curve into a half smile. "Good, 'cause I have plans for us."

"And what would those plans include?" I ask with my eyebrows drawn up in curiosity.

He shakes his head. "It's a surprise." The mischievous look on his face worries me, especially because I hate not knowing what to expect. It must be obvious. "It's just something for us to spend time together. Nothing more," he reassures me.

His declaration causes me to grow lightheaded with excitement. What the hell is going on with me? I would never have allowed this to happen before, and now I'm starting to see that with Nick it's happening a lot more than I can comprehend. Needing to take control of the situation, at least this one as best as I can, I ask, "What are you doing back here, anyway?"

He looks at me, puzzled by the question. "I thought we already worked that out. You're leaving with me," he says, sounding confident.

Shaking my head at him, I clarify my question. "I meant, what are you doing *back here*. You know you're not supposed to be back here," I say, looking at the door, once again wondering where the hell the security guard is at. I am really starting to question what it is he does around here.

Nick chuckles, bringing my attention back to him. "If you're wondering about the security guard, he's a really big fan and I might have promised him a couple of days' worth of tickets to turn his eye for all the times I come back here," he states, looking smug as he responds.

Rolling my eyes at him, I'm not surprised that he would stoop so low as to bribe someone to come back here. No wonder why the guard was never in sight when Nick was near.

Gathering up my files, I stack them neatly into a pile on my desk. From the corner of my eye, I watch Nick make his way around my desk to stand in front of me. His movement has me anxious from the anticipation of being near him. My anxiety increases when he lowers himself down in a crouching position so his face is directly level with mine. I can feel my chest rising and falling, matching my breathless pants.

He places his hands on each armrest of my chair, locking me in place. "I wonder what little wicked things you're thinking of with the look you're giving me." My eyes must look like saucers from how shocked I am by his words.

Snapping out of the seductive stupor my mind was completely lost to, I gently shove him away. "Get over yourself, Nick. Not every girl is going to throw herself at you," I proclaim.

His booming laughter vibrates throughout the room. "Good, because that's the kind of girl I'm looking for," he says, grabbing my hand and tugging me to stand. My chest crashes against his, allowing him to wrap his arms around my waist. If I weren't already in shock from being flush against Nick's body, his lips meeting mine would have easily sent me there.

Willingly, I open up to him, allowing his tongue access. The sensation of our tongues gliding against each other's sends me to another world. Seconds later, the feel of his lips pulling away leaves me mourning the loss of our connection. Opening my eyes, which had automatically closed, I find Nick seductively staring down at me.

"I've been dying to do that for days."

I'm trying to control my racing heart and my breathing, which is now practically to the point of hyperventilating.

"Why don't we get out of here?"

My head slowly nods in approval even though my mind is racing with doubt, still questioning what Nick's intentions are for the night. I have to remind myself of the deal I'd made with myself after Nick left the other night. It was finally time I stopped allowing my past to determine my future.

Nick leads me from my office and down the hallway to the exit. The entire time his hand is tightly clasped with mine and my inner school girl returns as we walk side by side. There was once a person who had helped me discover her, but it was the same person who forced me to lock her away for what I thought would be forever. It wasn't until Nick came into my life that she began to reluctantly reemerge. With a surreptitious glance, I find Nick smiling at me.

When we reach Nick's car, he leans against the passenger door, pulling me against his chest as he gives me a full-blown, make my knees weak, kiss. If he wasn't holding me, I'm pretty sure I would've collapsed to the floor. My hands automatically go to his shoulders, needing something to hold onto while my mouth receives and gives the kiss with as much enthusiasm as he's giving.

Breathlessly, we slowly bring the kiss to an end. "I missed you *so much* this weekend." His confession replicates how I felt. Placing one last kiss on my temple, he gently pushes me away. "Come on, let's get out of here. I don't want to do anything I'll regret," he says, sounding remorseful.

What the hell was that supposed to mean?

I climb into the car after he opens the door for me and wait while he enters on his side. Before he starts the car, he pulls out his phone and begins texting on it. I'm sitting in my seat, distracted by my thoughts, pondering the meaning behind his comment. Soon he's driving out of the building. I'm oblivious as to where we are going until he pulls into the same garage his car was parked in during the night he took me home from the club.

"Where are we?" I ask, confused.

Alarm bells ring in my mind. What exactly were his intentions when he mentioned a *"surprise"*?

"I thought we'd have dinner together," he answers with a heartfelt smile before exiting his side of the car and rushing over to mine.

"I'm not dressed for dinner, Nick," I say, looking down at my scrubs.

"You're perfect," he replies, tugging me out of the car and towards an elevator. Twelve floors later, the doors open to a hallway of apartment doors. Leading me down the hallway, he comments, "I know a restaurant would have been more romantic, but I selfishly wanted you to myself," he explains when we reach his door.

When he opens door, I notice the apartment is illuminated by the glow of candlelight. It's breathtakingly beautiful.

Walking inside the apartment, he leads me further into the room towards a table near a large glass window overlooking the city. "I figured dinner here at my place would be just as perfect."

The gesture makes me smile. My eyes turn to find the night sky brightened by the twinkling lights of the city gleaming through the window, and with the candle glow behind me, it feels majestic.

"I hope you're hungry because Julia has made a very delicious dinner," he remarks as he helps me into my seat at the table. I look down at the elegantly set table as he takes a seat. Within seconds, there are plates being placed in front of us.

"You really didn't have to do all this for me," I shyly reply, somehow feeling unworthy of the effort he's put into dinner. From the savory aromas wafting off the plates, my stomach is arguing otherwise and demanding I stay.

"I think your stomach would say otherwise," he says with a light chuckle from across the table, as if reading my thoughts.

"Let's eat," he orders already reaching for a bottle of wine sitting on the table. He grabs for my glass and before he takes it, I stop him. "It's okay, I don't want any," I inform him.

"Are you sure? It's vintage and would complement the steak very well."

"I'm sure. I'm fine with water."

He looks puzzled, but nods his head. "I'll have water as well, then," he says as he sets the bottle back on the table.

He reaches for his silverware, allowing me to relax. Unable to resist the mouthwatering feast in front of me, I too am soon lifting my utensils and cutting into the steak.

The conversation during dinner is kept light. The crazy weather Chicago has been blessed with, small stories of what we do to endure it. I'd at first feared he'd automatically begin asking me questions about my past, but surprisingly he never did, leaving me relieved. With the delicious dinner sitting in our stomachs, Nick is soon leading me to the couch so we can sit.

"Thank you for dinner. It was delicious."

"You're welcome. It's one of the reasons why I refuse to let my housekeeper go, regardless of all the raises she demands," he voices, following his gaze in the direction in which an older lady is now clearing the table.

"You're that bad, huh?" I laugh out.

Nonchalantly, he shrugs his shoulder. "Some days, I know I can be," he admits. "I've missed you being my therapist."

"I was barely even your therapist."

He brings his hand up to my face to tuck a loose strand of hair behind my ear, his thumb now slowly grazing my chin. "Taylor, you're the reason I keeping going. If not, I would have stopped showing up after that first day."

"It didn't seem that way at first," I complain. "Nick, what was the *real* reason why you didn't show up that morning I had you transferred?" I bravely ask, remembering the reason why I had him transferred. "The truth, Nick, not an excuse," I order.

He lets out a heavy sigh as regret overtakes his appearance. Running his hand behind his neck, he begins to massage it, a sight I've become familiar with when he's nervous. "You were right. I was hung-over that morning, but I didn't think you'd make a big deal about my excuse. It usually works with every-one else."

My resentment is high as I reply, "I never figured you for a liar, Nick, but you've proven me wrong."

He looks ashamed. "Taylor," he pleads, grabbing for my hand. My attempt to tug it away is unsuccessful. "I had every intention of going in. It meant seeing you, but I fucked up and made a terrible mistake. I'm still trying everything within my power to make it right. I swear."

The words hit me like an arrow straight to my heart, leaving me breathless and indecisive of what I should do. Believe him and forgive him, or walk completely away while I still have the chance? Oddly enough, I follow my heart and forgive.

"Don't lie to me anymore," I demand.

"Never again," he declares before pulling me forward and fusing our mouths together. His kiss is gentle, as if he's conveying his promise with just this one kiss.

My arms automatically wrap around his neck. His hands gently tug at my hips, lifting me towards him. Understanding his request, I straddle his hips, our lips never severing their contact. The kiss instantly takes away all the worry I had arrived with earlier.

I can feel my heart speeding with every second passing, growing excited with knowing I'm allowing myself to let go. Just as quickly, it comes to an end when the doorbell rings. Startled, I break our kiss as I blankly look down at Nick.

He looks toward the door with confusion as his housekeeper—who is apparently still here—greets the visitor. My wayward mind had completely forgotten she was still in the apartment. I'm embarrassed at the thought of how indecent we must have looked just a moment ago.

My mind doesn't have a moment to register the thought before there is bellowing coming from the foyer. "Nick is always willing to see me," says a female voice.

Jumping as fast as I can to climb off Nick, he's already standing to leave me sitting on the couch. Turning to see what he is so anxious to get to, a blonde is already lunging herself at Nick, pulling at his neck and kissing him fully on the lips. From where I'm watching, he doesn't make any attempt to push her away, only stopping when she pulls away with a satisfied smile on her lips. "I've missed you so much." Her softened purr disgusts me.

"What are you doing here, Tracie?" Nick asks her.

"I just got back from Europe and was lonely," she says,

running her hand down his chest towards his groin. It's taking all my willpower to not gag up my dinner. Nick looks down to her, seemingly confused for a moment, but just as quickly his head is snapping in my direction.

I'm shocked, unable to move as both their faces are now looking at me.

"Who is she?" the girl demands, her eyes shooting daggers at me.

"Nobody," I declare, finding the strength needed to make myself move. Marching my way towards the door, Nick attempts to grab me, but I side step around his hand and hastily walk straight out the door.

TEN

Skeletons of the past

Nick

"TAYLOR!" I SHOUT after her, but Tracie is firmly holding onto me with her arms still wrapped around my neck. Struggling to detangle myself from her arms, I watch Taylor walk out my front door, furious.

"Tracie, you have to leave," I announce, hating myself for taking so long to come to my senses.

"Who is she?" she repeats.

Using all my force, I finally manage to dislodge myself from Tracie's hold. Looking between the door and Tracie, who is still looking at me for an answer, I'm baffled.

"She's a . . . friend."

CLARITY

Tracie snickers. "Whatever. I should have known you wouldn't keep it in your pants while I was gone."

"There isn't anything going on between us!"

"I would hope so. The last thing I need is another cheating boyfriend."

Growling in frustration, I remember a girlfriend is the last thing I want at this moment. The words hit me like a brick, awakening my senses. They're the words I constantly repeat to myself to avoid this type of situation, but I know what I want now, and it's already walked out the door.

Without a backwards glance, I run out my front door and rush into the hallway. Slamming on the button for the elevator, it takes its sweet ass time to open. Looking up to see it's moving downwards, most likely with Taylor in it, I'm running to the stairs in hopes of catching her.

While rushing down the steps a dreadful feeling spreads in the pit of my stomach, knowing I won't catch Taylor in time at this rate. I pull out my cell phone and call the doorman, ordering him to stop Taylor before she can exit the building. Twelve flights of stairs on a still sensitive ankle takes longer than I would have expected. By the time I reach the lobby, it's empty. Running outside, Taylor is nowhere in sight. Frustrated, I walk back into the building, already taking my anger out on the doorman. "Why didn't you stop her like I told you to?"

"I tried, sir, but by the time I got your phone call she was rushing past me."

"Fuck!" I growl, fisting my hair in my hands.

Knowing she's most likely heading home, I hastily return to my apartment, taking the elevator this time. After knocking on the door, Julia opens it with apologetic eyes.

"I'm sorry, sir. She pushed her way through, even after I told her you were unavailable."

"It's okay, Julia. She left, though, right?" I ask, already making my way over to the counter to retrieve my keys and wallet.

"No, sir. She's in your bedroom," she answers. Shockingly looking at her, her eyes are refusing to meet mine. Stalking my way over to my bedroom, I find Tracie sprawled out naked on my bed, her legs wide open and her hands already pleasuring herself.

"Get out!" I bellow.

Stunned, she sits up, shocked at my demand. Gathering up her clothes, I throw them at her. "Put your fucking clothes on, Tracie, and get out!"

Grabbing for her clothes, her mouth is gaping open. "What is wrong with you?"

"I don't want you here."

"Why are you acting like this all of a sudden? Is it because of that girl?"

"How many times do I have to tell you? There is nothing going on between us. Never has. Never will be."

She looks at me as if I've lost my mind. "Why in the hell would you keep inviting me back to fuck you, then?"

"Exactly that. To fuck you. Nothing more."

Her eyes are welling up with tears and my heart fills with sympathy at the sight. "Tracie, I'm sorry if you thought other-wise, but you're not what I really want."

She looks towards my doorway as realization crosses her face. "You've slumped pretty low if that's what you're choosing over me," she argues, pointing at my door. I'm angered by her judgment of Taylor, but elect to keep silent instead of spewing my hateful words at her. I know I've done enough damage from the tears rolling down her cheeks. "Don't come crying to me when you realize your mistake!" she whimpers.

"I'll make sure not to," I announce, watching her dress, refusing to leave her alone. I'd rather escort her out, to guarantee she wouldn't be here when I return, than chance her still being here. Angrily, she stomps from my room and straight out my front door.

I don't follow the path she takes. Climbing into my car, I dig through my pocket in search of my phone. Looking through my contacts, it then occurs to me I don't have Taylor's number.

Shit!

There hasn't been a chance for me to ask for it.

The drive to Taylor's feels like the longest I've ever made. The traffic lights are adding to my frustration. The entire time my mind is thinking of ways to apologize to Taylor, how to reconcile yet another fucking mistake I've made with her. When I reach her apartment, I rush up the stairs and to her door, urgently banging on it. I'm determined to speak with her, regardless of how pissed I know she is with me. Instead of Taylor answering the door, it's a confused looking Katie staring back at me.

"Where's Taylor?" I ask, pushing my way around her and into the apartment. I can't risk Katie denying me the chance to see Taylor. Rushing my way to her room, I find it empty. Turning around, I see Katie scowling at me with her hands on her hips.

"What did do you do?"

"I fucked up," I answer, raking my hand through my hair.

Katie's eyes go wide. "You didn't try having sex with her, did you?"

"What? No!"

What demons does Taylor have that would warrant Katie championing her this way? Katie's question and Taylor's past references, leaves me to believe it has something to do with sex. It's probably why she wouldn't let me anywhere near her at first. Still worried from not finding her, I ask Katie, "Do you have her number?"

Katie's brow arches as she considers my question. Instead of giving it to me, she turns to walk away, leaving me standing in the room alone.

What the fuck?

Quickly following her, she's now in the kitchen searching through her phone and then raising it to her ear. I'm silently watching her, praying Taylor will answer. The disappointment on her face worries me.

"She didn't answer," she says, attempting to call again, but from the disappointed sigh she most likely received the same results. "She always answers my calls. It's a rule between us," she explains.

"You better tell me what the fuck you did to her to make her ignore my calls," she demands with angered eyes.

The fury in her voice adds to the guilt I've been carrying since the moment I went running after her.

"We were talking and a girl showed up." With the look she's giving me, she can tell I'm not being fully truthful. "She just showed up at my apartment and started kissing me while Taylor was in the room. I never intended for it to happen. Tracie sort of caught me off guard and I was confused as hell."

"You're an asshole!"

Sighing in defeat, I cannot argue with her. I feel like an asshole.

"Do you know where she might be?"

She's still glaring at me with narrowed eyes as she answers, "No. Taylor is . . . sensitive. That's the easiest way to put it. It's taken me forever to get her to trust a guy, and you go and do something to fuck it up."

"Why wouldn't she trust me?"

She opens her mouth as if she's about to explain, but shakes her head at me. "It's not my secret to tell. But I'm warning you," she glares at me, "you hurt her, and I will kill you!"

Her phones rings and I grow excited, thinking it's Taylor. Katie looks down at her phone. "It's not her. It's my date," she informs me before answering the call.

At that moment, the door opens and in walks Taylor. She still looks furious as she notices me in the room. Unable to resist, I rush over to her, engulfing her in my arms, her body immediately going rigid as I hug her.

"I'm sorry," I tell her.

She pushes me away without looking at me. "That seems to be all you're ever saying lately."

"Why didn't you answer my phone calls?" Katie reprimands as Taylor walks away and straight into the kitchen. She's expressionless the entire walk over, as if nothing has occurred.

She pours herself a glass of water before she replies. "I don't have my phone. It's in my purse that's in Nick's car."

"How did you get home?"

Not looking at me but at Katie, as she answers, "I was lucky there weren't any cops on the L tonight," she nonchalantly answers.

Shit. It hadn't occurred to me that her purse could be in my car. The guilt is now overpowering every ounce of my blood.

"Didn't you have a date tonight?" she asks Katie, still looking blank as she takes a sip from her cup.

"I do, but I don't know if I should go now." Katie glares in my direction.

Taylor gives her an encouraging wave of her hand. "Go. I'm fine."

"Are you sure?"

"Yeah, I already know he can't do anything to hurt me."

What the hell is that supposed to mean?

Katie returns to staring daggers at me. "I've warned you," she says, reminding me of her threat before grabbing her purse and exiting the apartment.

"What are you doing here, Nick? I would have expected you to still be back in your apartment."

"It's not what you think, Taylor."

Arching her brow in question at me, she says, "And what is it exactly that I'm thinking, Nick? Please, enlighten me."

Her reaction is both terrifying and confusing. Never in my life has a girl responded like she's currently doing. Take Tracie for example, she was still raging when she'd left my apartment. Taylor's reaction is the opposite, calm as if she's shutting herself off of all emotion.

"She's nothing to me. I swear."

She snickers at me. I'll accept it. It's better than nothing.

"It's clear she's more than nothing, Nick. She wouldn't have been throwing herself at you like that if she wasn't," she simplifies.

Sighing, I take a moment to choose the words for my explanation. "She's just a girl I had a couple of one night stands with. She's the one that wouldn't get it through her head that that's all they were."

"Poor girl," she replies.

"Taylor, what is wrong with you?"

She now looks taken aback. "What's wrong with me?" she asks.

"I mean. You're standing there acting like this was no big deal."

"How the fuck do you expect me to act? Do you want me yelling at you?"

"Yes."

"Why? It wouldn't change anything between us. There was never anything at all."

Stepping forward only makes her retreat. The fearful doe eyes I'm beginning to become familiar with are now on her face. It makes me stop, fearful of frightening her. Anger I will happily accept at this moment. Fear, never.

"I know that's what you think, but I swear it's what I was trying to change. I've seen it in your eyes since the day I've met you. You're not the type of girl who expects to be rushed. I was giving you time. I thought we were getting somewhere tonight, and then Tracie showed up and fucked it up for me. I'm going to repeat, there is nothing going on between her and me. There never was." Her silence is heartbreaking. She looks as if she wants to say something, but is refusing to do so. "Please, Taylor, just say something," I plead, hoping to encourage her.

"This is why I don't trust men. They couldn't care less who they hurt."

No longer caring how she'll react, I close the distance between us, taking her face in my hands and kissing her. For the first second she doesn't respond, but eventually her once rigid body relaxes as she holds onto me, her lips surrendering to my kiss. When we break apart, I feel a tear gliding down the back of my hand. She opens her eyes but keeps them downcast, refusing to look at me.

"My intention was never to hurt you, Taylor. It never will be, either."

Still not looking at me, she swallows. "I'm so confused right now."

Her confession makes me smile. It gives me hope.

"Please, don't push me away, Taylor," I plead. Her eyes finally find mine, and she still looks heartbroken, but a glimmer of hope is now in her eyes.

"I don't want to."

With a wide smile, I kiss her. I need her air to help me breath. She robbed me of every ounce of breath I had as I waited for her response. Pulling away, I know I've accomplished my goal when I feel her chest rising and falling, her face looking flushed.

Her lips start to tremble, causing me to worry. "What's wrong?"

"I'm scared, Nick," she whimpers. "I've never been more scared in my life of being hurt."

I feel as if I've been pierced through the heart from her confession. Keeping her tightly embraced in my arms, my mind is demanding answers as to why she feels this way, but my conscience is telling me to not rush her, or she may just push me away. The latter wins as she silently cries in my arms. Doing nothing more than soothing her to help calm her tears, she eventually pulls away and looks up to me.

"Oh, God," she says, looking embarrassed. "I'm so sorry."

I'm chuckling at her, hoping it she doesn't take offense. "It's okay." Taking a deep breath knowing I may risk her clamming up, I ask, "Taylor, can you please help me understand why you don't want to trust me?"

Her face goes pale and the doe eyes return.

"Alright," she sighs.

I should be thrilled she's agreed, but somehow the expression she's still wearing tells me I might just regret asking.

ELEVEN

Headstrong

Taylor

TAKING MY HAND, Nick leads me over to the couch, urging me to sit next to him. There's an urge inside of me to keep him at a distance. Instead, I scoot a little farther away so I'm at one end of the couch as I draw my knees up, feeling the need to comfort myself. His silence is calming and terrifying at the same time as he patiently waits for me to speak.

Sighing, he draws his body forward to rest his elbows on his knees, clasping his hands together. He tilts his head so he's still looking at me. "Does it have to do with this Josh fellow you were screaming about?"

The blood feels as if it's completely drained from my body

for the second time as I nod my head to respond. The sound of Josh's name leaving Nick's lips is repulsive.

"Is it going to be the reason that always comes between us?" he asks as he looks into my eyes.

"I hope not," I reply before bowing my head and resting it on my knees. I'm searching for the courage to explain everything to Nick. I feel his hand reach and tug me towards him, requesting I move closer to him. I grant his request and move to sit on his lap. He pushes my hair from my face, tucking it behind my ear before he wraps his arms around my waist.

"What did he do to you?"

Taking in a deep breath, I attempt to center myself before I begin. "I've only ever had sex once. It happened the weekend after graduation. He was my boyfriend. I should have known from the beginning it was too good to be true. He was the typical jock and I the book nerd nobody looked twice at, although he claimed he didn't see me as one while I tutored him. My infatuation of him took over and eventually we were dating. It'd only been a couple of months and I never allowed it to go any further than kissing. For some stupid reason, I believed he respected my decision," I declare with a halfhearted chuckle. "I should have known better," I repeat.

Nick begins rubbing my back, trying to further soothe me.

"We were at a bonfire in the woods when it happened. Everyone was drinking and I'd started drinking, too. I've been around a drunk all my life and I'm no stranger to how it affects your actions, but I didn't want to disappoint him. After a couple of hours he must have grown bored. So when he asked for us to leave, I thought he intended for us to go home, but he had other intentions."

By now, the tears are slowly starting to trickle down my cheeks.

"He took us further into the woods and the alcohol was already impairing my judgment. I didn't put up too much of a fight at first when he started kissing me. It wasn't until I was being lowered to the ground that the alarms in my head started going off. I kept asking him to stop, but he wouldn't listen.

"By the time I realized his intention, it was too late. He had me pinned underneath him with no way out. He was so heavy, no matter how much I tried pushing him off, I couldn't. I remember it hurting so much," I whimper. "After a while I realized he wasn't going to stop so I just gave up the fight and prayed he'd finish quickly," I say, now silently crying. "When he was done, he took me home and the entire time he acted as if it were no big deal. I was so disgusted with myself after it happened. I still am. That was the last night I ever saw him. I heard a couple of days later that he'd left to go visit some relatives in the south for the summer before leaving for college. But at that point, I could not have cared less. The farther away from me he was, the better."

"Please tell me you reported the fucker."

His question has rendered me silent.

"Taylor." The demand in my name has me flinching.

"No," I croak out. Feeling the need to put distance between us, I stand.

"You let him get away with it?"

I've become accustomed to hearing the same question. It came first from my therapist, when I first sought help for my nightmares, and then again from Katie. But I never regretted letting it happen until now.

"I would have left town the next day, but I had no money."

Nick stands up and begins to pace around the room. He's furious. Turning to face me, he stalks his way over. His actions have me recoiling as he nears me, but the sincerity in his eyes conveys it isn't me he's angry at.

"You shouldn't have had to run away, Taylor. He had *no* right to do what he did. He should have paid for his actions."

"Even if I would have tried reporting him, no one would have believed me. His family is one of the richest in town and has a lot of connections. They would have convinced everyone to believe his word over mine."

He stiffens. "You don't know that, Taylor. You should have tried." Having him point out my mistake is wounding. "Did you tell your parents?" he asks, further twisting the knife into the wound.

Shaking my head again, I say, "I only had my mother and she didn't care."

"How would you know?" He practically shouts in her defense.

I'm now furious as he reminds me of that dreadful moment she came to my room. "She knew what happened after I came home," I explain, remembering my mom's exact words from that night. "She would have preferred I end up pregnant so she could make money off of me."

My stomach is turning in disgust from having to admit the words. Nick's eyes go wide, but just as quickly return to looking sympathetic.

"It's my fault, anyway. I shouldn't have been drinking in the first place."

His hand on my hip tightens, as if angered. "Taylor, it wasn't your fault," he says, scorn in his face. "You told him no and he didn't listen. Drunk or not, he knew what he was doing. He took advantage of you!"

I wipe away the tear falling down my cheek. "It doesn't matter anymore, Nick." He looks directly into my eyes, and it's not sympathy I see, but concern. "It's never too late to try, Taylor. He deserves to pay for what he did to you. You don't deserve to pay for something that isn't your fault. " His statement is not a plea, but a demand I do something more.

"No." The one word has him furiously staring back at me. "Pressing charges against him would mean having to face him. I refuse to return to my past. It's my life, Nick."

"So I'm just supposed to continue being with you knowing someone else has violated you and that you refuse to do anything about it?"

He plunges the dagger still lingering in my shattered soul deeper into its wound. I was already broken before having to admit my faults to him.

"So that's it? You're just going to let him win?" His question is full of fury, reminding me of the reason why I've always pushed every potential suitor away.

"I'm damaged and broken, Nick. I will always be. If you can't accept me for how I am, then it isn't worth wasting your time on. My decision will never change."

"Somehow I'm beginning to believe you've given up."

"You've already seen what it's doing to me. I have *nightmares* from it! Imagine what would happen if I had to face him again. Is that what you want? For me to go completely insane, because that's exactly what would happen, Nick. I don't want to have to remember what happened. I just want to forget!"

Tears are cascading down my cheeks now. The pain and sorrow of speaking about it has taken over. Admitting I want nothing more than to forget should have me feeling shameful for giving up, but instead the admission has me feeling some sense of relief for standing up for myself. It's all I ever wanted from the moment I left that small town. To forget and never look back.

"So he just wins?"

"He only wins if I let the action of what he did to me rule my life."

"It should have *never* happened," Nick repeats.

"This is why you need to walk away, Nick."

We both remain silent after I state the words. A grim atmosphere overtakes the entire room for the next several minutes. My heart has always been broken, but knowing Nick may heed my words and walk away has me dreadfully holding my breath, preparing myself for the heartache to come.

"Is he why you've been pushing me away? Because you think that way of yourself?"

"Yes," I rasp out. "Trust is still the hardest thing for me to do. It's easier to not trust, than to have it broken," I announce to him, trying to swallow the lump that is sitting in my throat.

"That's all you've ever expected from me, isn't it? For me to break your trust?"

Closing my eyes, I laugh humorlessly. "You've already done it several times." He seems puzzled as he takes in my answer. "You don't take orders very well," I remind him.

He grins, the simple turn of his lips lightening the despair surrounding us.

"That was before I realized just how important you are." His confession has the dark walls surrounding my heart slowly shattering. "I'm a determined man, Taylor, and I'm determined to earn your trust," he declares.

"Why?"

Placing his hand on my cheek, he says, "I can't explain it, Taylor, but since the day I met you I knew you were different. You were someone I knew I couldn't let go of."

My once shattered heart is slowly mending. The sympathy he was giving is replaced with affection, and suddenly I want to fight to hold onto it.

"All I ask is that you give me a chance to earn your trust, Taylor," he repeats, bringing his lips to my temple. "I don't expect anything more until you're ready."

Quivering, the tears threaten to once again emerge. Instead of tears of despair, they're of bliss. Leaning in, I kiss him to push away the despair I've been harboring from that night. If it were possible, I'd use his lips to push my shame away as well. When he kisses me, I forget who I am. With one kiss the demons of my past cease to exist.

His arms are securely wrapped around me, making me feel protected, a feeling I wish to hold onto forever. My hands grip at his shirt, scared he'll change his mind and leave. Him doing so would only add to my nightmare.

Seconds later, my fear of the nightmare becoming a reality may come true when goes rigid. He pulls his head back and I dreadfully open my eyes. "Taylor, we better stop," he says, my heart sinking to the pit of my stomach.

Forcing myself to push the lump from my throat, I ask, "Did I do something wrong?" My heart begins to race, afraid he's changed his mind.

He looks at me with his eyebrows drawn down in confusion. "No, Taylor, why would you think you did something wrong?"

"Because you stopped," I say. He shakes his head slowly before kissing me gently. "I only stopped because I promised not to rush things with you." His answer leaves me satisfied and able to breathe again. I lay my head back down on his chest as he says, "You don't know how badly I want you right now and it feels wrong," he adds, running his hand up and down my back.

The disappointment of knowing how scared I am of his declaration is pitiful.

"Taylor?"

"Hmm?"

"Can I kiss you again?"

The request makes me chuckle. The thought that he's asking permission to do something as simple as kiss me makes me light up inside. Pulling my head from his chest, I shyly blush at him with a smile. "Yes, but don't ever expect me to ask if I can kiss you," I reply.

Throwing his head back to laugh, the sound replaces the silence of the room. "Yes, ma'am," he replies before slamming his lips against mine.

Trust is the hardest thing I've ever had to give, but with Nick, it finally feels worth trying for.

The darkness is surrounding me. The air smells of a man I'm unfamiliar with, but the feeling of his hard body is always pushing against me. Using every ounce of strength inside me, I push with all my might. This time, I'm determined to push him off, refusing to let him continue.

The sound of a loud thump triggers me to open my eyes, forcing them to adjust to the glow illuminating from the TV. turned on in my room. Taking in my surroundings, my mind registers I'm not in the woods of my dream, but my own bedroom. An unfamiliar groan comes from the floor near the side of my bed and I panic, my lungs letting out an excruciating scream. The opening of my door as Katie looks into the bedroom frightens me even more. Another groan comes from the floor, this time quieter than before, causing both our heads to turn into that direction. My eyes go wide as I take in Nick's form shielding his eyes from the bright light entering from the hallway.

"What the hell happened?" Katie questions, looking between Nick and me.

"I was tossed off the bed," Nick answers, rubbing at the back of his head. "It's okay, the floor broke my fall."

I gasp when I realize where the thump came from. "I'm so sorry!" I exclaim, already climbing off the bed to help him up. He's looking up at me with concern. "You okay?" he asks when deep inside I'm the one full of guilt.

"Did you have another nightmare?" Katie's voice demands our attention.

Sighing, I nod my head as I remember what I was dreaming of before I'd woken up. "I'm fine now, though," I tell her, knowing how worried she can get when they occur. Giving me a short nod, she closes the door, leaving me alone with Nick. Eyeing him as I kneel down at his side, he's still rubbing at the back of his head.

"I really am sorry. I don't know what happened."

He chuckles before sitting up and smiling back at me. "You're just rough in bed," he jokes, as if knowing how embarrassed I feel. He laughs along with me as he tugs me to sit between his legs. Engulfing me in his arms, he enfolds me tight against his chest, his lips kiss at my temple, sending a flutter down my spine. "Are they always that bad?" he worriedly asks, his voice low and full of concern.

Deeply sighing, I say, "Yes." The arms wrapped around my waist tighten as I lean my head back onto his shoulder. "You're still here," I point out, looking straight at the TV as it displays a commercial.

He chuckles again. "Yeah, I must have fallen asleep, too."

I can't resist smiling at the thought. After my confession in the living room, I'd asked Nick to stay just a little bit longer, deciding to watch TV in my room. We'd climbed onto my bed, and at first it felt odd to have him lying next to me. After a couple of minutes of simply lying next to him, I began to relax and must have fallen asleep. It could have also been that he chose to watch a game and I quickly grew bored.

"I better get going," he voices, making me go rigid. I don't want him to leave. It feels so good being in his arms, even if we're both sitting on a hard floor. "Do you have to?" I bravely ask.

His nose nuzzles in my hair and I feel him inhale. "I don't want to, if that's what you're asking, but I don't want to make you have another nightmare," he says, his voice low and full of sadness. "I felt you pushing me away from you, Taylor. It was because of me you were probably having the dream."

Sorrow has taken over the fluttering. For some reason, the fact that he knows why I've reacted angers myself.

"I hate this."

I hadn't realized I'd said the words out loud until Nick gently turns my face to look directly at him. "I don't have to leave if you don't want me to."

"Please stay," I courageously answer. He replies by gently kissing me before giving me a wide smile.

"Should we take our chances back on the bed or would it be safer down here? I don't know if my body can take another beating tonight." The statement makes my eyes go wide. Leaning my head forward and burying my face into my hands, I let out a small groan. His laughter rumbles through his chest and against my back.

Urging me up, we both climb back onto the bed and strong arms wrap around me, one at my waist and the other tucked under my neck, holding me at the shoulder. I'm being pulled closer to his chest and my face now rests upon his shoulder. Closing my eyes to allow my breathing to calm, I inhale the masculine scent that is uniquely Nick's. Behind the darkness of my closed lids, I take in his distinctive aroma, sending me to a state of relaxation.

Minutes later, my breathing has calmed, sending me back to sleep, but somehow it seems impossible. It's as if I would rather lie awake savoring the feeling of Nick's body comforting me than risk returning to the nightmare.

"You're not asleep, are you?" Nick's deep voice rumbles underneath my ear.

"Somehow I can't go back to sleep," I reply. His arm slowly starts to rub up and down my spine, blissfully adding to my calmed state of mind.

"Do you want to talk?"

Opening my eyes and lifting my chin so it's now resting on his chest, I'm able to stare into his eyes. "Depends on what you want to talk about."

His lips curve up into a smile, clearly understanding the message behind my reply. "What do you like to do for fun?"

"Sleep." He chuckles, making both our bodies shake. "Let me guess, yours is playing sports," I mock, adding to his laughter.

"Ironically, your idea of having fun is close to mine. I like to just relax. My life can be so crazy during the season with traveling and training, I rarely get time to myself. You'd think I'd have more of a break when the season is over, but I'm swamped with endorsement obligations to prepare for the upcoming season," he explains with an exasperated sigh.

"Did you always want to play baseball?"

Silence overtakes the room for a moment before he answers.

"I didn't really consider it until college. I almost didn't pursue it."

"Why?"

"My parents would have preferred I take over the family business. All Hunter males are bred from the womb to follow the footsteps of the previous successful Hunter," he grimaces. He doesn't need to further explain for me to understand the meaning behind those words.

"Enough about me. What were your dreams growing up? Did you always want to be a physical therapist?"

Anxiety overtakes my entire body. Nick wanting to know more about my past is not what I'd intended during this conversation. "No," I curtly reply, already sitting up to leave his embrace.

"Taylor?"

Looking over to the clock sitting on my side table, still avoiding his gaze, it's nearly time for me to wake up anyway. "I better start getting ready for work," I explain, climbing off the bed. "If you don't mind, would you please bring my purse up before you leave?" I ask, opening my door and heading to the bathroom without looking back for Nick's reaction.

Enclosing myself alone in the small room, my eyes shut to withhold the rising tears and the anguish from one simple question. I've vowed to never speak of my past, let alone allow myself to remember it, and it's a vow I intend to keep.

Almost an hour later, I'm ready for work and off to search for Katie so we can leave. What I don't expect to find is Nick still in my apartment standing in the kitchen.

"Where the hell is your coffee maker?" he asks, turning in a full circle, looking confused.

"We don't have one," I answer. "What are you still doing here?"

"What do you mean you don't have a coffee maker?" he asks, a scowl upon his face. "Everyone has a coffee maker."

"Try telling Katie that. She doesn't like the smell of coffee so I have to do without until I get to work," I grumble back. "Where is Katie?" I ask, noticing how she isn't in the room.

"She left a couple of minutes ago. I told her I would give you a ride to work, but you're going to be late because I need coffee."

"Me, too."

A smile is now replacing the scowl on his lips as he closes the distance between us, taking me in his arms. My arms automatically wrap around his waist, as if it's always been normal. His head lowers so his face is buried in my hair, his mouth next to my ear. "I would kiss you, but I have morning breath," his husky voice says.

Although my nose scrunches at the comment, shivers travel down my neck and straight to my toes as I relax into his embrace. Leaning my head onto his shoulder and simply standing in the spot with him holding me, it's almost painful to know I need to leave.

"We better get going," I sadly say.

Before long, he's driving up to the parking garage of my work building and parking his car. Taking a sip of the coffee that we'd purchased from the café up the street, the aroma helps push away the dread I've been carrying with me since we left the apartment. The fear of him asking for an explanation of my reaction to his question has been lingering with me since I'd left him in the room. Thankfully, until now, he hasn't asked, but it's bound to happen.

Nick lifts my hand and kisses the back of it, his smiling eyes looking back at me. "I have a game out of town this week. I won't be back until next week," he utters.

"Oh . . ." The word unconsciously slips out. "Well, thanks for the ride," I tell him, not knowing what else to say. He tugs at my hand, bringing my attention back to him before I have the chance to open the door.

"I was hoping we could have dinner together again when I get back."

Smiling back at him, I grow excited inside. "Sure, but if you don't mind, I'd rather eat at my place this time. I don't want a repeat of last night."

Rubbing the back of his neck with his other hand, he looks ashamed, yet it's clear he understands. "Sounds perfect."

Leaning forward to kiss him, the same hand that was holding his own neck is now holding mine in place, letting our kiss linger longer than usual. With our kiss ending, he keeps our lips a mere breath from each other, and his smells of coffee.

"So much for morning breath," I remind him. Normally the thought of kissing someone with morning breath would have disgusted me, but the taste of coffee beans mixed with the unique flavor of Nick's mouth is delicious.

"You sure you have to work today?"

"Yes," I reply, pulling away to open the car door, leaving him there in the parking lot. Taking one last glance over my shoulder before I enter the building, I find Nick is still gazing at me. Soon I'm sitting behind my desk and in my chair, my thoughts still lost in the my earlier conversation with Nick.

It was clear his only intention was to get to know me better, but I'd resorted back to my normal hardened shell of protection, as I'd always done in the past with anyone else. I've grown accustomed to distracting people, to keep from having to disclose too much of myself. Yet with Nick, who I'd told myself I'd try removing my guard, I was easily reverting back to my old ways. How was I ever going to let him earn my trust if I wouldn't trust myself to retract the walls around my heart? It seems like lately all I'm ever doing is asking myself questions.

Most of which I can't answer myself. Before long, the ringing of my office phone is breaking me from my trance.

"This is Taylor," I answer into the phone.

"I seem to have made the mistake of letting you walk away from me again without getting your number. How am I ever to stalk the one girl who holds my every thought if I can't properly text her?" Nick's husky voice delivers from the other end.

My overflowing smile is inevitable. The declaration he has made is the reason why it's there. There isn't a day that Nick Hunter hasn't overtaken my thoughts at one point, and somehow I predict it will only become tougher to resist.

"Well, that's a shame," I mockingly tease in return.

His familiar chuckle echoes in the room. Confused, my head snaps up to now find him standing in the doorway of my office. Replacing the receiver back in its place on the phone, Nick closes the steps between us to reach me. His usual pose of locking me in my chair is producing the usual reaction I've come accustomed to when he hovers over me.

"I refuse to leave you again until I have it, Ms.—" he proclaims, tilting his head to the side as if considering something. "You've never told me your last name."

"No, I haven't," I verify. "Maybe one day I will, but that's not today," I declare, reaching for his phone and entering my number before returning it to him. Taking the phone from my hand, he places a kiss on the corner of my mouth before turning to walk away.

"I'm going to take that as a promise," he announces before leaving my office without a backwards glance.

The reaction is expected, yet it's still wounding as the guilt sinks to the pit of my stomach. If I didn't learn soon how to break myself free from my protective shell, I may just end up enclosed in it forever.

TWELVE

Missing you

Taylor

PING . . .

The sound I've become so familiar with in the past week announces itself from my phone. As usual, I smile when I first receive it, but it doesn't last long. This past week has been nothing but exchanges of text messages between Nick and I, since he's currently traveling for his games.

On most days, I'm able to speak to him during my lunch break. It's the only opportunity I have to hear his voice during the day. Come 4 P.M., the phone goes silent until the next morning due to his traveling schedule, a circumstance I was unprepared for when Nick announced he'd be traveling this week.

Looking at the time on my phone before I open up the text message, it's almost time to leave work, causing a sigh to escape. It's another night without Nick. Opening up the message, it reads:

Why the sour face?—Nick

My head snaps up to find him standing in my doorway, a wide smile gracing his face when our eyes meet. Butterflies float throughout my stomach as he stalks his way over to me. Thank goodness Katie isn't in the office, because at this very moment, I want Nick all to myself.

Standing before he reaches my desk, my arms are already wrapping around his neck and pulling him down to me for a kiss. The last week of waiting for this one single kiss was torture. In every conversation we've spoken of it, and now it's become a reality.

He kisses me without holding back any emotion. Pulling away, our lips are barely an inch apart as he says, "You don't know how badly I've wanted to do that since the day I left." Our smiles returning with his comment.

Remembering how he mentioned he wouldn't return until next week, I ask, "I thought you were out of town?"

Casually shrugging his shoulder, he leans down to kiss me again. "You almost done for the day?" he murmurs into our kiss.

"My last patient of the day had to reschedule. I still have half an hour left before I can leave." I know it's not the answer he wanted to hear by the protested grumble he gives me. "Behave," I tease when he wraps his arms around me and begins kissing down my neck as I start putting my files into a neat pile. I'm giggling from the stubble on his chin when Sarah walks into my office a few minutes later. Clearing her throat, she gathers our attention.

Katie is the only other person from the office who knows

about Nick and me. I had intentionally wanted to keep it that way, but by the way Nick has my back flush against his chest and securely wrapped in his arms, it's clear we are more than mere acquaintances. Promptly releasing his hold around my waist, I feel him step back, putting space between the two of us.

She's looking between Nick and I with confusion when she states, "I came to remind you about the wedding this weekend. Don't forget." I'm already opening my mouth to reason how it's still unnecessary for me to attend when Nick inquires, "Wedding?" The curiosity in his tone leaves me cringing from the word.

Sarah perks up, excitement gleaming in her eyes. "My wedding is this weekend and Taylor has been trying to get out of attending from the moment I announced my engagement," she explains, now scowling at me.

"Sarah, you know parties aren't my thing. Look what happened at your bachelorette party."

She *tsks*, waving her hand in the air to push the reminder away. "That's different. You now have a date to keep you company," she claims, pointing the same hand in Nick's direction. "It's this Sunday, by the way." The reminder intended for him.

What the hell? She's now mirroring Katie in the matchmaking department. I don't even know where Nick and I are currently standing, something I still ask myself every day that goes by.

"I'm pretty sure Nick has better things to do than put up with me glowering the entire night," I claim, trying to defuse the subject, but Nick is already just as quickly responding, "I'm sorry, I can't, anyway. I have a game that day."

Her brows furrow. "But I thought you couldn't play?"

"We still have to be at the game, injured or not. I'm going to be gone all weekend," he says to me. Sarah's disappointment is sufficient for the both of us. A pang of sadness is internally taking over. He's only just returned and he's already going to leave again? Somehow the resentment is urging me to ask him why he's even here today, but another part of me is begging to hold onto him until the very last moment. I'm so damn confused at this point, my emotions scattered in every direction.

"You ready to go?" Nick's somber voice distracts me from my current thoughts.

"Yeah, let's go," I woefully reply, already leaving his arms and retrieving my purse. The walk to his car is made in silence. My bitterness slowly increases with every passing minute. It isn't until we've reached the car that Nick voices his concern.

Trapping me against his car before I can open the door, his arms wrap around my waist and the apprehensive look in his eyes is already giving me mixed emotions. "What's wrong?"

His gaze is searching for an answer as he waits.

"Why did you bother showing up today?"

With an uncertain tone, he asks, "What do you mean?"

"When do you leave again?"

Now understanding my meaning, he lets out a heavy sigh. "I scheduled my flight for early morning. Is that why you're so upset? Me having to leave again?" I don't know how to answer the question. I'm still trying to understand why I'm upset over this entire situation.

"Taylor, we had a night off in between cities and I really missed you. It's not uncommon for the players to sneak in visits with their family this way."

"I'm not family," I clarify.

Palming my neck to hold my head in place, he gazes down at me. "Do you want me to leave?" His brow arches high as he looks at me.

"No," I admit, now realizing how childish I'm acting. "I'm

sorry, Nick. I don't know what the hell is going on with me."

He cocks his head to one side. "If I didn't know any better, I'd believe you missed me," he smugly explains. Dropping my head against his chest in defeat, I hesitate to explain why I'm acting the way I am. "Yes, I did," I confess, pulling him tight against my chest. It took every ounce of courage to admit my feelings, but they left my mouth so effortlessly.

Time easily passes with him continuing to hold me in his arms. It takes the passing of several cars to break us apart. The entire car ride to my apartment is made in the same dreadful silence as the walk to the garage. With my mind full of possible reasons for my behavior, there's only one that keeps overpowering all others: the simple fact that I'm slowly starting to fall for Nick Hunter, and not having him near is making me miserable.

Nick

Swallowing the mouth full of food, I place the empty container on the coffee table in front of us. Taylor is soon doing the same as she releases a heavy sigh, looking just as full as I feel.

"As delicious as it was, I don't think I can take another bite," she protests, grabbing at her stomach and throwing herself back onto the couch next to me. The gesture makes me laugh.

"Told you it was the best in town."

"It was," she groans. "But you didn't have to pay for it. At least let me pay for half," she insists once more.

"Nope," I repeat for what must be the tenth time. I'm at the point of wanting to lecture her to stop asking.

"But you made dinner for us the first time."

"Technically, I didn't make dinner, Julia did. Second of all, you don't ever want to eat anything I cook. You may not live to see the next day. I can't cook for shit," I say, frowning as I remember my last failed attempt.

"You and me both," she laughs.

"Third, I would never make you pay for dinner."

She rolls her eyes in defeat before she chuckles with a smile. Staring at her, my mind is deliberately engraving her smile into my memory. It will have to sustain me until Monday. I'm still confused over what happened earlier. It was unexpected, yet still welcome. The moment Taylor admitted she was upset over missing me my heart pounded excitedly inside my chest. She's now shyly looking at me, a small irresistible smile on her lips. "Come here," I beckon her, already tugging her to sit in my lap. I've had the entire week to imagine how tonight would go. Between the weeklong text messages and longing to hold her in my arms, it's been pure torture.

"I've been thinking about what you asked me about my career. It wasn't until college when my coaches started pointing out my potential that I started pushing my limits. When I was offered a deal to play professionally in the minor leagues, I had to make a decision in life. Do as expected from my family, or pursue what made me happy." I don't need to finish the sentence when Taylor finishes it for me. "You followed your dreams," she proudly points out.

I nod my head in agreement. "They weren't necessarily dreams, but yes, I followed them. It took a couple of years, but eventually I was in the big league, playing with the big boys. It wasn't until my first injury that I realized how much of it I'd taken for granted."

"It took your injury to open your eyes?"

"No, it wasn't the actual injury, but a feisty little vixen I met on my first day of therapy that made me realize," I answer, quickly pecking her lips soon after. She wraps her arms around my neck as I kiss her, as if wanting to be closer, and I'm not going to protest.

"You're the one who decided to be an ass," she points out.

No matter what words she uses, her responses will always make me laugh. "Are you always this condescending with your patients?"

"You're not my patient, you're Katie's. And you should be grateful or else I wouldn't be allowed to have a personal—" she doesn't complete the sentence, leaving me to wonder what exactly she'd intended to say. "It doesn't matter anymore because you're almost done. You'll be back on the field playing with your balls again," she smirks.

Sometimes I wonder if Taylor realizes how dirty some of the words sound coming from her mouth. "How about you come to one of my games so you can watch me play with *my balls?*" I suggest, wagging my eyebrows at her.

From the roll of her eyes, she's picked up on the message I'd put behind my comment. "I can't."

Taken aback by her reply, I ask, "Why not?"

She's biting her lips and her eyes are looking everywhere but at my own. "I'm a Cubs fan," she states, my heart practically sinking to the floor.

My mouth drops open, speechless. She releases a bout of laughs, still leaving me puzzled. "Please tell me you're joking," I hesitantly ask, hoping it's the reason why she's laughing.

"Yes. I just wanted to see your reaction if I were a Cubs fan since I know it's the only other team in town. I couldn't care less what team is which since I don't watch sports at all," she claims, still giggling, making me playfully narrow my eyes at her.

Her laughter ends when she yawns hidden behind her hand, an apologetic look on her face. "Sorry. I haven't been sleeping well," she admits, alarming me. I'm about to ask her how often she's been having her nightmares, but she cuts me off by changing the subject.

"Only one more session with Katie and you'll be done," she reminds me. It's both bitter and sweet, knowing I'm almost done. "You would have been done sooner had you not had to delay your sessions because of your games this week."

The bitterness in her statement takes me right back to our conversation from earlier. Struggling to find the right words to continue where we left off, my train of thought is broken when Katie walks through the door.

"Hey, you're still here," she remarks, making her way to the other end of the couch and taking a seat.

"Did you ask him?" she asks Taylor.

If I weren't already staring at her, I would have missed the roll of her eyes. "I already told you, I'm not going to be mooching tickets off of him for you. You have the money to buy them yourself."

Waving off Taylor's comment, she says, "I know I do, but its box seats I want and those suckers are expensive. And you promised."

I'm questionably looking at both of them. Katie has her arms crossed over her chest with a pout on her face, while Taylor is piercing her with a glare. The sight is hilarious. Taylor lets out an exasperated sigh as she turns to face me. "Nick, Katie wanted me to ask you if you'd be able to get her box seats for your next game." Every single word is asked through clenched teeth.

Chuckling to brush off the pang of annoyance from the position she'd put Taylor in, I say, "You know you could have asked me yourself."

"I didn't want you thinking I was taking advantage of you."

"And how the hell do you think it'd make me look?" Taylor throws at her.

"You're the one kissing him, so it's easier for him to say yes to you."

"What the hell, you pimping me out for tickets now?"

Taylor's comment makes both Katie and I laugh. Taylor is now piercing me with a glare that has me clearing my throat to silence my laughter.

"The tickets will be at will call for you," I inform Katie, hoping my surrender to her request won't anger Taylor.

Katie stands with a satisfied smile. "Thank you, Nick. Good night, love birds. See you in the morning," she sing-songs over her shoulder on the way to her room.

"I don't know why she's thanking you. I'm the one who had to ask," she grimaces before stifling another yawn. "It must be late if Katie's home," she voices, reaching for her phone and checking the time. I'm hesitantly waiting for Taylor to tell me to leave, but Katie's comment has raised my hopes of staying the night. Before losing my courage, I bravely ask, "Is it okay if I stay with you until you fall asleep?"

She's nervously considers my question for a moment. "I'd like that," she utters. I don't know how I would have reacted had she denied my request, but knowing I'll be holding her in my arms a little bit longer replaces the worry I'd once harbored. I may only have the privilege to simply lie next to Taylor for another hour, but at this point, I'll take it. It's more than I would have ever expected when I first met her.

Following her to her room, I wait while she goes to the bathroom to get ready for bed. Minutes later, she's back at my side with a grimace similar to the one from earlier.

"Are you still mad about the tickets?"

Her pounding out the lumps in her pillow with more force than needed is my answer. "Taylor, it's no big deal. They always hold a certain amount of tickets for family and friends for when the athletes need them," I reassure her, hoping to cheer her up.

"Yeah, I'm pretty sure she was banking on that," she grimaces. "She just better not get used to it, because I refuse to let her use you."

"What if I let *you* use me instead," I say, the words uncontrollably come out of my mouth before I can stop them. I'm bracing myself for the wrath that may come from the comment.

"I'll keep that in mind for when I want my *own* box seats. Let me know when you play those Cubs," she teases, turning off the light.

I don't know whether to laugh or clarify how our teams are in two different leagues and how it would rarely happen, but I'm distracted from the thought of how my sexual remark didn't trigger Taylor to command me to leave, as it had in the past. With the darkness of the room surrounding us, she climbs into bed, allowing me to follow her. Entwining our bodies into each other as we had the last time I stayed the night, my hand begins gliding up and down her back as I smile. I listen as her breathing slowly calms. I'm gradually starting to fall asleep when Taylor's voice startles me awake.

"I never had any dreams growing up, but I do know there was one thing I didn't want to be," she declares.

"And what is that?" I ask, rubbing her back.

"My mother."

She tightens her arms wrapped around my waist and rubs her face against my chest, as if trying to find the perfect spot. Her answer has left me with more questions than before, but her answer has added another layer of understanding. I know there is plenty left to uncover, but hopefully with time and patience, I'll eventually peel them all.

THIRTEEN

Taking chances

Taylor

NICK WAS ALREADY gone by the time I had awoken the next morning. My heart immediately began mourning the loss of his arms when I'd reached over for him and found the bed empty and cold. When he had gotten up to leave was a mystery. Telling myself it was for the best that he left without a word was a lie in itself as well. However, as before, the text messages had resumed that same afternoon. Day after day, we would have our simple conversations throughout the day, but come night, they were absent. I kept telling myself it was due to his schedule, but the nights were beginning to be the most difficult for me. The nightmares were returning, some nights with full force, and even Katie struggled to awaken me. So far, I've had one every night since Nick left. I was beginning to fear falling asleep.

Tired, exhausted, and moody, today was not the day to enlighten me with a reminder of Sarah's wedding. While everyone was joyfully preparing to celebrate a new journey for my co-worker, I was sitting at home still resenting having to go. If I thought my Mondays were bad, today felt like a month full of Monday's bundled into one afternoon.

The wedding was beautiful in spite of all my protest to be there, but seeing Sarah happy, nothing else seemed to matter. It was her day, after all. I would just have to learn to push my childish manner aside for her. She'd chosen to have the reception outside, and with the sunset now hours behind us, the atmosphere was the perfect backdrop to her moonlight first dance with her husband. Preceding the first dance, everyone was ready to party. Everyone expect me.

Feeling anxious to leave, I'm brought to a complete halt when a familiar husky voice caresses my neck.

"Hey there, where are you going?"

My heart speeds up and my blood begins to race with delight. Swiftly turning, I nearly lose my balance, but Nick is quick to catch me, pulling me tightly to his side. The unique aroma of his cologne overtakes my senses, and it's the final piece needed to make my knees weak. I practically melt in Nick's arms.

"You're here. You said you weren't coming," I croak out, surprised with myself for finding my voice to state the obvious. Before I get a chance to finish, he's just as quickly cutting me off by commenting, "You. Look. Beautiful."

His warm breath and cavalier compliment warmly gliding against the skin below my ear hits me like a ton of bricks, sending every spark possible to rush inside of me. Failing to hide the blush now spreading across my cheeks, along with my bashful smile, I bravely take a step back to fully take him in. He's wearing a tuxedo, and even my absentminded ability for fashion understands it's designer. The suit is highlighting every inch of his body, leaving me now gushing with desire with just one look.

Desperately needing a distraction, I remember why I'd originally stood up. "I *was* going to find Katie to tell her I'm leaving," I admit.

"Why would you want to do that?" he asks, his eyes glancing in the direction of the dance floor. If he thinks for one moment I'm going to be heading in that direction, then he's in for disappointment.

"Nick, I don't dance," I point out.

His hand intertwines with mine as he begins looking over my shoulder. "Take a walk with me," he says, more a command than a request. I'm urged to walk at Nick's side.

"Nick, where are we going?"

The memory of the last occasion when a similar command was made has put a hindrance in my steps. The thought of Nick leading me to a secluded area is terrifying. As much as I'm slowly beginning to grow comfortable with him, the demons of my past will always have a reaction to isolated spaces. Because of those same demons, my feet are now rooted to the ground, and keeping me planted in my spot.

"Taylor?" Nick says, his voice full of worry. I'm staring at a set of blue eyes full of concern. Breathing deeply helps encourage me to push past my boundaries. Nick isn't to blame for the actions of my past and I'm tired of letting that said past control my life. If being alone with Nick in the dark of the night is one step forward to helping me slay those demons, then I'm willing to take the risk of what will come.

Swallowing my fear, I ask, "Where exactly do you want to go?"

Nick resumes our steps and leads us to a walkway illuminated by candlelit lanterns. Soon, we're standing not too far
from where we'd just left, but with enough privacy to conceal
us from passersby. The music can still be heard clearly, and as
if on cue, the chorus of Frank Sinatra's *It Had to Be You* begins. His arm wraps securely around my waist, tugging me tight
against his chest while he reaches for my hand. Our bodies begin swaying to the rhythm of the music.

"I should have known you'd find a way to get your way," I
say as I lean my head against his shoulder.

Swaying us a little faster so he can turn us in a full circle,
I suppress a giggle. "I love making you smile," he says into my
ear, making me shudder slightly.

"I bet you must do this all the time with girls," I remark.

"Is that what you think?" he asks, tilting his head as he
waits for my response.

"Yes."

"I've never done this before. I hate to dance, but somehow
you made me want to."

His answer surprises me, but the ambience of our surroundings just as quickly distracts me. Frank's smooth voice,
the feel of Nick's warm embrace, and my head gently resting
against his shoulder allows my mind to escape with the lyrics.
How unexpected that the words surrounding us are exactly how
I'm feeling with Nick at this moment. He's the only one besides
Josh who I've ever allowed this close to me. From the moment
he refused to be pushed away, I've known he would be the only
person to overpower what I felt for Josh.

Minutes later, the song is slowly ending and my heart is
wishing it wouldn't. Lifting my head to look at him, Nick is
staring down at me with a soft smile.

"You said you couldn't come tonight, yet you're here," I

point out. The thought has been lingering in the back of my mind from the moment he made his presence known.

"I left my game early and got on the first flight I could catch. It was a day game so I knew it would be possible. Plus, I couldn't stand being away from you much longer."

His confession goes straight to my heart, tugging at the strings of my emotions. Tremors course through my veins, igniting me.

Had you told me a year ago I'd be blissfully dancing with Nick Hunter at a wedding, I'd have checked you into the psychiatric ward myself. Yet, here I am, dancing with him in the moonlight.

He's taken by surprise when I reach up for our lips to meet. My fist is gripping Nick's coat for dear life to keep from tumbling straight to the ground from the weakness I'm experiencing from the kiss. Wrapping his free arm around my waist, he holds me up. I can feel the hard muscles of his chest against my forearms, the only barrier between us.

Sparks suddenly explode inside of me, like an endless Fourth of July night. As he slowly pulls away, breaking our kiss, he leaves me with my eyes closed, and my mouth wanting for more. My heart is rapidly beating out of my chest. I'm breathless, dizzy and light headed. All from this one kiss.

Opening my eyes to find Nick intensely gazing back at me gives me the courage to say, "I want to go home." The words are almost breathless, yet full of yearning.

Nick's eyes are full of understanding as he swallows before asking, "Are you sure?"

Nodding my head, my nerves are increasingly rising with the seconds it takes for Nick to pull away. With his arm still protectively wrapped around my waist, he leads us down the same path we came on.

"I should let Katie know I'm leaving or else she may worry," I comment, barely remembering I should do so.

It doesn't take long to find her. I simply needed to seek her out on the dance floor, where I thought she'd most likely be. Seeing Nick and I, she briefly breaks from her partner.

"We're leaving now," I tell her. At first, she seems disappointed by my comment, until she sees Nick. "Have fun," she remarks with a smile.

I don't know how to take her words, but regardless, I tightly embrace her to let her know I heard her. Pulling away, it's now Sarah who is at my side and she looks happier than ever, but it may be due to some alcoholic aid.

"It was a beautiful wedding, Sarah. Congratulations," I tell her, already hearing her sigh. "You're leaving already?" she whines. Glancing at Nick, her eyes light up in understanding. "I'll see you when I get back from my honeymoon," she says before hugging me one more time.

Minutes later, I'm waiting at the valet station with Nick, the entire time his hand tightly entwined with mine. It's still a strange and foreign feeling. It feels surreal, yet I no longer complain.

Nick

"Was it a beautiful wedding?" I ask Taylor as I drive us to her apartment. My thumb is brushing against her knuckles. The need to constantly touch her has completely taken over from the moment I first held her tonight. Our text messages were sufficient to keep me happy until I returned, but now having her physically next to me is better than the image I held in my memory.

"It's the only one I've ever been to, so I have nothing to

compare it to."

At first, her answer surprises me, but then thinking back to the few details she's given me, it would be typical since she doesn't like parties. Another factor that distinguishes her from other girls, she doesn't seek attention. The difference between them and Taylor, they would throw themselves at me, she was pushing me away. And if they weren't throwing themselves at me, I knew how to easily manipulate them to willingly give in to my request.

This is the first time that I've ever had to sustain self-control when it comes to sex. She was the one who opened my eyes to see how most men treated woman when they thought with their dicks. I was the typical male who'd only seen it as *sex*.

My eyes look back at her with longing as I see her nervous expression through the passing light. When she'd voiced wanting to leave, for a split second I caught a glimpse of desire in her eyes, but I'd just as easily pushed it away, not wanting to give myself false hope. I've heard those words plenty of times, but never would I have expected them from Taylor.

Regardless of what happens tonight, there's one thing I'm going to insist on, staying the night with her, even if it's just holding her as I usually do.

We reach her apartment and when I park the car, she turns to face me. "You coming up?"

Nodding my head with a smile, I quickly climb out of the car to help her out. The few steps it takes for us to reach her apartment door are making *me* nervous.

Inside, her arms wrap around my waist to pull me flush to her body and her lips are connecting with mine. The kiss is unexpected, but I'm just as happy to receive it. It's taking every ounce of willpower not to pick her up and take her to her room. The power of her kiss is sending every erotic thought to course through my mind.

Rapidly pulling away, I'm panting while I say, "Taylor . . ." The only word I manage to muster as her hungry eyes look back at me. My jaw is locked tight and my breathing is near a pant, forcing me to swallow to bring my urges under control. "I want you so badly, but you need to tell me to stop," I finally say, unashamed of how I feel.

"I can't," she replies, her eyes full of desire. It's the only response I need to know exactly what she's entailing and I'm in no state of mind to deny her request. I'll just keep reminding myself of the promise I've made. If she says, *stop,* I run. Because that's what it will take from this moment on to not scare the shit out of her.

FOURTEEN

Trust

Taylor

MY BODY IS lifted and Nick's brisk steps take us to my room, gently laying me on my bed after we enter. He removes his coat and climbs onto the bed. He hovers above me, as if hesitant to make any more movements. Reaching up with my hand, I tug his head down towards mine, needing him to kiss me.

Pulling his shirt from his pants, my hands make their way inside to feel the warmth of his ribcage. My mind is a mix of anxiety and anticipation, the latter overpowering my senses. His earlier demand is still lingering in the back of my mind, but regardless of how many times it's repeating itself, I still can't bring myself to stop him.

His lips begin kissing their way along my neck, leaving behind a trail of sparks electrifying my blood over every inch his mouth touches. One hand slowly creeps up high on my thigh, gently gripping it. For a moment my eyes close, the darkness rapidly sending me back to the memory of the forest, yet the feel of the hands gliding along my skin are not the same.

"Taylor . . ." The tenderness in my name brings me back to reality. Opening my eyes, I find Nick above me. "We don't have to do this if you're not ready," he voices.

"Please don't stop," I whimper, demanding he continue.

He pulls me into a sitting position, leaving me puzzled. Tugging me to straddle his waist, I heed his request. It's strange how I've come to love sitting in Nick's lap, yet being in this position feels even better. My arms automatically wrap around his neck as I lean forward to resume our kissing. The kiss instantly takes away all the worry I felt just moments ago. My hands fist his hair, while his hands are fiercely gripping the sides of my waist, pulling us closer together. Even with the barrier of Nick's pants, I can still feel the hardness that is growing against the middle of my thighs. As my core starts rubbing against his awakening erection, my blood starts to heat with a want I've never known.

"God, Taylor, you're torturing me here," he growls into my mouth, nipping at my bottom lip. "You don't know how much I want to keep going, but I'm not going to force you to do anything you don't want to do," he says before he stops to look me directly in the eyes.

The excitement coursing through my body makes my heart race as his eyes search mine for any sign of refusal. There is no way that would happen, though. I wouldn't be able to live with myself if I did. His hands reach for the hem of my dress, but suddenly stop there.

Gabbie S. Duran

"Is it okay if I take this off?" he asks, his question full of concern, seeking permission first and foremost. Reaching down, it's my hands that tug my dress over my head. I'm straddling him now in only my bra and the mere scrap of my thong, while he's still fully clothed. Needing to remedy that, my fingers slowly start unbuttoning his shirt and soon I'm opening it, allowing my hands to skim across his bare chest.

Bravely, I push my center up against his hips, causing the hands on my waist to tighten as he lightly groans. His jaw is tight and the obvious strain to keep under control is radiating from his face. Feeling the urge to take his strain away, I lean down to kiss his neck. The throbbing of his vein under my tongue beats harder as I graze my tongue across it.

With strained words, he says, "Taylor, I'm going to lay you down," as if needing to explain his every move.

Nodding my head in approval, our bodies gradually descend back onto the bed, while internally I'm crying out for him to hurry. He hesitantly hovers above me before leaning down to gently mesh our mouths together. Lifting up to look directly into my eyes, the concern radiates clearly from him, as if he's waiting for me to say stop.

My arms wrap around his shoulders, silently encouraging him to continue before the heat of his tongue touches my sensitized skin, sending a stimulating tingle all the way down to the tips of my toes. I'm burning up in a flaming heat, and with haste my hands are urging him to take his shirt off.

Pulling himself from my embrace and kissing his way down my body, the heat of his tongue glides down the valley of my breast to my abdomen, my body reacting by arching up to him, requesting more. My hands reach down to grip his head as he trails his mouth lower until I let out a gasp, realizing what he's about to do.

"Taylor," I hear, his husky voice brings my attention back to him. "Are you okay?"

My face must be three shades of crimson from the embarrassment of my reaction. Now biting my bottom lip, I'm calmly nodding at him. He brings one of my legs up towards him to remove my shoes.

"As sexy as you are in these heels, the last thing I need is you clawing my back with them."

I'm completely baffled by his comment, not understanding exactly how that would happen as he removes my underwear. He lifts my legs up and over his shoulders. His head disappears between my legs and my earlier gasp is nothing compared to the shocking moan I let out when his mouth meets my heated center. The warmth of his mouth against my core makes me buck my hips up to meet the demands of his tongue, and I grab onto his head again, needing something to hold onto as he slowly starts to lick his way up and down my center lips. My feet are pushing into his shoulders, helping to leverage against his mouth. My whimpering has now turned into out of control moans as his mouth starts sending me into a spiraling vortex, pleasure rushing up and down my body.

His mouth is wickedly torturing me, bringing me to the verge of climaxing. Seconds before I reach my completion, I just as slowly come back down from the pinnacle. My moaning has turned into a pleading whimper, nearing a cry of frustration. As I believe he'll continue his torturous act, I am no longer able to resist and am propelled into a spiral of sensations I've never felt before, one of powerless desire as I begin to convulse.

As I'm lying there exhausted and trying to get my breathing under control, I can feel my heart pounding against my chest. I open my eyes to find a smile on Nick's face, clearly satisfied with himself. I watch him slowly remove the remainder of his clothing, his eyes entirely locked with mine. Taking in every inch of his naked body, eventually I find the bulge between his legs. Stunned and slightly frightened, I become hesitant of what will come next.

Searching his pants for his wallet, he removes a condom from it, holding it in his hand as he comes back to join me on the bed. I'm shivering. Not from the desire I once had, but from anxiety.

"Taylor," he mutters, looking into my eyes. "I'd never do anything to hurt you, but if you don't want to do this then I'll understand."

Gazing back up at him, I admit, "I'm just scared." I tremble as I hold back the tears threatening to emerge.

Understanding, he nods before he crawls back into bed. "If you ever need me to stop, just say the word and I promise I will. Do you understand?" The tenderness in his voice pushes all fears from my mind as I nod my head.

He reaches down to tenderly give me a kiss and I instantly forget what I was scared of as I pull him down on top of me. He reaches behind my back and unhooks my bra, pulling it off me, leaving my chest bare to him. Working his wicked mouth on my breasts, my hands grab onto his hair as I let out a moan. He leaves my breast, bringing his mouth back to mine, hungrily kissing me. I can feel his hand start to skim against my side down to my thigh as he wraps my leg around his hip, making me pull him tighter against my core, gliding himself back and forth against my center.

"Nick, the condom. Now," I demand against his mouth.

He laughs, lifting his body to sheath himself, leaning back down seconds later. The anticipation rises within me, my breathing becoming labored from eagerness to have him inside of me. Tenderly, he kisses me, his lips sensually relaxing me before I start feeling him pushing between my thighs.

My legs willfully fall open to allow him between my thighs. "You ready, baby?" he questions into my mouth, but instead of verbally relaying my response, I grab onto his waist with my hands and pull him forward, the tip of his penis right at my entrance conveying my answer. He places his hand underneath me, lifting my hips up while he slowly pushes himself forward and into my core.

My eyes clamp closed and he suddenly stops. "Taylor . . ." I swallow hard, mentally and physically waiting for the pain to come. "Baby, look at me," he gently demands.

My eyes open to find him intensely staring down at me, a silent command to keep my gaze locked onto his. "I don't want you closing your eyes this time. I want you to know who is making love to you." His deep voice is full of control.

He inches into me, my core giving him resistance with each inch. Bringing himself to a standstill, I'm fearful he's changed his mind. "Relax, baby, I don't want to hurt you," he says, sinking further into me. The memory of the discomfort and pain emerges and regardless of how much I try to obey his command to relax, I can't.

As if sensing my discomfort, he bends down to fuse our mouths together, the distraction of his kiss pushing away any discomfort I feel. Pushing the final inches connecting us as one, I gasp and grab onto his shoulders, making his body go rigid.

"Baby, you're so tight. I'm afraid to hurt you," he whispers, placing a kiss below my ear. "You need to tell me when you're ready for me to move," he says, his voice sounding strained.

I lift my hips up and start rocking against him, my core starting to blaze with the eagerness for him to move. He pushes forward, rocking his hips and I throw my head back and moan from the pleasure he's giving me. Wrapping my legs around his waist to pull him tighter to me, I begin to find a rhythm, matching him thrust for thrust.

Pulling my hips tighter, he thrusts harder against my core, intensifying the pleasure coursing through my veins. The sensation rises higher and higher with each minute. Throwing my head back as I tightly close my eyes, the darkness is overtaken with a spark igniting throughout my entire body, spiraling me out of control.

Screaming my name as he pumps his hips faster, he goes rigid above me once more. I can feel his labored breathing fanning against the bare skin of my neck. Slowly opening my eyes, I find him looking down at me with worry while I slowly recover from the earth-shattering universe Nick has sent me to.

"You okay?" he breathlessly asks, smiling down at me.

"I think I'll live," I laugh out.

Gently kissing me before he rolls both our bodies, he drapes mine across his chest and tightens his arms protectively around my waist. Placing my head down onto his chest, the thumping of his heart drums into my ear, slowly sending me off into a peaceful slumber.

FIFTEEN

Dessert is always best

Nick

THERE'S A BODY half draped across me. Normally I would push it off. I've had plenty of girls wake up at my side in the morning. I'm not ashamed to admit I allow them to stay the night. I consider it easier to request another round of sex with no questions asked in the morning, but my number one rule is *"Do not cling."* The circumstances are different this time. It's me who is pulling this girl closer to my side. The warmth of her body is nearly a necessity at this point. Her familiar smell is addictive and has me craving more.

Taylor stirs in my arms, startling my breath to hitch. I'm fearful she'll push me away. Instead, she lifts her chin to rest on my shoulder.

"Good morning," she rasps out, a contented smile following the words. Grasping her tighter in my embrace, I place a kiss upon her temple.

"Good morning," I reply.

The sound of an alarm announcing itself at our side alerts me it's time for Taylor to get up. The thought of knowing I will have to surrender my hold on her body is disappointing.

"Will you hand me my phone?"

Doing as she requests, she turns off the alarm, returning us to the silence we were laying in moments ago.

"I don't want to get up," she protests. The laughter I let out shakes both our bodies. "You can call in sick," I jokingly suggest.

"I can't do that," she muffles into my chest. "I've already called in sick this month. I'd get fired if I do it again."

The statement leaves me once more in my disappointed state. Sighing along with her, I have to relinquish my hold to allow her up. Tugging at her comforter to wrap herself in it, she sits at the edge of the bed, slowly turning to face me as she nervously chews on her lip.

"Are you going to act shy now, Ms. Taylor?" I tease.

A faint glow of sunlight illuminates through her windows, allowing me to catch the slight blush of her cheeks. "You have nothing to be shy about," I tell her. She continues with her silence, worrying me. With dread, I ask, "Do you regret last night?"

Turning to face me, her eyes are wide. "No!"

"Then what's wrong?"

Once more, she's blushing as before. "I just don't know how to act," she conveys, shamefully looking at the floor. "I've never had sex with someone."

"I mean, last night . . . Last night was the first time I've ever willingly had sex with anyone," she corrects.

Reaching for her hand, I tug her to close the distance between us. Tucking her between my legs and wrapping my arms around her waist, her back is to my chest, allowing me to comfort her. She looked so vulnerable when she made her confession. Knowing I was partially to blame for her reaction is upsetting.

"Thank you," I sigh into her ear. "I know how hard it was for you to trust me, Taylor, and I swear I'll continue to do whatever it takes to keep that trust."

She slightly turns her body to better face me. The sincerity in her eyes has now replaced her weakness. Her lips meet mine, tender at first, as if hesitant. I force myself to push away the hunger that she is awakening. I can feel her smile as she pulls away. "Have you always been this cavalier with every girl you meet?"

"No," I truthfully answer without a pause. "They weren't worth my time."

She's taken aback by my response. "What does that say about you?" Her head is cocked to the side as she waits for my response. Repeating my words in my head, I realize it would sound chauvinist if I respond in such a way. "It's because they weren't you."

She considers my answer for a moment. "And what exactly am I, Nick?"

"You're someone worth pursuing."

She gives me a deep sigh as if unsatisfied with my answer. "I better start getting ready for work before I'm late." Standing to head over to her dresser, she rummages through it.

She leaves me sitting and wondering for a moment what I have said wrong.

"You sure you don't want to reconsider that sick time?"

With her back still facing me she heads to her closet next and grabs a set of scrubs off a hanger. "I can't do that to my patients. Besides, it's Monday, which means I'll see you later today," she reminds me.

"You should be excited. It's your last day today," she adds over her shoulder as she walks out of the bedroom, leaving me alone with my thoughts.

It's killing me knowing we have to leave the bed today, but I need this last appointment to get me back onto the field. I never thought I'd be dreading the completion of my physical therapy when this all began. My last day is also a reminder I won't be seeing Taylor anymore during my sessions. I'm no longer finding an excuse to avoid them, but the opposite; I've come to look forward to them. One final appointment and I'm back to doing what I love.

Hearing the shower turn on makes me grow hard again, knowing that she's going to be lathering her naked body soon. Shit, I'm surprised I'm not in there with her right now. But if I were to go in there, I'd make her late. I would end up making love to her again in the shower.

I have to keep repeating her earlier statement.

"I'm her first . . . The first man she's ever made love to."

How time has changed. It was only a month ago when I couldn't get Taylor to allow me to be near her, let alone touch her. Yet, she trusted me with her entire body last night.

Letting out a deep breath, I stand from the bed to dress. My heavy heart lightens when an idea pops into my head. Hopefully, with enough pleading, I can make it happen.

It isn't long before she's exiting her room, looking stunned when she finds me waiting for her.

"I take it your giving me a ride?"

"I wouldn't have it any other way."

Her brows arch high. "Lucky for me, you like coffee. So no complaints from me," she says, making me smile at her. "I'm paying, though."

"No, you're not," I argue. From the narrowing of her eyes, I can tell this morning my little firecracker will soon return.

My phone rings as I enter the therapy room ten minutes before my scheduled appointment time, another odd habit since I met Taylor. I've rarely ever shown up early to anything I have scheduled. Looking down at the phone, I sneer as I push ignore on the screen, not feeling the urge to speak with my mother at the moment. Knowing she'll try calling again, I quickly turn off my phone so she doesn't disturb me for the next hour.

My eyes find the stability ball I remember seeing Taylor sitting on the very first day I laid eyes on her. It was the first of many times I've seen her bouncing on the ball. Wondering why she prefers sitting on the ball instead of the chairs provided in the room, I'd asked Katie about it on one of our most recent appointments.

"It relaxes her," she answered, adding a shrug of her shoulder, as if not fully understanding the reason herself.

Since the day I met Taylor, I've never looked at a stability ball in the same way. Making a mental note to buy one for our own personal use, I look around the room to verify I'm alone before I head straight to see why she enjoys it so much. As my ass lands on it, I practically roll off the thing, forcing me to catch my balance. How the fuck does she find this thing comfortable if it moves all over the place? It takes a couple of seconds, but eventually I'm bouncing on it myself, fully understanding why it's relaxing.

"You better not pop my ball." Taylor's voice breaks my thoughts as she walks her way over to me. Her eyes find mine with a mischievous twinkle in them. "As you can see, Mr. Hunter, you've gotten your request. I'll be your sports therapist for the completion of your therapy." She smirks.

"Lucky me."

This morning as I'd strenuously waited for Taylor to shower, I persuaded Katie to trade spots with Taylor for my appointment. It wasn't an easy task convincing her. She'd pointed out how I'd be putting Taylor's job in jeopardy now that we were seeing each other, but I was persistent and promised to be on my best behavior. I wanted to leave my therapy knowing her hands were the last ones on my ankle.

Taylor's presence in front of me has me returning my attention to her. Her eyes are gazing down at me, not doing a very good job of hiding the hunger in her eyes.

"Baby, if you keep looking at me that way I'm not going to be able to keep myself from pulling you down on top of me," I huskily growl up to her. "Trust me, I'm pretty sure this ball would make for a really challenging sex position, but I like challenges."

Her eyes narrow down into slits. "One night . . . I give you one night and you become all cocky," she scolds.

Holding my hands up in surrender, I say, "You win. No sex on the ball, then."

"Get your ass up on that table so I can check your ankle and get this over with," she orders, returning to the stern Taylor I once knew her to be.

Doing as she commands, I quickly glance around the room to make sure we're alone. Reaching for her wrist, I tug her forward. "Can I get you to be this bossy next time we're in bed?"

She pulls herself away, expressionless as she looks at me. Swallowing, I'm afraid that I might have pushed our teasing too far.

"You seem pretty confident there'll be a next time."

Silently questioning whether she's teasing or stating a fact, I'm panicking at this point. With Taylor, anything is possible. The smile creeping up on her lips allows me to breathe.

She leans her body closer to mine. "If you're a good boy and follow instructions today, then maybe you'll get your reward," she hums into my ear.

Pulling her wrist from my grasp, she reaches down for my ankle, fully returning to her therapist demeanor.

Before I can reply to her proposal, another therapist is entering the room with a patient, depriving me of the chance to pursue the subject. The quick glance of Taylor's eyes when she looks up accompanied by the slight tug of a smile informs me she knows exactly what she was doing. This girl has accomplished what no other girl has managed to do, have me strapped by the balls.

What the hell is happening to me?

Regardless of the reasons, it's what I've been searching for; I just hadn't known it and there isn't anything I wouldn't do to keep it this way.

Forty-five minutes later, she's wishing me a professional goodbye due to the abundance of other patients and therapists around. Exiting the therapy room, I'm quickly following her back to her office.

"Nick, what are you doing?" she asks, her voice hitching with hesitation as she turns around to face me. Walking in her direction, I can no longer resist keeping my hands off her.

"Don't worry, baby, I promised to be a good boy back here, but I do need to ask you something," I say as I wrap my arms around her waist.

"My parents are in town for a charity event this week and I have to meet them for dinner tomorrow night. I was hoping you would come with me."

"I don't think that's a good idea, Nick."

Pushing her away from me, my brows are drawn down in confusion. "Why wouldn't it be a good idea?"

"I'm not the type of girl you bring home to your parents, Nick," she croaks out before her eyes find the floor.

I force her head up with my finger so she will look at me. "Taylor, you're the perfect kind of girl to bring home to my parents," I tell her, hoping to push her doubt aside. "It's not that big of a deal, Taylor. It's just dinner," I reassure her.

She's skeptically looking at me, her expression conveying denial to accept my request. Leaning down, I kiss her. The sweet taste of her kiss has become my weakness. I can't get enough of them. Feeling her body relax against mine, I slowly end the kiss to plead this time. "Please, Taylor, it would really mean a lot to me." She takes a heavy breath, giving me hope.

"Okay," she answers, making me feel a sense of triumph inside. "But, I really don't think this is a good idea," she mutters.

I give her a wide smile. "Stop worrying, Taylor. Everything will turn out fine," I confidently reply. "Now, how about dinner with just *me* tonight?"

The humor in her eyes has returned. "Is it just dinner you want, or dessert?"

Wagging my brows at her, I say, "I've always liked eating my dessert first." My voice drops low as I add, "And I know I can find a way of making you want the same."

Her laughter vibrates throughout the room and is music to my ears. "As long as there's chocolate. The real kind, not the kinky stuff I know you're thinking about," she lectures as she wraps her arms tight around my neck to pull me down to kiss her.

Now she has the possibilities floating through my mind. She may not be keen on the idea at the moment, but I've proven I can be a *very* convincing man.

SIXTEEN

Always doubtful

Taylor

I DON'T NEED an alarm to wake me this morning. My nightmare of a dream has me frightfully awakening. Gasping for air, I go rigid, fearing I'm still trapped as an arm wraps around my waist, pulling me to a hard chest. However, the voice delivering comforting words into my ear do not match the darkness of my nightmare.

"Taylor?" The gentleness in which my name is said is opposite of the monstrous growl belonging to my dreams.

Forcing my breathing to calm, I answer, "I'm alright." I try to sound convincing even though I still feel frightened with every breath I take.

"You scared me," he whispers against my skin, tightening his hold as he conveys the words. The gentle feel of Nick's lips placing a kiss on my shoulder helps push the lingering demons aside.

"Was it just as bad as the last two times?"

His question surprises me. I would have never expected him to keep track of the moments they've occurred. Swallowing the lump still lodged in my throat, I answer, "No. This time I couldn't see his face. I could only hear his voice."

There's a moment of silence before he hesitantly asks, "Do you want to talk about it?"

"I would prefer not to," I automatically answer, as I've always done to anyone who's asked the question in the past.

The disappointed sigh he lets out forces the guilt I'm holding inside to build. "It's not you, Nick. I just don't like telling anyone about them," I say, knowing it's not the answer he's seeking.

"Then you're not having them because I'm staying the night?" he asks, hesitation laced into every word.

Turning to face him, the darkness encasing the room keeps me from clearly making out his features. But knowing I'm directly facing him gives me the courage to say, "Some nights are good and some are bad," I admit. "I don't think my nightmares will ever go away, but knowing you'll be here when I wake up helps push my fear of falling asleep aside. That's more than I've ever hoped for since they began." He pulls me close so we're mere inches from each other.

The comfort and security of being enveloped in his arms unexpectedly awakens the same desire as the previous night. With the sun slowly rising behind us, notifying me it won't be long before my alarm goes off, I plan to take advantage of what little time I have left with Nick.

Lifting my leg to pull him to me, I kiss him. His hand squeezes my thigh, an indication he's still holding onto the restraint he's been containing since last night. Deepening our kiss helps push the terrifying thoughts of my past from my mind and replaces it with a desire I'm still discovering.

"Taylor, we should stop. You're probably still sore this morning," Nick mumbles into my mouth while pulling away and kissing a path down my chin. He may have made the suggestion, but the tantalizing kisses grazing across my skin say otherwise.

Lifting my head, I say, "I thought you had kissed it better last night." Remembering where his mouth had been before we'd fallen asleep does nothing but fuel my desire.

"Taylor . . ." he warns as I push myself up against the erection prodding between my legs.

"Are you sure?" His eyes search mine for any sign of uncertainty.

The question has me smiling at how considerate he's been, a sentiment I would have never expected from Nick. I pull him down for a kiss, and within seconds I'm trembling as desire courses through my veins.

Our hands gradually start removing clothing, returning to feel every inch of each other's skin with every layer removed. Wrapping my legs around his waist to pull him into me, he groans, making me laugh. He's hard against my core and I'm surprised he has the willpower to pull himself away to sheath himself. But within seconds he's back on top of me, nipping at my neck, his teeth grazing my skin, driving my senses wild.

Slowly, as if still cautious of his actions, he fully enters me, remaining motionless when he's buried himself to the hilt. His eyes hesitantly search mine for a moment before he gradually starts rocking his hips. Blissful jolts of pleasure travel through my veins. Every rhythmic thrust of our hips drives me closer to the pinnacle of completion. I can no longer resist letting go. Moaning his name, I explode with the all too familiar ecstasy Nick has helped me discover. The continuous rocking of Nick's hips increases in speed, making me rise once more. The explosion is much more powerful this time as we both scream out in unison.

Bringing our bodies to a slow stop, we're both drenched in sweat, both breathless and satisfied, as we lie still entangled in each other's arms.

Pulling away to hover above me, he says, "Good morning."

Giggling, he rolls our bodies so I'm draped across his chest. I'm delightfully exhausted and all I want to do is fall back to sleep. My eyes find the clock on my bedside table and take in the time.

"Shit, I'm going to be late. I'm never going to hear the end of it from Katie," I say, scrambling off the bed in search of my clothes.

"Damn straight you won't. Hurry up!" I hear Katie exclaim from outside my door, making me wonder just how much she can hear since our walls are thin. Through my peripheral vision, I can see Nick already dressing.

"You're not going to take a shower?" I ask, scrunching my nose at the thought.

He stalks the few steps needed to reach me and embraces me in his arms. "If I take a shower with you, you'll definitely be late for work."

Wrapping my arms around his neck, I ask, "And why is that?"

My body is gently lifted off the ground, bringing me eye level with Nick. "Because I'm going to do things to you in the shower that will make you late," he states. His husky voice sends a shiver down my spine. If I weren't already lifted off the floor, his response would have me floating in mid-air.

Katie's distinctive knock is pounding on my door, reminding me of the time.

"You're right. I can't risk being late."

Sliding down Nick's chest, a gleam of hope sparks in his eyes. "There's always the weekend," he points out. The declaration has me laughing.

"Only you would think of a silver lining," I tell him, making us both chuckle as I rush off to take a shower.

When done, I rush to the kitchen, walking past Nick sitting on the couch. I've somehow expected him to still be waiting, as he's done in the past. On the way, I grab my purse to start digging through it, quickly finding what I need. Next, I'm grabbing for a glass to fill it with water. From the corner of my eye, I catch a glimpse of Nick walking towards me. Coming to stand directly behind me, his arms link around my waist and his face leans in to nuzzle at my neck, the slight stubble on his face tickling me.

"Whatcha got there?" His chin rests on my shoulder as I proceed to toss a pill into my mouth and swallow it down with a gulp of water.

"My birth control pill," I answer when done.

He stiffens behind me before I rapidly spin to face him. "You're on the pill?" he asks.

Nodding my head, although still confused, I say, "It helps regulate my period. Why?"

"You've been making me glove up this whole time when I could have been feeling every inch of you?" Confusion courses through me with the look of disappointment he's delivering.

"I make you glove up because I don't know who you've

been with." He looks ready to answer, but he isn't allowed to re-ply due to my hand now held high to silence him. "I don't want to know, either," I mention, the words bitterly coming out as I unwillingly imagine Nick with other girls. Especially the most recent that showed up at his door.

"What about you? Have you been tested?" he asks.

Annoyance slowly builds inside of me, but the resentful-ness he's also stirred is the reason I answer. "I got tested when I went in for a pregnancy test after I was raped. I needed to make sure I wasn't going to have the bastard's baby or be left with some damn disease from what he did. Thankfully, I was left without either."

His eyes sympathetically look down at me, but it isn't his pity I want. To be honest, I don't want anything from him at this point. "I better get going or else I'm going to be late," I say, already pushing him away as if he's to blame for my now bit-ter attitude. Grabbing for my purse again, I walk my way over to the door, Nick closely behind me. Locking the door when we both exit, I shove myself past him and out of my apartment building, quickening my steps when I'm outside.

"Taylor . . ." Nick demands my attention, but I ignore him. The cause of my resentfulness is still lingering inside of me. Halted to a stop when Nick takes a hold of my arm, he forces me to face him. "Where are you going?"

"I'm going to work."

"I thought I was giving you a ride."

"I'd prefer to take the L today."

My answer is like a slap in the face as he looks down at me with shock.

"What did I say to make you mad?" he asks, the same sin-cerity conveyed in his eyes as he'd had in the kitchen. The tears are slowly starting to build and I forcefully push them down, refusing to surrender to the memory.

"It's bad enough I have to live with the nightmares of what he did to me, but I hate having to explain my actions because of what he did." My jaw is tightly locked as I suppress the tears still threatening to emerge. The tender touch of his palm brushing against my cheek helps push some of the tears away.

"Don't let that asshole do this to you, Taylor. You're only letting him win when you do."

Swallowing the lump still lodged in my throat, a gloomy silence stands between us before Nick pulls me to his chest and tightly wraps his arms around me. Surrendering to his embrace, I need his comfort to push away the demons that have returned.

"I'm sorry," I regretfully reply for my reaction.

"I'll forgive you if you let me give you a ride to work."

The offer makes me laugh into his chest, but it isn't until a few minutes later that we are taking the steps leading to his car. The tension follows us on the drive to my work, but it isn't until we are pulling up to my building that the subject is deflected in another direction.

"Don't forget about dinner tonight. I'll pick you up around seven."

"Are you sure about this?" I ask, still hesitant.

Grabbing my hand to tug me to him, his lips gently meet mine and I can feel the smile on his lips. "Everything will be fine. It's just dinner."

Sighing, I decide to withhold the choice words lingering on the tip of my tongue. "See you at seven," I say, feeling anxious about tonight. Pulling away so I can exit the car, I walk away without a backwards glance, and a heavy heart.

Is it too late to reconsider stepping in front of a bus?

Nick

The lab technician withdraws the needle from my arm with a smile on her lips. It's a flirtatious smile and I plan to take full advantage of it.

"We'll mail you your results within the week, Mr. Hunter."

Holding my hand against the gauze that is wrapped around the crook of my arm, I flash her with a smile as I ask, "Can I have them before I leave?"

"Not usually," she answers.

"What do I need to do in order to get them before I leave?" I plead as I lean in closer to her, purposely dropping my voice in a low, seductive tone.

Her lips shyly curve up in a smile and the evident blush in her cheeks is a sign my antics are working. Nervously biting her lip as if considering my request, she lets out a deep sigh. "Do you mind waiting a couple of hours? It's the fastest I can promise," she informs me.

Pulling back, still flashing her with my smile, I say, "Of course. You're the best." I pause to glance down at her nametag. "Alice . . ."

A glow spreads across her cheeks as she gathers the vials of blood she just finished withdrawing. "We'll give you a call when the results are ready." She leaves the room with a brisk step in her walk.

She leaves me with a smile as I contemplate all the possibilities those results will bring.

SEVENTEEN

Parents

Taylor

I'M SO DISTRACTED that I don't notice when Nick walks into my office. The sound of the closing door is what breaks my concentration, making me look up in the direction of the door. The sight of him leaves me breathless. My heart begins pounding against my chest while my mind contemplates the reasons why he'd need to shut the door.

I'm curiously looking at him as he begins to stalk in my direction, holding up a document in his hand.

Curiosity gets the best of me. "What is that?"

"This, Ms. Taylor, is what you requested of me."

My face draws back in clear confusion. I know for a fact

I've asked nothing of Nick. He doesn't stop until he's standing directly in front of me as he places the document on my desk. Instead of looking at it, my eyes are locked firmly on his, waiting for him to explain himself.

My eyes draw up as he leans down and locks me firmly into my chair.

"I went and got tested this morning, and according to this paper," he says, tilting his head at the direction of my desk, "I'm all clean, which means I get to feel every inch of you from this day forward." Leaning down so his lips brush my ear, he whispers, "Without having to glove up."

My heart suddenly halts. The fact that he got tested all on his own is the reason why my excitement grows.

"There is no longer an excuse to have anything between us and I plan to take full advantage of it tonight." His warm breath causes a wave of shivers to shoot directly down in between my legs where it hits me like an electric jolt.

I'm pretty sure my underwear is soaked from the pooling liquid suddenly forming below. He places an open mouthed kiss below my ear, instantly causing me to moan from the sensation. The kisses continue along my jawline until his mouth finally meets mine. I'm sitting here trying my best to keep myself under control, but I can't. The memory of this morning is currently replaying in my mind.

"Later, Taylor. I plan on finishing this later."

A strangled whimper escapes my mouth, adding to Nick's laughter.

"Dinner first," he adds.

I'm now grimacing into our kiss as he reminds me of our original plans. "I want to give you a ride home, but I know if I do we'll never make it to dinner."

"I wouldn't mind going straight home to plan B."

Smirking at me, he asks, "What exactly is Plan B?"

"You. Me. My bed."

Closing his eyes and letting out a strangled groan, he takes a deep breath before snapping them back open. "Neither would I, but I doubt my parents would be happy if I didn't show up."

I sigh from his remark. Katie walks into our office, forcing Nick to pull away. "I'll see you at seven," Nick remarks, turning to walk away from my desk and giving Katie a quick wave goodbye before he exits.

"Did I interrupt something?" Katie mischievously asks. The teasing wag of her brows has me rolling my eyes. Picking up the document left behind on my desk, my eyes quickly scan the page for the results.

He *is* in fact clean.

"What's that?" Katie curiously asks, walking over to my desk.

"Nick's results."

"Results?" she asks, holding out her hand for the document. I surrender it so she can see for herself. Seconds later, her brows are arched high as she looks down at me. "He went and got tested?"

"Yes. And before you ask, no, I didn't ask him to do it."

"Damn, Taylor. That boy has got it bad for you."

"Him getting tested does not mean he *has it bad for me.* It only means he's like every other typical man wanting to get laid. He's just preferring to do it without a condom."

She snickers. "Believe what you want, Taylor, but he didn't have to do it," she states before dropping the paper back onto my desk.

My eyes follow her movements as she heads back to her own desk and concentrates on her computer. The entire time my mind wonders about the true reason why Nick decided to get tested. The only person who can give me a *definite* answer has already left the room. Until then, I'm left asking the same question that is constantly on my mind. *What the hell am I to Nick Hunter?*

What the heck was I thinking when I agreed to go to dinner with Nick and his parents? I've only just met the guy a little over a month ago and he already wants me to have dinner with them? I must have been out of my mind when I agreed. But when he looked at me with those pleading blue eyes of his, I couldn't deny him; there is no winning when he begs. Lord knows he's done enough to try to make me happy; the least I can do is grant this one request. The only problem is this request is the biggest one when it came to—Shit. I still don't know what to call what is going on between us.

What exactly do you call two people having sex together?

Friends with benefits?

What have I gotten myself into? It's too damn soon to be meeting his parents.

Letting out a frustrated groan as I go through my lame and practically empty closet, I hear Katie come into my room. "I thought you'd need help so I brought over some options," she cheerfully says with an armful of dresses. I'm instantly thankful that she's my roommate.

Since Katie has a limitless budget when it comes to shopping, I trust her to have something that might impress Nick's parents. As we make our selection, I start to feel more confident that I'm going to satisfy Nick. The last thing I want to do is make the wrong impression on our very first meeting. Who am I kidding? I don't want to make the wrong impression. Period.

This time there's no argument from my mouth as Katie preps my hair and make-up, and in record time I'm ready when Nick is knocking at the door. My stomach is in knots and I'm ready to heave from the nerves. Making sure to take deep breaths as Katie lets Nick in the apartment, I stop breathing all together when I see him.

With him standing in front of me I nervously ask, "Do I look okay?"

"You're the most beautiful thing I've ever seen."

As my breath catches in my throat, he leans in to kiss me. All earlier doubt has completely vanished. He leaves me breathless when he ends our kiss.

"I'm tempted to take you to the room and tear this dress off you."

"Whoa there tiger, that dress she's wearing happens to be one of my favorites and the last thing you're going to be doing is ripping it," Katie chastises from the entrance of the apartment, still holding onto the door.

"I can't make any promises," Nick replies, taking my hand to lead me out of the apartment.

"Why do I have a feeling you're willing to risk Katie's wrath?" I ask on our way to his car. Stopping when we've reached the passenger side, his eyes bear down into mine. "Because it would be completely worth it to get what's underneath it."

Smiling at his response, I say, "As long as you don't rip it off until *after* dinner."

"Deal."

The playfulness is replaced with silence. Tension overtakes the ambiance inside the car the entire drive. Eventually, he brings his car to a stop, and as the valet helps me exit the car, I take in my surroundings. He's driven us to one of Chicago's most upscale restaurants and I begin to panic. I've heard of this restaurant, but never imagined I'd be stepping foot in it. How am I to guarantee I won't make a fool of myself?

My self-doubt has fully returned.

Nick wraps his arm around my waist, leading me into the building, every step I'm full of nerves. Composing myself as best as I can as we enter the building, I tell myself, Nick is a wonderful person so why would his parents be any different?

I'm instantly proven wrong when we are led to a table where an older couple is already seated. The moment their eyes take me in, they scowl. The lady's eyes are critically analyzing me, the unhidden contempt on her face notifying me she's disappointed in what she sees.

"Nicolas, is there a reason why you've invited a dinner guest with you tonight?" The question entirely aimed at me.

"Mother, this is Taylor. Taylor, this is my mother Regina and my father Harold," he conveys, clearly ignoring her comment.

Politely holding out my hand towards her, I say, "It's nice to meet you." She stares down at my hand with disgust, never offering her own hand. Just as quickly, I pull my hand away, feeling dejected.

She looks over to Nick as she delivers her next words. "Having to hear about your liaisons is one thing, but to insult your father and I by bringing one to dinner is beyond disrespectful."

"Mother," Nick barely manages to get out before she's silencing him with her hand. "Don't. You've already done enough," she says, now looking at me.

The insult causes a lump to form in my throat and it's preventing me from speaking. Even if I attempted to do so, what good would it do to defend myself? She's already made her assumptions about me.

It takes Nick's father loudly clearing his throat to distract us. "Why don't we all take a seat and try to enjoy the evening as planned?" he says as Nick's mother lets out an audible gasp.

I'm still standing, contemplating whether I should leave. At this point, it'd be the best for all of us. Instead, I'm urged by Nick to sit as the waiter pulls out my chair. The only other seat available is across from me, leaving me feeling vulnerable without Nick at my side.

I sit there in a trance, trying to ignore the awful glares coming from my right as his mother's eyes continue to bore into my soul. I keep repeating how I'm doing this for Nick and no one else.

Eventually, the conversation turns to topics in which I am not included, leaving me with no other choice but to sit and endure feeling incompetent. When the food arrives, I'm lost in my own thoughts, counting down the minutes until our departure, when Nick's father chooses to address me.

"Taylor?" His questioning tone throws me off guard, making me snap my head up in his direction.

"Look at her, she can't even respect us enough to pay attention to our conversation. Where on earth did you find this girl, Nicolas?" Regina furiously complains.

"Mother," Nick snarls in her direction.

"I'm sorry, Nicolas, but your father did ask her a question and she's clearly ignoring him." Her voice sounds like nails on a chalkboard. "What kind of manners were you raised with, young lady, that you cannot be polite enough to answer a question when it's originally asked?"

Gently placing my fork down, I summon the best smile I can muster.

"If you'll please excuse me, I'm off to the ladies room."

Every word is forced as I attempt to convey honesty in my statement.

"Of course," Nick's father replies, standing along with Nick. His mother prefers to stay rooted in her seat, clearly uncaring of how rude she appears.

"I'll walk you," Nick suggests.

"That won't be necessary. I'm sure your parents would like to continue their conversation with you."

I don't give Nick the chance to argue before I turn and head off towards what I believe would be the restrooms. When I'm no longer in their view, I take another hallway, which I know will lead me to the exit. It doesn't take long before the brisk breeze of Chicago's air hits me full force, helping push most of the torment from the night aside.

The valet is already trying to flag down a taxi, but I walk right past him, knowing I wouldn't be able to afford the fare home. Lucky for me, the small clutch Katie lent me contains my pass for the L. It may take longer to get home, but sitting in a crowd of strangers would be much more pleasant than enduring the venom I've been receiving.

Nick

Glancing down at my watch once more, I realize it's been fifteen minutes since Taylor excused herself to the restroom. The moment she walked away, I instantly felt her loss. My mind was screaming to ignore her request to not follow her and instead lead her out of the door, but I'd known deep down inside she needed the time to herself.

My entire life, I've endured my mother's wrath, which is why I'm able to easily ignore it. Looking over to my father, I have to wonder how it is he's managed to bear being married to her for so long. Then I remember how he was practically forced to marry her to merge the families' companies. It wasn't strange to do then, and is still expected of me now. It's one of the burdens my mother never failed to heave in my face as she constantly reminds me of the responsibility my brother had failed to live up to.

He was supposed to marry one of the daughters of my father's business associate, but instead had chosen love—a love that had come to betray him for money. Instead, it left my mother hopeful I would take his place and marry her instead. But to do so would mean to leave my career, something I was unwilling to do.

Unable to resist, my eyes look down at my watch and my patience evaporates. "I'm going to go check on Taylor," I inform my parents.

My mother's response does not surprise me. "If we're lucky enough, she's drowned herself in the bathroom."

Ignoring her crude comment, I head to the ladies' room to patiently wait for Taylor, hoping to mend what little of the night that is left. Two minutes later, a woman is exiting and instantly flashes me with a mannerly smile. In the process, she has completely opened the door, allowing me a peek inside. In the short time the door is open, I can see there is no one else in there. When I've waited long enough and I'm alone in the hallway, I bravely enter the facilities. Boldly taking my chances, I bend down to check under the stall doors to find them also empty, alerting me that Taylor is obviously not in the restroom.

Rushing out of the ladies' room, I walk as fast as I can towards the exit. Outside, I look from left to right, not seeing her anywhere. The valet is standing in front of me, patiently waiting for an order.

"Did you see a girl? This high," I say holding up my hand

to my shoulder. "Lace black dress, brunette hair?"

"I tried flagging a taxi for her, sir, but when I turned around she was already gone."

Shit. She's already left.

"Thank you," I reply, handing him my valet ticket. I'm not going to trouble myself with going back inside. My main concern is Taylor.

While waiting for my car, my thoughts are in turmoil, struggling to find the correct words I'm going to face Taylor with. I already know she isn't going to easily forgive me for tonight, but I will try my best to make it up to her.

If that woman wasn't my own mother, who I loved and respected dearly, I would have stood up and walked out of there with Taylor a long time ago. She didn't deserve to be treated in that manner. Had I known my parents were going to be so rude tonight, I would have just blown them off and spent the night having dinner with Taylor at home.

The entire drive to Taylor's apartment my heart is racing, my mind still battling with what to say. My night didn't go exactly how I thought it would and how it ends will depend on Taylor's reaction.

As I pull up to her apartment complex, I immediately see her already nearing her building, allowing me time to park my car and rush over to her. Meeting her at the entrance, her eyes are furiously regarding me. "Leave me alone, Nick. Just stay the hell away from me from now on," she says, hurt clear in her voice as she opens the door and steps inside.

Following her to her apartment, I force myself inside before she can shut the door.

"I'm sorry about tonight, Taylor. If I'd known they didn't want you there I wouldn't have taken you," I say, regretting the words the moment they leave my mouth.

The sharp intake of her breath makes my heart drop to my stomach. "Why did you, Nick? Was it to prove to me that we will never be equals? If that was the case, it didn't take dinner with your parents to prove it to me. I knew it the moment I laid eyes on you."

"No, Taylor, that's not what I meant." I reach out for her, but she steps back, bringing her hand up to warn me to stop.

"I told you from the beginning I wasn't good enough for you, but I was stupid enough to believe it when you said I was. I should have stayed away, but I was a fool who opened up her heart and trusted you."

Her words have completely gutted me.

"Never again. Just get out, Nick. Take your mother's advice and walk away while you can. It'd be best for the both of us," she says as tears stream down her cheeks.

"Taylor, please."

"It doesn't matter, anyway. I'm nothing to you."

"How can you think you're nothing to me? You mean more to me than anything in this world."

She wraps herself in her arms, shaking her head in denial. "If you cared you wouldn't have allowed me to be torn apart by those people."

Her words sting like a slap in the face. Every word is true. I try approaching her, wanting nothing more than to hold her in my arms, but it's impossible as she retreats from me. "They're right. I'm just another one of *your conquests.* I've known it since the beginning and I know it now."

"Taylor, now you're just talking nonsense."

"All you've ever cared about is getting in between my legs!"

My rage emerges with her words. "That's a low blow. Even for you, Taylor," I growl out. "Why would you say something like that?"

"We're two different people, Nick. It was never meant to be."

I want to argue, but she cuts me off. "I think you should leave," she states, the fury in her statement returning me to the state I'd arrived in.

Dread.

Worry.

Regret.

As much as I want to force her to listen to me, I know it's the last thing I should do.

"I'm leaving tonight, but only to give you time to calm down. I told you once, Taylor, I wasn't giving up on you and I'm saying it again, this time with a promise. I'm not giving up on you.

"I love you, Taylor, and there isn't anything in the world that would change that," I say before turning and leaving her apartment. She slams the door behind me, making me turn around to face it.

"I'm not giving up on you, Taylor. Never."

EIGHTEEN

Redemption

Nick

THE MISERY COURSING inside of me does not compare to how I made Taylor feel tonight. I'm ashamed of myself for not defending her sooner. I know I should have, but my arrogance kept me from acting upon it, an act that is costing me dearly now that she has pushed me away. I know no one is to blame but myself.

The drive to the hotel to confront my parents feels never-ending. It's as if every red light has sided on their behalf to keep me from getting to them sooner. The entire time my determination is fueled by the image of Taylor's shattered expression.

Soon enough, I'm pulling up to the valet station of an impressive hotel. I don't waste a second as I step out of my car, nearly taking out my anger on the poor valet boy as I yank the ticket from his hand. Stalking my way past the registration desk, I already know which room they're going to be in. It's the same as always. My mother is a creature of habit and insists on reserving the same room.

The ride up in the elevator is another delay, fueling my wrath. Marching my way to the presidential suite, I bang on their door, demanding entrance. Their butler answers, greeting me with his usual curt nod as I brush past him. I find my mother in the living room, reading a fashion magazine without any regard to my presence as I stalk my way over to face her. The only indication she gives in acknowledgement of my presence is an arched eyebrow as she continues to stare down into the pages in front of her.

"Where is Dad?" I ask, searching the room for him, but finding him absent.

Still staring down at the object in her hands, she answers, "I left him downstairs at the bar, most likely drinking his sorrows away thanks to your little escapade," she lectures. "I expect you're here to apologize for your behavior tonight."

"My behavior? You're the one who should be apologizing!"

Now both her brows are arching as she glances up at me. "We've raised you better than to behave the way you did tonight. You were the one who left us sitting at the table to most likely run after *that* girl you embarrassed us with."

The rage inside of me takes over. "I'm done! I've put up with enough of your shit mother. All my life—" Before I can finish my lecture, she stands up, fury now replacing her once blank eyes.

"You've done nothing but bring disappointment to our family by defying your duties. We have only two sons, yet neither can do what is required of them. "

"Have you ever asked whether we wanted to do it or not?"

"It isn't a choice. You're a Hunter, Nicolas, and you have Macintyre blood coursing through your veins as well. You don't have a choice. It is expected of you!"

"That's all you've ever told me, but it's not what I want."

A disappointed sigh leaves her lips. "Nicolas, how much longer are you going to believe that swinging a bat and catching a ball is more important than pursuing what is your legacy?"

"Until the last day I can do it. I've done nothing but try to satisfy your every demand. Regardless of what Nathan and I have done, it's never been good enough for you. I've probably lost the only girl I've ever had feelings for tonight because I did nothing but sit there and allow you to spew your venom at her."

With a wave of her hand, she dismisses my statement. "Her walking away is for the best. She isn't good enough for you. She will bring nothing to this family."

"I don't give a shit what she has or will bring!"

"Tell me, Nicolas, how much do you really know about this girl?"

"It doesn't matter what I know or don't know." I say the words to mask the sting of her question. There is so much I don't know about Taylor. She refuses to fully open herself up to me. But to admit that fact to my mother would only bring mockery upon myself.

Feeling the need to further mend the mistake I've made tonight, I resume my battle with my mother. "I don't care what you think of her, but you better pray to God Taylor forgives me for your actions tonight, because whether or not I ever see you again depends on her."

"How dare you choose her over your family."

"Family would never make me choose between the woman I love or them," I growl back at her."

"You wouldn't dare defy me, Nicolas."

"Try me," I reply before stalking my way past her without a backward glance.

"Nicolas!" The shouting of my name is ignored as I walk straight out of the suite. I'd expected to leave with a feeling of satisfaction, yet I feel far from satisfied. The realization of what my life has always been came to me in that brief moment.

All my brother and I have ever been to my mother are pawns in the game of chess she's played all her life, bred to succeed and obey. We both began to defy her commands as adults, preferring to follow our own dreams. I may be a disappointment in her eyes for not following my father's footsteps, but at least I'm doing what I love.

Now, if I can only say I'm currently happy in life, it would be satisfying enough. I was happy two hours ago when I held Taylor in my arms, but the damage I've managed to create between us has torn that apart. There is only one way to bring my happiness back, and it is Taylor.

I hadn't intended to confront my father. Upon exiting the elevator is when the thought occurred to me. Entering the hotel bar, I quickly find him, sitting alone and looking miserable. Unlike my mother, it's as if he's sensed my presence and turns to face me. The strained smile I receive guides me to him.

"Hello, son." The guilt in his greeting is also opposite of what I had received from my mother.

"Father."

I've never called my parents *"Mom and Dad"* as most children do. I've only ever formally addressed them. I was raised to respect my elders, using ma'am and sir to address anyone in our world of power. I was taught to hold my tongue, never to speak back to my parents, and had never dared to until tonight.

Taking a seat at his side, he gives me a curt nod. "Would you like a drink?"

Refusing his offer, he turns to request a refill of his empty glass.

"You disappeared on us."

"I went after Taylor. She left."

"I apologize about tonight. It shouldn't have happened."

Nodding my head in agreement, I stay silent, unable to respond just yet. The only sound between us is the clinking of the ice in the glass he's swirling in his hand.

"I told Mother tonight was the last straw. I don't think I can ever forgive her for what she did."

He stares off into the distance, lips flat. "I can't blame you, son."

His admission should bring me satisfaction, but it doesn't.

"Did you know I wanted to be a pilot when I was a child? The infatuation began when I was young and we'd board our jet to fly to our destination. I'd imagine myself in the pilot's seat flying us around the world. I never got to follow my dreams."

"You could have if you wanted to."

He doesn't seem convinced by my words. "It was different then. I was expected to follow the path laid out in front of me."

"As I am?"

Now finding my eyes, he looks shocked. "No," he declares. "I'm proud of the man you've become. You followed your dreams."

If my heart weren't in pieces because of the situation with Taylor, it'd be beaming at the moment.

His mouth forms a smile. "I really like this girl. She's . . . different."

"Yeah, she is. She's like no one I've ever met before. She's a little firecracker."

"I bet. She looks it. She's earned my deepest respect for tolerating as much as she did tonight."

His reminder of my loss has my darkened mood returning.

"She'll come around," he says, sounding confident it will happen. I wish it were as easy as he makes it sound.

"Tell me, where did you meet her?"

I recall the moment I first met Taylor clear in my mind. It's the reason for my smile. "She was my original sports therapist, but it didn't last more than a week before she had me transferred." His brows arch with curiosity. "She refused to put up with my shit."

"Is that so?"

"I just couldn't let it be. I don't know," I say with a sigh. "She's different," I repeat my father's words. "She didn't care what my name *was* or *how* much money I had."

"Maybe that's why you're drawn to her."

"When I'm not with her, I don't feel complete."

"You're in love," he declares.

I'd already known that, but hearing my father point it out makes it feel real.

"Yes, I am."

A silence lingers between us. Again, the only sound is the clinking in his glass as he twirls it.

"I really miss our conversations."

"So do I," he draws out.

"You're not around long enough to have them anymore," I bitterly let out.

"It's my fault," he admits. "But I plan on remedying that. I don't want to live my life being a stranger to my own sons. I want to know what's going on with their lives. It's a shame my son is dating a pretty girl and I have no clue who she is," he teases.

"If it makes you feel any better, Taylor didn't know, either."

He's questionably looking at me. "I was an ass and never got around to clarifying how much she meant to me until tonight, but it was too late."

He cringes with me when I finish.

"If there's anything we Hunters have ever proven, it's how hard headed we are. We don't know how to take no for an answer," he says with a wink.

His declaration leaves me hopeful.

I was going to do everything in my power to earn Taylor's forgiveness. As my father stated, I'm a Hunter, and it's in my blood to refuse the answer *no*.

NINETEEN

To forgive or forget?

Taylor

DECEIVE . . . TO MISLEAD by a false appearance or statement; delude.

A dictionary isn't needed to remind me of Nick, my shattered heart was doing the job for me.

It's been four days since I last saw Nick. Four *full* days since he deceived me that dreadful night. It's when my soul discovered the *true* identity of Nicolas Hunter.

Regardless of his attempts to beg for forgiveness, my heart is too wounded to consider the thought. He began with phone calls, which I only deterred to voicemail. Seconds later, they were followed by a text message. I also ignored those after the first one.

"I'm sorry, Taylor. Please, just talk to me."

The days feel endless. I've tried hard to push the memory of Nick behind me, but my heart won't allow it, and the memories are branded in my mind.

I tried hard from the beginning to push him away, but I failed to make him understand that nothing good would ever come from him chasing after me. He was persistent, a trait I valued in him. But falling hopelessly in love with him only to have him shatter my already wounded heart was the result.

Forcing myself to focus on my patients and their needs helped make the days flow easier. It gave me a momentary distraction throughout the day.

After crying the last tear I allowed myself to cry for Nick, I forced myself to shut him completely from my mind. It wasn't easy, but unfortunately I had help. The nightmares had returned, this time with a deeper intensity than before. These were different. I wasn't waking up screaming for anyone to get off me, I was now begging for someone to stay . . . Nick.

Regardless of my begging and screaming, he would turn and leave. I would wake up crying, wishing it weren't true. I knew they were simply dreams, but they still felt real.

I could practically smell him, feel the warmth of his skin against my hands, and taste of his mouth as it kissed me in return. Then just as quickly, he would drift away.

It was easier not to sleep than to have to endure the nightmares, the result taking a toll on me mentally and physically. I was more distant than normal, and at times, I would avoid anyone and everyone if possible. I've resorted to taking the L to and from work to avoid having to face Katie. I didn't want my broken heart to be the cause of me saying something I may regret.

Arriving home at the end of the day, I'm barely walking into my apartment when Katie stomps her way from her room. She stops at the end of our hallway, glaring directly at me.

"Where were you?" she demands. "I tried calling you but you still have your phone turned off."

I'd informed her the day I silenced it. She wasn't happy with my decision, but understood.

"I went to get coffee."

"You need to get over your little tantrum already and turn on your damn phone," she scolds. Normally a lecture like this would make anyone cringe, but not me.

"Why?"

Katie throws her hands up with an exasperated sigh. "You didn't get home on time and I started freaking out, that's why."

"I'm sorry," I apologize. "I'm home now."

She growls at me, full on growls in exasperation

"Taylor, I get it. He acted like an asshole, but it doesn't mean you have to completely shut out the rest of the world." She continues to lecture as I walk into the kitchen. "And I bought dinner. So you better eat it or I'm shoving it down your throat!" she shouts over her shoulder before disappearing down the hall into our bathroom. Within minutes, I hear the starting of the shower.

With a raised brow I stare down at the deli sandwich sitting on the counter. I'm far from having an appetite. To be honest, I haven't had one in days. Grabbing the sandwich, I place it in the refrigerator so it won't go bad. Maybe Katie will eat it for lunch tomorrow.

Returning to the living room, I throw myself onto the couch. I slump into the cushions to rummage through my purse for the object she was lecturing about. Turning on my phone, I wait. As expected, it immediately begins to ping. Surprisingly though, it takes minutes for it to stop.

My text messages from Nick say . . .

"I have one brother, his name is Nathan. He's three years older than me."

"I was raised in New York City, spending all my summers in the Hamptons until five years ago."

"I never had a dog, but always begged for one. I never got it. My mother never wanted the dander or mess in her house."

"My favorite color is blue."

"I have no middle name."

"My first car was a Porsche. I wrecked it two months later."

"My first kiss was with a girl named Mindy, who slobbered more than kissed. I won't tell you who I lost my virginity to because I know you could care less, but I also remember the girl's name in case you change your mind."

That last text has me scrunching my nose at the phone.

"I broke my arm falling out of a tree when I was six. My mother grounded me for a week for disobeying her order of not going outdoors and getting dirty."

"My nanny's name was Barbara. For the longest time I had a crush on her, until I found her kissing our cook. Our cook was a woman."

This one makes me smile as I bite back my laughter.

"When I discovered my love for baseball, I dreamed of playing for the Yankee's. Now I despise the team."

Now I'm chuckling.

"My childhood best friend's name was Tom. I told Tom all my secrets. Tom was a very good listener. He was also my imaginary friend."

This text I can tragically relate to.

"I once spotted a girl from across the room. The sight of

her left me breathless, especially when she lifted her head and stared into my eyes."

There are no words to express how I'm feeling after that text message, but I continue reading.

"This same girl was constantly in my thoughts. I couldn't get her out of my mind. She consumed me, day and night."

This text message makes me feel the same as the one before it.

"Her name is Taylor . . . and I love her."

It's the last text message, and the one that leaves *me* breathless.

Holding my phone while my mind recaps each text message, my injured heart is slowly mending.

Why?

A simple, yet complicated question, which continues to repeat itself in my head while I read through the messages once more.

This time though, I deliberately take my time to read each one. My heart is gradually feeling the need to respond as I absorb every word written. When finished, my vision is obstructed by the tears that have built. I'd told myself I had cried enough tears for Nick this past week and I wouldn't cry anymore, but I'm finding it difficult to obey my own decree as the tears slowly trickle down my cheeks in defeat.

My selfishness to refuse to allow anyone in my heart had eventually hardened it. Yet Nick had somehow managed to find his way in. The heartache I've been carrying since I'd pushed him to leave has left me feeling as if it were a mistake. But can I truly believe I'll be able to excuse and forget Nick's faults if I do forgive him? Somehow, it feels I may be failing myself if I keep telling myself *no*.

My thumb brushes the screen of my phone, contemplating

my next step. Bravely, my fingers find the response box and cautiously type the next words.

"Wilson. It's my last name, but I hate it because it's a reminder of a father I never had."

I push send while I still have the courage to do so. My heart is now hastily beating as I sit and wait for a response. Seconds turn into minutes, minutes that sluggishly tick by with no response. My once rapidly beating heart is starting to sink into the depths of my stomach, the rejection from the silence eating away at my emotions.

Katie's footsteps force me to pull myself from my thoughts. Blinking away the remainder of my tears as she walks into the living room, she takes a seat on the other end of the couch. Katie turns in my direction as if preparing to say something, but suddenly pauses as she furrows her brow. "What's wrong with you?" she worriedly asks.

I swallow the tears that have built, still unable to answer.

"Tell me," she demands.

Not knowing how to explain the cause for my anguish, I scroll to the beginning of the text messages and hand her the phone instead. A minute later, she's looking at me with a confused look upon her face. "When did he send these?"

"I don't know. I got them when I turned on my phone."

She considers my response for a second. "I don't get it. Why would he send you random sentences about himself?"

"Maybe he thinks if he shared secrets about himself I would, too."

She looks down at my phone, a hint of a smile curving her lips.

"Apparently it worked," she says, referring to the response I'd sent him.

Taking the phone back from her hand, I contemplate if

there is any way to take my own text message back. "No, it didn't. I sent it ten minutes ago and he hasn't responded. It's obvious he doesn't care anymore," I grimly reply.

"What time is it?"

Looking down at my phone, I say, "Seven thirty-three, why?"

"He's not going to respond anytime soon." There's already a hollowness piercing at my emotions, but Katie's comment deepens the wound. "He's playing right now," she further explains.

Reaching forward for the remote sitting on the coffee table, she brings the television to life and flicks through the guide until coming upon the sports channel. Pressing enter, it now displays a baseball game. As she mentioned, the image on the screen is projecting the White Soxs in the midst of a game.

"Look, there's Nick," Katie comments, pointing at the screen, but all I see is an enlarged image of the stadium before it focuses on the batter. The player hits the ball, a pop as the ball makes contact with the bat sounds from the speaker of the television. Just as fast, the camera is zooming in on the ball as it speeds down the field and I instantly recognize Nick on the screen. He dives for the ball, throwing it to second base. The second baseman's hand reaches forward to catch the ball, turning to throw it to the first baseman. The receiver catches it, tagging the running batter coming in his direction out. The crowd cheers with excitement as the camera's view returns to Nick. The commentator is now praising Nick for his excellent play as he runs his way off the field.

Days' worth of sorrow have completely vanished with just that moment of viewing him. My breath has hitched, my heart has returned to erratically beating, and my insides begin to turn giddy from only those couple of seconds I was able to view him before it leads off into a commercial.

"Why is it going to a commercial?"

"It always does that in between innings. It gives the teams time to warm up without us having to watch them."

I sit, impatiently waiting for the game to return. Just as I've begun to lose my patience, the game comes back on. Nick reappears on the screen as the first batter. The faint chorus of the song "Wild Ones" is playing throughout the stadium as he walks up to the batter's diamond.

"Why are they playing that song?" I ask Katie, perplexed as to why those specific words would be played for Nick.

"They always play a specific song for each player. It's usually one they choose. It's like a signature song for them." My earlier giddiness has vanished. "Taylor, they've been playing that song for him for a while. Don't take it too serious."

"Easy for you to say. You're not the one who would be considered part of his *wild side*," I remark, my eyes locked onto the screen in front of us.

Nick lowers himself into a crouched stance as he readies himself to hit the ball. The pitcher looks behind his back as he brings his right hand up to his glove. His right knee is brought up towards his chest and he throws his body forward as he releases the ball. It flies through the air straight ahead of him in Nick's direction as he throws his first pitch. It lands in the glove of the catcher and the crowd groans in disappointment. Nick steps back a moment, swinging the bat in the air before he returns to his earlier stance, preparing to hit the ball. The pitcher throws the ball again, this time it makes contact with Nick's bat, but zooms to the side of the field. I expect Nick to run, but he keeps himself at the diamond instead.

"Why didn't he run to the base?"

"It's a foul ball. He isn't supposed to run," Katie explains.

I have no clue what she means by that answer, but my eyes have never left the screen of the television. They've been focused solely on Nick. The pitcher readies for another pitch. This time when he delivers the ball, Nick is quickly jumping back as it swooshes by him. Continuing to keep my eyes locked on the TV, I can see Nick's body language in reaction to the last pitch; he's clearly irritated. Once more, he's readying himself to hit the ball, but when the pitcher delivers the pitch, it's now striking Nick's thigh.

"Holy shit!" Katie shouts at my side. I'm gasping into my hands as I watch Nick drop his bat and rush to the pitcher. The pitcher mimics his move and is meeting him halfway as they throw themselves at each other and begin fighting. Both teams are soon following onto the field as the crowd erupts in a chorus of roars. In my mind, I'm predicting the teams will help separate the two players, but I'm proven wrong when the mass of players begin to participate in the brawl. The overwhelming cheers and hollers from the crowd are only encouraging them to continue, when in my mind I'm wishing they would just stop.

I've completely lost sight of Nick in the mass of players who have all begun to blend together in the center of the field. Fists are aiming in whichever direction they can swing. Players are pulling and yanking forcefully, trying to outdo the opponent. Within minutes the brawl is ending, but Nick is forcefully being dragged off the field, disappearing into a passageway in the dugout. The announcer is speaking, but my astounded mind is still trying to process what has occurred. The disappointed groans and boos of the crowd can be heard clearly through the speakers of the television.

"Where did he go?"

"Nick was suspended for the remainder of the game."

"Serves him right," I comment, more at a non-existent

Nick who is nowhere for me to lecture.

For the next couple of minutes, replay after replay of the battle is repeated, throwing me into an angered state of mind. My phone pings in my hand distracting me from the chaos on the screen I'm staring at.

I would have never guessed Wilson.—Nick

You've got some nerve, I comment back.

Almost immediately my phone is pinging with a response.

For replying?—Nick

For causing a fight! I just as quickly reply.

Please tell me you're in the stands so I can come get you.—Nick

My eyes go wide as I gape at the phone.

You wish, I sourly respond.

He surprises me when my phone begins ringing and Nick's number appears on the screen. Without a second's pause, I answer.

"I was watching the game on the TV and only because Katie put the game on," I say, blaming her. "And I can't believe you actually started a fight. Are you crazy? You could have injured yourself again," I lecture into the phone. "What the hell is wrong with you?" I ask, breathlessly ending my lecture.

"Are you done?"

"Yes, I'm done," I throw back at him, irritated.

I hang up on him, infuriated by his question.

Taking my frustration out on the phone, I toss it down onto the couch in between Katie and me. The phone begins ringing again. Still aggravated, I stare at it, refusing to answer.

"You're not going to answer it?"

"No," I furiously mumble back to Katie. She surprises me by picking up the phone and answering it herself. My hands reach out to try to take the phone from her, but it's too late as she begins speaking into it.

"She's pissed." I watch her as she listens into the phone, her head slightly nodding and agreeing to whatever it is he's saying. "It's your head, not mine," she replies, leaving me confused when she hangs up the phone.

"What did he say?"

"He wants to know why you didn't answer the phone."

Childishly crossing my arms across my chest, I keep silent while directing my eyes at the commercials.

"What else did he say?"

"I'm going out," she answers, standing up from the couch and turning the television off before she begins walking away.

"That's not what he said," I retort, following her down the hall and into her bedroom.

"No, it's not, but I have a date and I'm already late."

"No you don't!" I shout at her retreating back. "Katie, if you don't tell me what he said, I'm going to beat it out of you."

She turns, her eyebrow arched high. "Weren't you just lecturing Nick about fighting?" she teases. The fury in my eyes is what has her answering my earlier request. "He's coming over."

"What?" I shout back at her. "I thought you were on my side?"

Sighing, she walks over to stand in front of me, her hands reaching up to rest on my shoulders. "You've done nothing but mope around for the last week. I'm tired of it. You miss him. We both know that. I may not be happy with what the douche did, but I could hear it in his voice, he's just as miserable as you are."

"So?"

"So you guys need to figure your shit out." I shake my head in refusal, but Katie catches my attention again by shaking my shoulders. "Yes, you are," she argues. "And I *do* have a date, which I'm now late for."

She shoves me out of her room, leaving me no choice but to retreat to my own. I sit on my bed, waiting as the minutes gradually pass by. Sometime later, Katie peeks her head inside, informing me she's leaving and wishing me luck on her way out. My eyes grow heavy from lack of sleep. Too weak to resist, I soon fall asleep.

A heavy knock on the door startles me awake. With my heart beating erratically, I take leaded steps towards the door. I hesitantly open the door to find Nick's remorseful eyes staring back at me.

"Can I come in?" he timidly asks.

Granting him access, my hands grip at the door to keep myself from reaching out to touch him as he brushes by me. Closing the door after he enters, I turn to find him standing directly in front of me. His hands engulf my face, bringing his lips down onto mine. I reach out to grip his waist, pulling him to close the gap in between us.

Days' worth of sorrow and grief are still present in my mind, but my heart has already surrendered to his kiss. The warmth of his tongue gliding against my own is a presence I've been deeply craving for these past four days. The feel of his body against mine is a comfort I hadn't known I'd longed for until now. The tenderness in his touch is just as familiar as it had been from the last time I had seen him.

Our kiss comes to an end and my mind is silently whimpering from the loss of his lips as he pulls away. His hands are still possessively digging into my hair to hold me in place.

"I missed you so much, Taylor. I'm sorry."

"You've already said that."

"I know, but . . ." He sighs, sounding frustrated. "What do I have to do for you to forgive me? Whatever you ask of me, I'll do it," he pleads, his hands gently tightening in my hair, as if refusing to let me go.

My mind knows I can't risk forgiving him just yet, but my heart is begging otherwise. All from his one kiss. Tears are ready to emerge and I blink them away.

"I don't know," I croak out.

"I swear, Taylor, if I could turn back time I would never have let it happen."

The admission swells my heart, but how will I ever know if his words are truthful?

"Please . . ." he pleads, kissing my temple. Pulling away, I look directly into a pair of eyes full of remorse and sorrow.

"I don't know if I can handle having my heart broken again," I truthfully admit.

"I won't break your heart."

"You don't know that," I say as I pull away.

"Yes, I do." I doubtfully stare at him, unable to believe his words. "I don't know what you've done to me, Taylor, but I've never felt this way about anyone. Ever. I don't want to know what it would feel like to completely lose you."

I swallow to keep myself from admitting he has the same effect on me. I've known it from the moment we first bickered.

"Can we just go back to the beginning?" I ask.

Letting out a sigh of relief, he says, "As long as it's not too far back where I have to wait to kiss you. I don't know if I can endure having to wait to earn your trust all over again."

"It's too late," I respond.

He stiffens. "If I have to earn your trust a hundred times over, then I will." Pulling me close to envelop me in his arms, the warmth of his body has me melting into his embrace.

Turning back time seems like the most logical answer at this point, but it's impossible. Regardless of what he says or does, I know things will never be the same.

TWENTY

Hopeful

Nick

WITH MY ARMS tightly wrapped around Taylor, I keep asking myself if I'm dreaming. Holding her still feels surreal. For the past week, I've only experienced it in my dreams. I want nothing more than to stay asleep, to be able to hold onto her. I'd come to believe it was all I had left. Brushing my nose against her hair and inhaling her sweet smell, I realize I've missed it just as much as holding her.

"Why did you start the fight?"

"He hit me first," I laugh out. Jerking her head back, she glares at me.

"Now you just sound like a child," she reprimands.

"I was pissed. Not at him, but at myself. It was just easier to take it out on him."

"Was it worth getting kicked out of the game for?" she asks, sounding irritated. Unfortunately, her fury makes me smile. I've come to love the furious side of Taylor. It's what drew me to her.

"Can we not talk about that? I want to talk about us."

Her lips go flat and her eyes are looking anywhere but at my own. She's avoiding my question. A drawn out silence gradually starts to overtake the room, worrying me.

"Taylor," I croak out, pulling her attention back to me.

She pushes herself away from my embrace, leaving me with a sense of loss from her now absent body. "I don't know what to do, Nick. Did you honestly think you would just be able to come over and I'd easily forgive you?"

The blood drains from my face from her question. It's a sign she isn't willing to forgive me.

"I can't help but think your parents were right." Her statement both angers and pains me.

"They're not the ones who would make the decision for me, Taylor."

"You led them to believe they can. You never once spoke up during dinner!" she throws back at me. My mouth opens to dispute, but I'm quickly cut off before I have the chance. "It was then you should have been saying those words, not now. Not when it's too late."

"Don't say that," I desperately plead as I step towards her, but she retreats, moving further from my reach. "I went back. I did tell them. You're all that matters now, Taylor." Her eyes stare back at me with uncertainty.

Stepping forward to catch her before she can react, I look directly into her eyes as I say, "Stop thinking you're not worth anything, Taylor. You're worth more than you'll ever know. What's it going to take for you to understand that?"

She swallows as her eyes become glassy, but she blinks to keep from shedding her tears. Instead, she tries pulling away but my lips are already descending down onto hers, hoping to kiss her agony away. She responds by gripping onto my forearms, pulling me to close the small gap between us. When we end the kiss, she slightly shakes her head.

"I can't be with you wondering how long it will be before you break my heart again."

"I already told you—"

Before I have a chance to finish, she argues, "I believed you in the beginning and I trusted you then."

She's right. My own selfishness made me determined to earn her trust and when I'd done so, I'd just as easily taken advantage of what she'd hesitantly given me.

"I'm so sorry, Taylor," I shamefully let out. "I know I don't deserve your forgiveness, but I'm asking you to at least give me another chance."

Her hands are gripping my wrists, as if contemplating whether or not to pull my hands away. Instead, her hands tighten, a sign she's still struggling with her decision. A nerve-wracking silence fills the room as I await her answer.

She gently nods her head, allowing me to breathe in relief. The entire time I waited for her answer, I was left with a sense of heaviness, fearing she'd deny my request. I pull her against my chest, feeling as if the weight of the past week has finally lifted from my shoulders. It may only be the beginning of the battle to earn her trust again, but knowing she's giving me the chance has made me more hopeful than when I'd last left her.

Her head is now resting against my chest as my arms securely wrap around her body. She lets out a heavy sigh followed by an exhausted yawn. She's struggling to disguise it behind her palm, but watching her makes it contagious.

"I'm sorry."

"I woke you when I got here, didn't I?" I ask, remembering her sleep filled eyes when she answered the door.

She answers with another nod, struggling to keep her eyes open as she lays her head back down against my chest. The sight of her fatigue hadn't gone unnoticed in the brief second I'd taken her in before she allowed me inside her apartment. But the need to hold her, to kiss her, had completely distracted me.

"Would it be selfish of me to ask to stay the night with you?" I bravely ask. Her head yanks back as she looks at me with uncertainty. "I just want to hold you, Taylor. Just like in the beginning." My statement seems to help calm her anxious mind, but she's still impassively looking at me, making me feel uneasy.

I'm preparing myself for her to say *"no"* as she relinquishes her hold from my waist, but surprisingly she reaches down to take my hand and leads me towards her bedroom. I shut the door behind us, enclosing us in the darkness before she tugs me in the direction of her bed. She releases my hand before I hear the rustling of clothing and the sound of a creak from her mattress.

Removing my shoes, socks, and shirt, but leaving my pants on, I climb in next to her to lie down. Her legs are bare, her body only covered with a shirt, explaining the earlier rustling I'd heard. I can't resist my smile when she entangles her body with mine. Placing a kiss on her temple, I feel her breathing slow, alerting me she has quickly fallen asleep.

Sleep eludes me for another hour. The adrenaline of the night is leaving me to stare off into the distance of the room's darkness, my mind drifting off to the possibilities of what could have been the outcome of tonight.

Taylor twitches in my hold, startling me from my thoughts. My mouth finds the hollow of her neck in an attempt to calm her, allowing me to taste and lightly kiss along her soft skin. It reminds me of how sweet every inch of her has always tasted against my tongue. Feeling content with Taylor in my arms, I feel her body tremble and this time she lets out a soft whimper. I've felt her this way before, right before she awakes from a nightmare. I tense, preparing for the worst.

Taylor

I arch higher, thrusting upwards to meet Nick's lips. His hands are skimming against my skin, provoking my desire to rise with every inch that he touches. He lifts his head, greeting me with his teasing smile, a mischievous twinkle in his eyes. It's the same gaze every time he brings me to the brink of completion. My mind knows what's coming. It's mentally prepared for the loss I will soon feel. But as always, I can't pull myself awake. I'm silently screaming, begging, for him to stay.

My arms reach out for him, still begging, crying. I scream for him not to leave, but my plea is useless. I have no voice. Only a silent cry escapes my lips as his retreating steps put distance between us. I follow, hoping to catch up to him. He's within grasp. My arm extends as far out as it can stretch, but he's not close enough for me to reach.

It's useless.

He's gone.

A sense of loneliness has replaced the comfort of his arms, filling the hollow of my shattered heart. I can blame no one but myself. Falling to my knees, I continue screaming, unable to contain my sorrow any longer. Darkness overcomes me and I welcome it. It will replace the agony I've brought upon myself.

"Taylor . . ."

Nick's familiar voice is calling out to me.

Searching, I'm alone, still trapped in my nightmare. My crying intensifies from the agony of being teased.

"Taylor, baby. Wake up."

The voice pulls me completely from the nightmare. My hands aggressively grip the sheets of my bed. Gasping, my lungs demand I fill them with air.

"Shhh, it's okay, baby. I'm right here. I'm not going anywhere," he murmurs, rubbing his hand up and down my back to comfort me.

"Come here," he requests, already lifting my body to turn and straddle his waist.

I hear his words, yet I'm still doubtful. The palms of my hands find his face, feeling, needing to confirm he's real.

"You're still here?"

"Where else would I be?"

"You left me." It comes out as a whimper.

"Taylor, I told you I wasn't giving up on you." The meaning of his words still has me baffled as I remember his promise. He pulls me to his chest, closing the small gap between us. "What were you dreaming about? It wasn't your usual nightmare, was it?"

I'm afraid to admit the truth. His next question keeps me from answering.

"How long have you been having them?"

"Since the night you left." Laying my head on his shoulder, the sound of his beating heart comforts me back to a serene state.

"Will you tell me about them now?" His deep voice is just as comforting as his touch. "You were begging me not to leave.

I want to know why you would think that."

I don't want to speak of the dream, but my conscience is telling me I should no longer keep secrets from him. It wouldn't be fair after all the text messages I'd read earlier.

"It's not about him," I inform Nick in case he thinks I'm still dreaming of Josh. "They're about us. It starts with us having sex."

"Making love," he corrects. "I don't think I've ever had sex with you, Taylor." His statement lightens my heart.

"It starts with us *making* love," I correct my earlier words. "Before we finish, you leave. It's the same every time."

Soft lips meet the hollow of my neck. "That's never going to happen, Taylor. Nothing will ever pull me away from you."

"You keep saying that, Nick, but it's hard for me to believe."

"Tell me why you're so afraid, Taylor." I can hear the desperation in his voice. "Is it because of your dreams?"

"It's hard for me to believe anyone would care for me. My own mother made me feel more like a burden than her daughter."

He's silent for a moment. "I'm sorry you had such a shitty life, Taylor, but that won't change the way I feel about you," he says, feathering kisses against my temple. "And I'll always be here to pull you from your nightmares."

Burying my face in the crook of his neck, I inhale his unique scent, a smell I've so greatly desired. My lips find the smoothness of his skin, gently trailing kiss after kiss along his shoulder. His body stiffens, the soothing of his hand on my back coming to a halt.

"Taylor," he slowly draws out in a warning.

"Nick," I tease against his skin.

Knowing he's here, a reality and not a dream, is tempting.

Against wanting to admit it, my heart and mind have longed for him this past week.

Kissing my way up his neck, a quiet groan travels up his throat, vibrating against my mouth. The taste of his skin is nothing compared to the dreams I've had these past few days.

"Baby, you're torturing me," he groans out. His lips begin to mimic my movements.

Our lips finally meet and open up to share a kiss. Pushing my tongue into his mouth and feeling the warmth of his tongue sliding against my own kindles a flame I've missed. The sensation is still new, but I'm coming to discover it's one I enjoy, especially with Nick.

I can feel the bulge between his legs starting to harden against the thin material of my underwear. Our chests are rhythmically rising and falling together. The spark Nick always ignites inside of me has combusted into a fire burning through my veins.

Nick's voice breaks our kiss. "Can I take your shirt off?"

Without answering, I reach for the hem of my shirt then lift it over my head. Soft, warm lips return to my skin, kissing their way across my collarbone to the valley of my breasts. His long fingers find the clasp of my bra, slowly working their magic to remove the piece of material. My nipple is enclosed in the warmness of his mouth as he suckles and pulls at one before he moves onto the other, a reminder of my dream. Just as fast as the thought is brought to mind, the kneading of his large hands on my butt pulls me back to reality. He tugs me harder against his evident arousal. My hands have somehow found their way in between our bodies to the button of his jeans.

"Taylor, are you sure about this?" He sounds doubtful, but him helping me push down his jeans doesn't match his words. In the process, I remove my underwear, the only barrier left between us.

"This doesn't mean you're forgiven," I say against his lips while climbing back on top of him. We both let out a moan as our bodies connect.

The hands on my waist are guiding my movements as I rock back and forth. My hands grip his shoulders as my moans increase and my body quickly climbs higher, pushing me closer to the familiar peak I've only dreamt about for the last week. My fear of Nick stopping causes me to voice it aloud, fearing the last few minutes are nothing but a continuation of my dreams.

"I'm not going anywhere, baby," Nick growls into my ear.

Meeting each one of his thrusts, I can feel myself nearing my climax. Days' worth of lacking Nick's touch has me on the edge of completion. His thrusts become faster, determined to push me to my peak. The sparks of desire build. Unable to hold my control, I surrender to the explosion of pleasure bursting inside of me.

Between my thighs, Nick's thrusting increases its pace and moments later he's grunting my name as he finds his own release. Exhausted, our bodies come to a stop as we both gasp for air. I'm trembling from the aftershocks of my climax, unable to move.

"That was intense," Nick breathes into my neck.

I cannot disagree. My breathless pants keep me from responding. He lays us down onto my bed, his hands adjusting my body to drape across his chest. His arms securely wrap around me as I lay my ear against his shoulder.

"Goodnight, Taylor," he whispers to me. I could do nothing more than contently sigh while the thumping of his heart sends me back to sleep.

TWENTY-ONE

Only time will tell

Taylor

WRAPPING THE TOWEL around my body, I pad my way back to my room. The brisk cool air of the apartment causes me to grow cold for a brief moment. That is, until I enter my bedroom to find Nick sitting on my bed. The sight of him sends me back to last night.

Clad only in his jeans, his bare chest is slightly propelled upward by his hands resting behind his head. His longs legs are stretched out and crossed at his ankles. Add his striking blue eyes gazing straight in my direction and he's the perfect vision of a cover model enticing his viewers. My mind fills with sinful thoughts as I remember every detail of when we made love.

"You keep looking at me that way and you'll be needing to take another shower soon."

"You're the one who's the tease."

Pushing myself to break eye contact, I turn towards my closet to grab a pair of scrubs. Seconds later my towel is yanked from around me, leaving me to stand naked in the middle of the room. Turning around, I glare at Nick as he sits on the edge of the bed holding my towel behind his back. I reach for the towel, allowing him to wrap his arm around my waist and tug me forward so I'm standing between his legs.

"How am I the tease?" he laughs out before burying his face in the valley of my breasts. Pushing on his shoulders in an effort to escape his embrace only allows for his mouth to latch onto one of my breasts.

"Nick," I breathlessly say as he continues his torment. "You're going to get me fired if I don't get to work. You've already made me late."

Had it not been for Katie pounding on my door, I most likely would have never woken up this morning. The week of restless nights had taken a toll on my sleep. And last night, after Nick and I made love, I was finally able to enjoy a night of peaceful rest. So much so I'd slept straight through my alarm. Although, I'm beginning to think I didn't entirely sleep through it since I found my phone lying near Nick's hand when I was startled awake. Nick had tried pulling me back to bed while protesting for Katie to go away. He'd quickly fallen back to sleep, giving me the chance to sneak from his embrace and take a shower.

"You sure you wouldn't rather stay home so we can make up for our time apart?" he asks, kissing his way up to my neck.

My hands gently grip his shoulders to keep from collapsing to the floor. The warm breath cascading across my bare skin is making my knees weak.

"Nick . . ."

My phone begins to ring.

"Ignore it."

Using every ounce of strength to push him away, I start searching for my phone. "I can't. Only a hand full of people know my number, so it must be important," I explain, finding it beneath the covers.

"Hello," I hesitantly answer.

"Taylor, are you almost here?" my boss asks, sounding concerned.

My boss's voice is like an ice bucket on my carnal desires. Pushing Nick away, his eyes are disappointingly pouting at me.

"I'm leaving in a minute. I'm sorry," I answer while rushing to put my underwear on.

"I was worried about you. You haven't arrived and I wasn't able to reschedule you're ten o'clock appointment. Are you going to make it on time?"

Pulling the phone from my ear to take in the time, I see I still have an hour to make it to work.

"Yes, of course." He lets out a reassured sigh before we end the call. "I have to go," I say to Nick before putting on my bra.

Standing, his lips find mine to give me another one of his signature breathtaking kisses. "I'll give you a ride," he says after pulling away.

Nick may look heart-stricken from not convincing me to stay home, but I'm silently whimpering inside for the same reason. It hasn't been a full twelve hours since he knocked on my door and we're already exiting with our still unresolved relationship. But I know if I approach the subject now, I'll never make it to work in the promised hour.

I love the way you smell. I've come to love it more than the smell of coffee.

I push send on the text message before I lose the courage to send it to Nick. Even with stopping for coffee, he got me to work within the hour. Inhaling the aroma of the dark liquid makes me realize there was now something to trump what was once my most favorite smell. The vibration of my phone distracts my thought.

I love the way you taste.—Nick

The sentence makes me smile as I read it. Just as quickly, I receive another message.

Especially between your legs.—Nick

My eyes turn to saucers as an ache builds in the same spot he's indicated. Before I have a chance to answer, Katie is entering our office.

"You almost done? I'm hungry," Katie whines from her end of the room. In my peripheral vision I can see her rubbing at her stomach, making me chuckle.

"Almost," I tell her, making sure to exit out of my text messages.

"Damn, my lips are chapped," Katie groans. "I forgot my lip gloss. Can I borrow yours?" I look at her with confusion. "Chapstick, then?" she laughs out.

Grabbing my purse, I search for the Chapstick at the bottom of my purse. My hand brushes up against the small pouch of my birth control and my heart nearly sinks to the floor. I can't remember the last time I'd grabbed for this pouch. Pulling it out and opening it up to check, my eyes go straight to the last day I'd taken them.

No . . . No . . . No . . . This can't be happening.

"Taylor?"

"I don't have one," I lie. "I'm sorry, Katie. Can we have lunch together tomorrow?" I ask, throwing the pills back into my purse and abruptly standing. I don't wait for her answer, already rushing out of the building and down the street to the local pharmacy.

The entire time my heart is pounding out of my chest. Entering my destination, I head to the back of the store where the pharmacist is located.

"I need a morning after pill," I blurt out to the female standing behind the counter.

She's sympathetically looking at me. "They're in aisle eight with the feminine products."

Turning, I walk towards the aisle she's directed me to. I soon find them, but the price is a roadblock in my plans. My trembling hands reach up for the plastic encased security box containing the pill.

For minutes I stand in the aisle, contemplating my plan. With the decision made, I return to the counter to pay for my purchase. Pulling out my credit card, I hand it to the girl along with the box, knowing it's the only method of funds to pay for the item. She must have noticed my pale expression when I placed the plastic box down on the counter, for she is now giving me a sympathetic smile.

When my purchase is paid for, I tuck the small brown paper bag into my purse. My steps are unhurried as I return to the office. My wayward mind has made time pass quickly and I arrive just in time to receive my first patient after lunch. My entire afternoon is spent rushing from one patient to another, leaving me no time to return to my earlier thoughts until the car ride home with Katie.

It's then I also see Nick's new text message.

Your place or mine tonight?—Nick

I don't know how to respond to the message just yet.

"Does Nick play tonight?" I ask Katie.

"Yeah. I think it's the team's last game before they travel. Why?"

"He's asking whether it's his place or ours tonight."

"I would prefer his so I can get some sleep tonight." I stare at her with incomprehension. "You're loud," she teases.

I turn to face her, my mouth gaping open from embarrassment. "It's okay, Taylor. I'm happy for you. Maybe he's tired of camping out at our place," she muses.

Remembering what happened the last time I visited his apartment, I type my response.

My place.—Taylor

We still haven't come to a resolution from last night, and I still have my earlier dilemma to deal with. My hand tightens its grip on my purse, knowing exactly what it contains. A heavy heart has overtaken my entire body with every minute leading us to our apartment. Entering our apartment, I go directly to my bedroom.

Two hours later Katie finds me sitting on the edge of my bed, the box I'd purchased earlier sitting in my hands as I stare down at it. I'm still contemplating whether to take it or not. I've had plenty of time to make the choice, but the doubt of whether it's the best decision has been lingering with me from the moment I left the pharmacy.

"You've been in here since we arrived. What's wrong?" The concern in her voice has me turning to face her.

"I don't know whether to take it or not." I hold up the box for her to view.

"But I thought you were on the pill?"

Her question has me cringing from knowing what I will

answer next. "I forgot to take it this week. I hadn't thought about it until this afternoon when you asked me for Chapstick."

"Wasn't he using a condom?"

"He got tested, remember? And, we were in a bit of a hurry," I blush, remembering how impatient I was to have sex with Nick.

Her chin points down in the direction of the box. "Is that why you hightailed it out of the office this afternoon?" Nodding my head to answer, I'm now staring back down at it, too.

"I always told myself I wasn't going to have kids. I didn't want to turn out like my mother. Every moment she could she never failed to remind me that I was a mistake because she was stupid and didn't use birth control. I was always afraid I'd make the same stupid mistake she made. It's why I stayed a virgin until . . . until." I can't get the words out. I shudder as I'm forced to remember the incident.

Katie rapidly moves to stand in front of me, kneeling down to my eye level.

"Don't say it," she commands. "You have no reason to feel ashamed of what happened, Taylor." It's as if she has read my thoughts. "And you'll never be like your mother."

"How would you know?"

She has a hint of a smile on her lips as she grabs for my hand holding the box. "Because you haven't taken this pill yet. You're not selfish like her. You're already trying to protect something that may not even exist, Taylor."

I sit, trembling as I remember my emotions on the walk back to work. I kept telling myself I would be killing my unborn child. Could I be selfish enough to follow through with the action?

Looking to her for the answer, I ask, "What do I do?"

"It's not my decision to make, sweetie," she rasps out.

My eyes are now clouded with the tears that have been building. My throat is just as full as I keep forcing myself to swallow them down.

"What if Nick doesn't want kids? It wouldn't be fair to force him to raise a child he never wanted. I know for sure I can't afford to raise a baby on my own." Before I can continue with my speech, Katie interrupts me.

"Even if Nick walked away, Taylor, you'd still have me. I would be here to help you raise that baby."

I find myself doing something I've never done before. I reach out to hug her. I've never been someone to show my emotions. It wasn't until Nick walked into my life that I began to do so. Whether I choose to admit it or not, he's brought about a drastic change in me. He's helped me evolve into the person I'd always wished to be. It's the reason why my decision is so much harder. Could I bring myself to possibly kill something that is a part of him? If it even exists?

Another minute later we're both pulling out of our hug, tears in our eyes.

"Thank you, Katie," I croak out, wiping at my nose.

Katie grabs for the box, turning it to read the instructions on the back.

"It says here you have forty-eight hours to take it. Maybe you should wait and talk to Nick first. I hate to admit it, but he should have a say in the decision as well."

My heart sinks as her words register in my thoughts. All I can wonder is *how is Nick going to react?*

I guess I'm going to get my answer tonight if he does obey my text message and meets me at my apartment. There is nothing left to do but wait and anticipate how Nick will react. But in my heart, I know I've made my decision. I refuse to be like my mother, but only time will tell if that will ever happen.

Nick

Taylor opens the door with a grief stricken appearance. The sight pushes away every ecstatic emotion I'd come with. It's a recollection of when she'd opened the door last night. As I'd done then, I step forward, pulling her to my chest, feeling the need to push away the anguish I know she's harboring inside.

"What's wrong?" I ask against her temple as I hold her.

She stays in my arms for only a brief moment, as if savoring my comfort before she pulls herself away.

"We need to talk." The tone in her voice has me feeling apprehensive. It has me fearing she's doubting her decision to forgive me.

She moves around me to close the apartment door, and without glancing back to me proceeds to walk down the hall in the direction of her room. Cautiously, I follow her with my emotions spiraling out of control before they start sinking in despair. Once I've stepped into her room, she closes the door behind us and turns to face me. She wraps herself in her own arms before her eyes find the floor.

"Taylor, you're starting to worry me," I croak out.

She looks up to me before saying, "If it makes you feel any better, I'm worried myself."

"What is that supposed to mean?"

She's doubtfully shaking her head. "Nick—"

I don't let her finish what she would have said as I step forward, taking her face in my palms, needing to hold her. Somehow knowing if I risk taking her into my arms, she will most likely retreat.

"Taylor, please don't tell me you regret last night. I wouldn't be able to walk away from you again. I refuse to."

Wide eyed, she responds, "No, Nick. This isn't about last

night," she replies, but just as quickly she's nervously biting her lip as she considers her next words. "Well, technically it is, but it isn't about me forgiving you."

I'm elated, but confused. "Tell me what's wrong?"

"I forgot to take my pill," she blurts out.

Her statement has me smiling. "That's it? You're stressing over forgetting to take *one* pill?" I laugh out.

"It's not just one. It was the whole week." My inner amusement has died, leaving me dumbstruck as her wistful eyes stare back at me. "We had sex last night. Unprotected sex," she clarifies.

My palm drops from her face as if stricken by a current of electricity. "So what does this mean?" I ask, still pondering her words.

She's staring directly into my eyes as she answers, "It means I might be pregnant."

The words feel like a hammer slamming into me, knocking me completely senseless. All I can do is stand there, silent, unable to respond.

"I'm sorry, Nick. I swear, I never meant for it to happen, but—"

"Don't," I stop her. "What do you plan to do?" I ask quicker than I would have expected.

She's returned to gravely looking at me. "Before I tell you, I need to know where we stand."

"What does that have to do with your decision?" I irritably throw back at her, causing her to flinch. I hadn't meant for it to come out so brash, but my mind is still trying to process the possibility that I may become a father soon.

"What's the point of telling you what I plan on doing if we aren't even a couple?" she argues in return.

"Why do you keep thinking that, Taylor? I've already explained how I feel about you. And to answer your question, I see us in a relationship, now answer mine," I demand.

She walks over and takes a seat on her bed before she answers. "I bought a morning after pill this afternoon," she explains, but pauses. She hasn't yet said another word, but my distress evaporates with her comment.

"Did you take the pill?" I ask, somehow fearful she already has. If she took the pill, there wouldn't be a child to question any longer. For some agonizing reason, the thought has me uneasy as she takes her time to answer.

Hanging her head as if ashamed, she replies, "I couldn't do it."

Closing my eyes, I let out the breath I'd been holding, the weight of those seconds escaping with that breath. Opening them, she's woefully looking up at me.

"If I *am* pregnant and you want nothing to do with me or the baby, I'll understand. I promise I won't ever bother you for anything, but I wouldn't be able to live with myself knowing I took the pill," she whimpers out before burrowing her face into her hands. It's what I need to hear to make me move. Crouching down in front of her, I force her hands from her face and look into her sorrow filled eyes.

"I would never make you raise our baby on your own."

"But I'm not going to force you to stay with me, Nick."

"You wouldn't be forcing me to do anything, Taylor. I've already told you plenty of times I wasn't going anywhere."

She trembles in front of me as she blinks away the tears building in her eyes. She swallows as we silently stare at each other for a moment.

"Are you mad at me?"

It takes me a moment to answer, only because I'm carefully choosing my words. "I'll admit I'm scared, but not mad." She gives me an understanding nod as she sucks in a deep breath.

"I meant what I said. I won't force you to stay. It's not your fault this is all happening," she reminds me.

Her admission has my heart quickening. The fact that she'd easily let me walk away if it were my choice has reminded me of why I've come to love her. Her stubbornness, and her will to fight for a child she may be carrying because she refuses to hurt it, shows she's worth keeping, even if she refuses to see it in herself.

Leaning in to take her in my arms, I say into her ear, "You're crazy if you think I'd let you deal with this alone." The arms wrapped around my neck are returning my embrace, notifying me she approves. It's all I need to know she's stuck with me for a while, regardless of the outcome.

TWENTY-TWO

Control

Nick

MY LIPS BRUSH up against Taylor's head while my nose takes in the fragrance of her hair. She tightens her hold on my chest. Most of the nights she slept with her back against my chest, but only moments ago she turned so she can rest her head on my shoulder, a content moan leaving her lips when she gets comfortable. Being awake this early in the morning is not routine for me, but my mind has been in a constant turmoil from the moment we climbed into bed. Sleep has eluded me at this point.

Most of the night was spent recalling our conversation from last night and the predicament Taylor and I are in. Her stirring has caused me to fully awaken, returning me to my thoughts from earlier.

Taylor's alarm begins ringing from her phone, alerting us it's time for her to awaken. I'm not as lucky as the morning before when I reached for her phone first, easily shutting it off before she was aware. This time she finds it and turns it off before turning to face me. A faint glow of sunlight is peeking through the crack of her curtains, illuminating her smile as she locks eyes with me. Selfishly, I don't want her to get up out of bed just yet. I want to cherish what extra minutes I can with her before she has to leave for work.

"Good morning," she whispers, still groggy and half asleep as she struggles to keep her eyes open. Leaning down to kiss her nose, I reply, "Good morning, sunshine. Anyway I can convince you to stay in bed with me today?"

She half-heartily chuckles. "Is this going to be a routine question every morning?"

"I hope so."

"I wish I could, but I can't," she mumbles into my shoulder, already sounding as if she's beginning to fall asleep again. I should just let her fall back to sleep, but I would hate for her to get upset at me for letting her do so. Kissing her temple, I sit up, taking her body with me, making her grumble in protest. Rubbing at her sleep filled eyes, she lets out a yawn.

Her eyes take me in before she speaks. "I'm sorry you're stuck sleeping in your clothes lately," she says, referring to the jeans I'm currently wearing. At least she allowed me to remove my shirt while we slept. Her comments cause my thoughts to return to right before we climbed into bed last night.

"Nick, is it okay if we just sleep tonight?" she had hesitantly asked.

"Isn't that what we were going to do?" I joke.

She'd grown serious to a point that her body stiffened as

she stood at the side of her bed with no intention of moving. It was then I understood her hesitation. Making my way over to her and placing my hands on her hips, I said, "Taylor, you're the one in control. Always will be." Her body relaxed and she gave me a contented nod before turning to climb into bed. I followed right behind her, molding her body to mine before we drifted off into sleep.

I suffered through the majority of the night, trying to force away the hard-on that threatened to emerge every time Taylor stirred in my arms. My desires have yet to catch up with the fact that I'd assured her we'd do nothing more than sleep. It was easier in the beginning, when I was gaining her trust, to just simply hold her. But from the first time I made love to her, it was proving more difficult than I'd expected to return to that state of mind.

Breaking my own thoughts, I ask, "How about we just stay at my place tonight so we don't have this problem tomorrow morning?"

There's a brief silence as she considers my suggestion. "It's closer to your work, which means we can sleep in longer," I say, trying to bribe her. Her eyes light up before I lean forward and kiss below her ear to help convince her. I feel her lightly shiver. "Is that a yes?"

She leans her forehead into my shoulder. "Yes," she mutters. It's not an excited *"yes"* but I will take it. She yanks her head back and asks, "Wait, don't you have to travel?"

Cocking my head in surprise, I ask, "Are you sure you're not becoming a sports fan?"

A hint of a blush creeps up her cheeks. "I had to ask Katie," she shyly admits.

Her admission has me chuckling with her.

"I have tonight off before I have to travel tomorrow," I tell her. Then, pushing my luck, I add, "Want to come with me?"

She rolls her eyes as she stands up. "I have to work Nick, and I'm *not* calling in sick."

I let out a disappointed groan. "Why do you always have to be so difficult?" I tease.

"Come on. We have to leave soon or else I'm going to be late for work."

I don't have to wait long before she's returning to her bedroom, already dressed and quickly packing her bag.

Staring down at the small backpack she holds in her hand, she encourages me to hurry.

"Let's go, I need my coffee," she urges.

"Are you sure you should be drinking coffee?"

Her brows furrow in confusion. "Why not?" she asks, but just as quickly realizes the reason for my question. "Are you going to be one of those individuals putting me on every restriction possible if I *am* pregnant?"

I'm torn as how to answer the question. Is it strange to want to protect something that is a part of me when I'm not even sure it exists?

"We can get you decaf if you want," I suggest trying to redeem myself.

"Forget it. Let's just go before I'm late for work," she scowls, but from the tone she uses, I know she isn't happy about my suggestion.

Quickly catching up to her before she can open the door, I turn her to face me.

"No, I wouldn't have to put restrictions on you because deep down inside I know you would make the right decisions yourself," I inform her.

Her lips go flat before I reach down and gently kiss her.

"I would," she replies when I pull away. "But if you ever

suggest decaf again, I may just strangle you," she says with a sarcastic smile on her face, making me laugh once more.

Taylor

The first thing I do when I reach my desk is pull open the drawer holding my treasured supply of chocolate that Nick gave me weeks ago. I may be denying myself caffeine as a precaution, but I don't have the strength to deny myself chocolate when I'm aggravated.

Savoring the milk chocolate as it melts on my tongue, my thoughts drift to the day they were delivered. Every morsel I've eaten since then reminds me of Nick. Looking into my purse for my phone, I proceed to send off my first text of the day.

Chocolate now reminds me of you.

I send it off and seconds later receive a response.

Does it taste as good as me?—Nick

Better, I tease.

Now my feelings are hurt. :(—Nick

Since I'm still in a playful mood, my fingers automatically type a response.

If you're a good boy, maybe I'll kiss them better tonight.

This time I'm hesitant to push send. The intercom announces my patient has arrived, and before I can give it any further thought, I push on the screen so he will receive it. Tossing my phone into my side drawer, I proceed with my day. How I've developed the brazenness to send such messages to Nick is still a mystery to me. Knowing it's a simple text and that I don't have to verbally announce the confession makes it easier to say. It's also the bravest I've ever been when it comes to flirtatious responses, another act in which Nick has managed to create in me.

My entire day goes by quicker than I would have expected. I'd kept my promise of a rain check with Katie, even going as far as picking up the tab to make up for my ill-mannered behavior the day before. She understood the reason for my actions, but my conduct was inexcusable since she is my best friend. Her forgiveness leaves me carrying on the remainder of my day in a cheerful mood. It's when my workday comes to the end that my thoughts return to my message from this morning. Nick has yet to respond and it's starts to worry me that I may have been a little too bold with him.

As if my mind can conjure him, I find Nick in my office sitting in my chair behind my desk. His eyes meet mine and his lips go up in a mischievous smile. He's chewing on one of the prized confections he'd sent me.

"You're lucky I like you, or else there would be war for you eating my chocolate."

His brow arches in a challenge. "Since you hurt my feelings this morning, I figured the chocolate would perk me up," he smirks.

"Is that so?" I ask, already at his side and leaning on my desk. My arms cross over my chest seconds before his arms reach out to jerk me over. I'm now standing in between his legs as he uses his thighs to lock me in place. I use every ounce of willpower to not smile down at him.

"What are you doing here so early?" I ask, looking towards the clock to find I still have fifteen minutes to go before I can leave.

"Weren't you the one complaining in the beginning I was always late?" He looks down at his hand that is holding the chocolate, as if analyzing it. "Plus, I heard chocolate cheers people up and I knew you still had some," he explains, taking a bite. His eyes peer up at me through his lashes and his lips slightly curve up to one side. "I don't see how it does." His response has me rolling my eyes.

He reaches for my top, pulling me down so our lips are only a breath apart.

"I would much rather you cheer me up," he huskily says.

"What did you have in mind, Mr. Hunter?" I say in return.

His groan is satisfaction to my ears.

Leaning down, I kiss him.

The mix of Nick's unique taste of his mouth and the sweetness of the chocolate is torture to my senses.

The clearing of a throat has me jumping back and pulling away from Nick. Cringing, I slowly turn to face the person who made the sound.

"Ms. Wilson." The reprimand in my boss's tone indicates he isn't happy to have found me locking lips with Nick. He looks past my shoulder as I walk over to accept the envelope he extends in my direction. He turns to place another on Katie's desk before he looks over his shoulder with a faint smile on his lips. "Have a good evening, Taylor," he says before exiting the room.

"You are going to get me fired," I tell Nick as I glare at him.

"Good. Maybe then you'll have more time to spend with me," he smirks then takes another bite of chocolate.

"I don't know what to do with you sometimes, Nick," I absent-mindedly reply while I walk back to my desk to retrieve my purse. Nick stands and pulls me into his arms.

"I could think of several things you could do to me." He nuzzles near my ear.

"I bet you could, but they won't be here."

The vibration of his chuckle striking against my neck has me stifling a moan as he keeps me wrapped securely in his arms. Remembering I value my job over my new found desire encourages me to push Nick away.

"We should go or else you're *really* going to get me fired." As intended, the words allow me to fully make my escape.

"You really know how to kill a guy's mood," Nick grumbles. His comment makes me smile, knowing I've won this battle. But from the smirk still on his lips, I know it won't be long before I surrender.

Cringing at the sound of the elevator's ping, I recall my last experience in this building when I had rushed out as fast as my legs would take me, vowing to never return. Yet, here I am. He begged me to begin trusting him, and to do so I would have to believe he was telling me the truth.

The hand linked with mine gives me a reassuring squeeze before we take the first step off the elevator. A buzz travels down my spine from both the dread of having to enter his apartment again, and knowing this time I will actually be staying the night, a request in which I mentally prepared myself for the previous time I was invited.

"Are you hungry?" Nick asks as he shuts the door behind us. Shifting my backpack from one hand to the other, I give him a quick shake of my head. "Let me give you a quick tour of the place."

Nick leads the way and I timidly follow him down a hallway to the rear of the apartment. Holding a door open, he waits for me to enter first. Entering himself, he places my bag down on the floor.

Taking in the room, it's obviously his. A large bed is in the center, black and grey tones are the preference of choice for his décor. My eyes automatically stay focused on the bed. The moment my eyes spot it, my mind goes to images of Nick with other women, especially the woman who interrupted us my first night.

Turning to face him, I ask, "Do you have any other rooms?" He looks perplexed by my question. Glancing one more time at the bed, I say, "I don't want to sleep in the same bed you had sex in." My statement catches him off guard, rendering him speechless. "I know it's stupid, but—" I stop, carefully choosing my next words. "I'd just feel more comfortable sleeping in a guest room if you have one."

"Are you serious?" he asks, his voice laced of bitterness. I don't bother answering but find myself already exiting the bedroom, needing to escape. "Taylor, where are you going?"

Stopping as I enter the living room, I'm full of trepidation from the tone he's used to catch my attention. "Maybe this was a bad idea, Nick," I inform him, already regretting I'd agreed to this idea.

"Why are you acting like this? It's just a bed," he defends, extending his arm out to point back to his bedroom.

"A bed that God only knows how many girls you fucked in it!" I throw back at him.

He looks astonished by my statement. "Are you really going to hold that against me?" His tone rises with each word. "I was no saint before you met me, but just like I don't hold your past against *you,* I wish you wouldn't use mine as an excuse to run," he defensibly lets out. His eyes are furiously narrowing down at me, clearly challenging me.

"We all have ghosts in our past, but don't expect me to sleep in the same bed you had sex with them in," I retaliate now narrowing my own eyes back at him.

I can see his jaw tightening, but he remains silent. I've never been in a situation like this.

"I'm sorry, Nick. I don't want to be compared to anyone else. It's why I always insist we sleep at my place," I admit, dropping my gaze to the floor between us.

"I never once treated you like someone from my past and I never will, Taylor. But you have to start putting *both* our pasts behind us if you want to make this relationship work."

He's left the decision up to me. The weight of his declaration has me seeing reason, afraid it may all come to an end any moment.

"Do you have a guest room?" I ask again, hoping he'll say he does.

A smile slowly rises on one corner of his mouth when he answers. "Yeah, I do. I haven't had anyone besides my brother stay in there. Alone." I smile inside while he stalks his way over to me. My arms automatically lock around his neck as he takes me in his arms. "I know you said you weren't hungry, but do you mind if I order in? I'm starving."

"Sure," I mumble into his chest, trying to push my mind from my current thoughts.

Hours later, the comfort of Nick's arms has me drifting off to sleep faster than I would have expected. We'd finished dinner hours ago, but I used every excuse possible to avoid heading to bed. Now, I feel myself being carried to bed.

"The guest room, remember," I mumble, keeping my eyes open to ensure he keeps his word.

"Yes, I remember," he answers before turning into a bedroom that isn't his. He gently lays me down onto the bed.

"I'll go get your bag," he says before I hear his footsteps retreating from the room. Using the minute I know he'll be gone, I quickly begin to undress from my scrubs. Climbing under the sheet, I use it as a protective barrier around my half-naked body as I sit and wait in bed in only my bra and underwear.

A few minutes later I hear him return. The bright glow of a light causes me to wince as my eyes struggle to adjust to the bathroom light.

"Sorry," Nick apologizes as he shuts the door, leaving it cracked open just enough to blanket the room in a soft glow. He returns to my side, handing me my backpack containing my clothes. He's wearing a pair of workout shorts and nothing more.

Grabbing it from him, I begin rummaging through its contents for my sleep shirt. Putting it on, my eyes find Nick patiently waiting before he heads over and turns off the light. Holding open the blanket, I feel him climb in at my side, molding our bodies together.

His warm breath grazes against my neck as his deep voice whispers, "Goodnight, Taylor," before placing a kiss just below my ear.

I lay in Nick's arms, relishing the comfort I know I will be missing after tomorrow.

TWENTY-THREE

One step forward

Nick

"WHERE ARE YOU going?" I playfully tease, pulling Taylor back into bed. Her laughter pulses against my chest. My arm is firmly wrapped around her and my head is resting on her temple. She gently pushes against my chest and I groan, refusing to relinquish my hold on her.

"Nick," she says, her protest coming out muffled. "You're going to make me late."

"Shhh. I'm trying to return to my dream," I tell her, throwing my leg over the lower half of her body. "You were moaning instead of protesting."

It's the closest I've come to my erotic thoughts being satisfied in the past two nights. My mind was begging I strip her of her shirt and rake my tongue over every inch of her last night.

It was clear that she wanted nothing more than to sleep when we'd climbed into bed. It was her sign of refusal. Instead, my dreams were the only satisfaction I received.

Remembering in vague detail what had occurred in my dreams, my cock is already hardening.

"Nick!" she protests again, pinching my side with her fingers. "Get off me," she muffles once more.

I laugh at her failed attempt, still holding her tight. She continues to struggle, pushing with all her might against my chest. The shoving is no longer playful. Her body is frantically trembling in my embrace.

"Get off me!" she yells this time, sounding panicked. The tone has me stiffening. Lifting myself off her, she scrambles away, practically running from the bed and straight into the bathroom. The door slams behind her, leaving me to blankly stare at it.

Standing up from the bed, I follow her, finding the door barricaded when I turn the knob.

"Taylor, let me in," I say, knocking on the door.

"Just give me a minute," she mumbles from the other side.

"I'm sorry, Taylor. Please. Just let me in," I beg again, but all I receive is silence. Attempting to push at the door once more, I'm still unable to open it. Patiently, I wait, mimicking her silence in hope she'll open the door. Minutes later, my request is granted when the door cracks open.

Her tear-stricken eyes stare back at me. "I need to use the bathroom," she informs me. I look at her with confusion, wondering why she would tell me that small detail. "I don't want to go pee in front of you," she adds.

I give her a curt nod and turn to walk towards my own

bathroom to give her some privacy. The steps taking me to my room feel shameful, full of regret for what I've done.

How is it Taylor can make me feel like the most appalling person from one simple act? An act, which in most relationships would have been seen as playful, loving, could have resulted in us making love. Instead, I had her trembling in fear and rushing as fast as she could to escape me.

Reaching my bathroom, I lean down onto the counter, my head dropping in shame. My stomach is rolling and full of a sickening dread that she will retreat and shut me out as she had the first time this happened. Closing my eyes in an effort to shove the feeling aside does nothing but recall the memory of that day as it replays behind my closed eyelids. Her frantic and frightened screams were similar to the ones only moments ago. Only this time, it was me causing those screams.

"Nick," Taylor mutters from the doorway, breaking my thoughts. "I'm done," she relays, sounding apologetic.

Her eyes are bloodshot, evidence of her crying. Her arms are protectively wrapped around her as she leans on the door-frame. Her shoulders are hunched forward as she averts her eyes momentarily towards the floor before peeking back up to look at me.

Cautiously, I step forward, fearful she'll cower away. When I'm mere inches from her, she unwraps herself and reaches out for me, closing the distance between us. She leans into me and rests her head against my chest. Kissing her temple, the weight of my worry evaporates.

"I'm sorry, Taylor."

"It's not your fault, Nick. It's mine." She pauses to take a deep breath. "I need to learn to stop being so afraid," she croaks out.

I could do nothing but remain silent. There are no other

words than the ones I've said before. To repeat them would be to remind her of her past.

"Do you want to take a shower with me?" I ask, using the question to break the dark mood we're still surrounded in.

The feel of her head nodding against my chest brightens my smile. Gently pulling myself away from her embrace, I proceed to turn on my shower before turning to find her shy-ly removing her shirt, her arms returning to wrap and conceal her underwear when she notices me gazing at her. With a silent chuckle I step forward, cautiously grabbing onto her arms.

"Do you need some help?" I ask near her ear, knowing how she likes it when I tenderly kiss the crook of her neck. She delivers my prize and shivers from the contact.

A gentle nod of her head has my hands wrapping behind her back to unsnap her bra and pulling it forward to drape off her body as I step away. Her eyes stare up at me as I skim my fingers down her sides to hook into her underwear. Kneeling, I pull them down. My hands skim up the sides of her legs, a cluster of goose bumps arising where my fingertips brush her thighs. Our eyes never break their connection, adding to my de-sire and impatience to make love to her.

Standing in front of her, her hands reach out, pushing down at the waistband of my shorts until they are in a puddle at my ankles, resting besides her clothing. I watch as her eyes drop down to take in my obvious erection that has been pushing against her stomach. I'd tried desperately to contain my desire for her, but it's physically impossible when I'm next to Taylor. She can be fully clothed and my mind is still racing with erotic thoughts. But to have her fully disrobed in front of me has me starving for her body.

"Someone's excited," she mocks, glancing down to my erection standing at full salute. Her finger grazes down the length of it before I feel her hand wrap around my shaft. Lifting up on tip-toes so her mouth is near my ear, she murmurs, "Poor thing."

Her tongue darts out to lick her lips, causing my cock to jump from the sight. Before I can react, she releases her hold on my shaft to step around me. My eyes follow her as she pauses to look over her shoulder before stepping into the shower.

"You coming?" she hums.

"You better believe I'll be coming soon," I mumble under my breath as I follow her into the shower. How she succeeds in pulling control over the simplest of actions has me perplexed. I could only think of one explanation, but it's the same words I've been desperately hoping to hear from those lips.

Entering the shower, Taylor's back is facing in my direction as she starts rinsing her body. Stepping up behind her, my arms automatically wrap around her, pulling her flush against my chest. Her head leans back to rest on my shoulder, allowing me to begin trailing kisses up her neck as my hand slides down her abdomen.

"Want me to rinse your body?" I huskily ask into her ear. She gasps when my hand begins to stroke her between her legs. Without waiting for her to answer, I grab the bar of soap and begin gliding it across her stomach and up her breasts, making sure to cover every inch of her chest before I pull away and start washing her legs. She turns to face me as I stand then takes the soap from my hands.

"My turn," she says with a smirk. My resistance is holding on by a thread as she begins washing my chest, gradually lowering her hands. Her eyes are locked with mine the entire time, playfully mocking me as the smirk remains on her lips. I let out a groan when she reaches my cock, her slippery hands grasping it in her palm, gliding slowly up and down. Restraining her movements by clasping my hand around her wrist, I glare down at her. "Taylor, you're playing with fire there," I warn her through clenched teeth. Closing my eyes, I picture ugly old ladies and nuns cursing me to hell to keep from exploding any second.

"I like your fire," she says as her warm breath glides against my ear.

"Taylor," I repeat, now picturing the entire Yankee team. Unfortunately, it does nothing as she gives my cock a rough squeeze, and it's the final straw. "You asked for it," I growl, grabbing her thighs and picking her up. With her back now against the wall, I wrap her legs around my waist and plunge forward, completely forgetting I told myself to be gentle with Taylor. It causes me to come to a halt, but her satisfied moan, and the tightening of her legs encourage me to move.

Her lips meet mine, passionately kissing me while I thrust in and out of her, returning to my earlier images to keep myself from exploding. From the tightening of her core around my shaft, she's nearing her pinnacle. Her frantic cries inform me she may be just as close. Parting from our kiss, she's now screaming, "Harder, Nick. Please!"

Those are words I never expected to hear from Taylor's mouth. With her nails now digging into my shoulders and her body meeting each one of my thrusts, I am left no choice but to grant her command.

She lets out a piercing wail seconds before I feel my own climax coming. Remembering I have no protection on, I urgently pull myself from Taylor's body, releasing myself all over her stomach. I'm still holding her up against the wall with what little strength I have left as we both try to catch our breath.

"God, Taylor," I breathlessly say against her temple as I place a kiss upon it. "I lo—" I cut myself off before I can finish saying the words. We both silently stand against each other, catching our breath before I pull myself completely away from Taylor's body, releasing her legs and allowing them to drop to the floor. Grabbing for the soap once more, I return to rinsing her body and removing any evidence I've left on her. The entire time silence has overtaken the room, both of us fearful we'd say the wrong thing.

"Are you alright?" I ask, concerned I may have been too rough with her. "I didn't scare you, did I?"

She stares at me as she slowly smiles. "It was perfect." Her palm reaches up to pull me in, demanding I kiss her. The pent up tension from my concern evaporates with our kiss. I can still feel her smiling when we pull away.

"I'm not a fragile flower, Nick," she says, shyly looking towards the floor. "I really liked it."

I let out the breath I didn't know I was containing. "I'll remember that for next time," I tease, placing an open mouthed kiss below her ear. She shoves at my chest, alarming me back to my earlier state. "Shit! I'm going to be late."

The frantic look in her eyes as she starts rinsing her hair has me laughing at her. Her hand comes up to swat at my chest. "Nicolas Hunter! I will make sure you are not able to walk on that ankle for another month if you don't hurry up!"

Still laughing, I make a mental note: never anger a person who can cause bodily injury.

Rinsing myself when she's done, I peek over my shoulder to find her staring down at my ass. Her eyes go wide when I catch her, making me grin from the blush forming on her cheeks. She may be a feisty little firecracker, but she's mine.

"See, got you here with ten minutes to spare," I gloat as I help Taylor from my car. Pulling her into my arms, I whisper, "I'm really going to miss you."

"How long this time?" Taylor whines into my chest.

"Ten days," I answer, already dreading every day I will be away from her. "How much longer until the season ends?" she asks.

"Hopefully not soon," I reply. She yanks her body back to scowl at me. Leaning down, I kiss the frown from her lips. "I'm hoping we go all the way."

She looks confused. "I'm predicting we'll make the play-offs, but I'm aiming for the World Series." By the confusion on her face, I know she still has no clue what I'm speaking of. "I'll explain during our phone calls. It will give us something to talk about while I'm gone." She doesn't look as excited as I would have liked her to be. "You know, you can always ditch your day job and come with me," I suggest with a hopeful smile. It doesn't work.

"You would love that, wouldn't you? For me to be your groupie," she teases

"Groupies are for rock stars. You'd be my own personal fan girl, with your own jersey and everything."

"Do I want to know if any other girls have had the privilege of that position before?" she asks, her brows raised high in curiosity.

"There hasn't been one," I answer before kissing her again for good measure. "I'm beginning to think that question will always be asked."

Dropping her eyes to the ground, she says, "Probably."

Yanking her flush against my chest, I kiss the top of her head. "Most of the answers will be no, Taylor. I've only ever had a handful of relationships that were more than one-night stands, and most of them were in high school. So this is new to me, too," I admit.

There is a drawn out silence after my answer. "I'll make sure you remember me every day," I comment, already contemplating ideas of how to make it happen.

She says nothing to my response, giving me the opportunity to reach into my pocket and retrieve a key. Handing it to her, she asks, "What's this for?"

"It's the key to my apartment."

"Why do I need a key to your apartment?" she asks, already trying to hand it back.

I close her hand around it, refusing to take it back. "It's yours to keep." She's about to argue, but I stop her by placing my finger on her lips. "Just keep it while you think about it."

She nods her head and looks down at her phone before letting out a disappointed sigh. "I've got to go," she mumbles the dreaded words I do not want to hear.

"I'll text you."

She gives me another silent nod before she stands on her tip-toes and quickly gives me a peck. I watch as she walks away, leaving me feeling empty without her.

TWENTY-FOUR

Arduous hope

Taylor

"WHAT IS THAT?" my first patient of the day asks as I massage his knee.

Looking up to him, he's squinting his eyes, as if trying to get a better look at something on my neck. Releasing his knee to reach up for my neck, I don't feel anything.

"What are you talking about?"

He scoots forward on the exam table, his finger pointing forward to poke at my neck. "It's a big red spot."

Heading over to the mirror on the wall near the weight machine, I search for the spot in which he was poking at. My eyes go wide and my face is now blushing the same crimson red as the hickey staring back at me. Immediately, I cover it with my palm as if it would make it disappear. Closing my eyes and mentally cursing Nick, I pull my hair out of its ponytail and use it to conceal the blotch. Turning back to face my patient, I now have a fabricated smile on my face.

"I burned myself with the curling iron this morning."

He looks at me with confusion. "But your hair isn't curled."

Dammit. Why can't this twelve-year-old be more gullible?

"Straightener," I correct myself. "Let's finish you up," I add, trying to distract him. He argues no more after I pierce him with a glare, but his eyes periodically glance at my neck.

As soon as I'm done with him, I march as fast as I can back to my office. Finding Katie sitting at her desk, I rush to her and pull my hair aside to show her my neck. "Fix it!" I command.

She looks at me with bewilderment. Pointing my finger as close to the spot as I can imagine, her eyes go wide. "Holy shit. That thing is huge!"

I have to breathe deep in order to refrain from verbally saying the words coursing through my mind.

"What do you expect me to do?"

Waving my hands in the air, I say, "Don't you know how to get rid of these things?"

"No, I haven't dated any vampires recently," she mocks.

Stomping my foot on the floor, I yell, "Katie!"

She's now chuckling up at me. "Calm your tits, woman," she replies as she opens her desk drawer and retrieves her purse. "I've got some foundation that may help." I feel as if I can breathe normally once more, until she adds, "But it won't make it disappear. That won't be gone for at least a week."

Groaning from the realization of her comment, I'm already conjuring the words I will be cursing at Nick when I speak to him. Five minutes later, with layers of make-up caked on my neck, I retrieve my phone to find a text message from Nick. Katie leaves to attend to her waiting patient with a playful wave of her fingers.

I miss you already. -Nick

Angrily, I begin typing my response.

I won't be missing you for the next couple of days.

I'm expecting to receive a response via text message, but instead my phone begins to ring. Checking my surroundings to make sure no one is around, my finger finds the answer button.

"How dare you leave a hickey on me?" I snarl into the phone.

"Oh—"

"Don't act stupid. You did it on purpose, didn't you?"

"Not intentionally. Things got a little out of control," he explains. I growl into the phone, earning me a chuckle. "I'm sorry, Taylor." I can almost hear the pout along with his words. "If you want, you can give me one when I return."

My name is announced via the intercom, cueing me to end the phone call. "I've got to go, Nick," I say, rubbing at my temple.

"Taylor?" he quickly says into the phone to catch my attention. "I *really* am sorry." This time the apology sounds genuine.

"No more hickeys. They're gross," I say into the phone before I end the call. My earlier resentment has completely vanished and is replaced with my heart feeling heavier than this morning. Ten days is too . . . damn . . . long.

I'm in the middle of a therapy session when my stomach begins to cramp. It begins with a simple twinge, but as the minutes pass it progresses into full-blown cramping. My appointment ends thirty minutes later and I immediately rush to the ladies room. It's then I see the answer to the question I've been impatiently waiting for. It takes me several minutes before I can move. My mind is silently processing the results. My reaction is far from what I expected of myself, feeling neither disappointed nor excited over the result.

The announcement of my name being paged over the intercom has me returning to the present and reaching under the sink where we keep an ample supply of feminine products for our personal use. After taking care of my personal business and quickly washing my hands, I exit the bathroom and return to my workday. It isn't until I am through with the therapy session that I am able to take a short break and return to my desk. I sit for a few minutes, the entire time trying to process how I will inform Nick that I started my period.

Reaching into my desk to retrieve my phone, my mind races with possible ways to text Nick with the much-awaited answer, but my heart refuses to allow me to type it out. It's only fair I tell him in person. Knowing it will not be until Sunday that we are face to face again will test my patience, and my sanity. Instead, I find myself asking for reassurance.

What time are you coming home Sunday?

It's still early in the day so Nick should be able to respond, but the wait has me nervous he may not answer. Minutes go by and just as I'm about to give up hope, the sound of the ping I've been desperately waiting for echoes in the room.

Not until late because of my day game.—Nick

That's fine. I'll leave the door open.

My place, I quickly text next, remembering how he gave me the key to his apartment.

Miss me that much?—Nick

The question has me grinning. Of course I miss him. Every

night I sleep alone without his arms tightly wrapped around me leaves me worried the nightmares will return. Nick's presence in my life has alleviated the episodes, to a point where I'm now dreaming of him instead of my past. I'm fearful I've come to depend on him to keep them absent. What will happen if Nick and I were to go our separate ways at some point? That thought is a waking nightmare.

I miss you every minute of the day.

It's been over a week since I've seen Nick. His traveling has returned us to text messages as our only form of communication. The day begins with me awakening to an adoring greeting in which he'd sent the previous night, and the evening ends with me delivering a similar message to wish him a goodnight. When he's able to sneak away, he will call me during my lunch break. We've had to work around both our schedules, but the minutes I'm fortunate to hear his voice leave me with the strength to proceed throughout the day. The lonely nights are ruthless, though.

Saying the words through a text makes me feel more confident. My smile has widened, my heart is fluttering, and the vision of him receiving the message is coursing through my mind. The announcement of my next patient has my visions breaking and returning to reality. I can already predict a restless night, but tomorrow may just be similar if my nightmare becomes a reality.

Nick

I'm practically racing through the streets of Chicago to get to Taylor's apartment. I'd insisted she wait for me at my apartment today, but she stubbornly kept refusing. She still doesn't feel comfortable in the space, using the excuse she preferred to wait at her own apartment. I've granted her request since I was traveling, but I've come to the conclusion she will be staying with me while I'm in town. No questions asked. If we are going to make this relationship work, even with the distance put between us every so often, then she is going to have to compromise on our living arrangements. If it were up to me, she would have been permanently moved into my apartment by now.

The thought makes me silently laugh inside. Never would I have imagined I would be envisioning *living* with a girl, let alone be eager to claim I'm in a relationship. Yet Taylor has me envisioning our possible future.

Reaching her apartment. I rush to her front door after parking my car. Quietly knocking on the door, she immediately opens it, an excited smile upon her face as I scoop her up and kiss it from her lips. Kicking the door shut with my foot, I carry her down the hall.

Taking a seat on the bed, I position her so she's straddling my hips, refusing to release my hold on her. It's been too long since I've been able to hold her. I don't know if I will be able to let her go for the next couple of days. With my mouth grazing against the bare skin of her shoulder, the arms wrapped around my neck pull me closer to her body.

My hands glide inside her shirt, finding and grasping her breast. "I've missed you so much," I confess. She rewards me with a whimper that goes straight down to my cock hardening between her thighs.

"I've missed you, too." The sincerity in her words quickens the beat of my heart.

"I can't wait to be inside you," I growl in her ear, already attempting to lift her shirt, but she abruptly pulls her arms from my neck and stops me.

Confused, I pout up to her. "What's wrong?"

"We can't have sex," she states, nervously biting her bottom lip.

"Why not?" I'm almost whining.

Her broken-hearted expression has me stiffening in worry. "I started my period," she answers just below a whisper. My once beating heart momentarily stops. A feeling of dread and sorrow I was not prepared to receive courses through my mind.

"I got it yesterday," she explains.

"So, you're not pregnant?" I ask. I've been thinking the question from the moment she gave me the news, but I couldn't find my own voice to ask until now. Dropping her head, she nods without looking into my eyes. Lifting her chin with my finger, I notice her eyes are glassy as they gaze back at me.

Silence overtakes us both. There are no words to say that could comfort us both at this point. From the moment she announced she may be pregnant, we've both been avoiding the subject. There was no purpose in discussing the situation when we had no accurate result as to whether it existed or not. Now there isn't anything more to discuss.

Leaning back onto her bed, I pull her body with me, laying her across my chest and comforting her. Seconds turn into minutes. Minutes turn into an hour before she's pulling herself up and off me.

"You tired?" I ask, knowing from the exhaustion in her eyes she is.

"Yes, I was about to start getting ready for bed," she says.

"Want to stay at my place tonight?"

"I don't think that's a good idea, Nick," she replies as she stands up from the bed.

"Why not?"

Her back is facing me now, but from the way her body stiffens, I know she's debating how to answer.

"Taylor?" She turns to look at me, the determination on her face advising me my battle with Taylor is about to commence.

"What's *really* going to happen between us, Nick?"

Out of every possibility as to what I thought she would say, I never expected her to ask that specific question.

"What is that supposed to mean?"

She lets out a heavy sigh. "I've been thinking. Maybe me getting my period was a good thing."

My earlier dread was still lingering as we lay in bed. My thoughts had wandered to an unforeseen future with Taylor, but with those words, she has me doubting my own thoughts.

"What was the first thing you wanted to do when you walked in that door?" she asks, her arm stretched out towards her own front door. "You walked in here determined to have sex."

"Yeah, so? I've missed you."

"Is this how our relationship is going to be from now on? Just sex? From the beginning it's been one fucked up thing or another. The only thing filling in the gaps is sex," she declares.

"Is that how you see it?"

"Think about it, Nick. I'm fucked up in the head from a past that will never let me live a normal life. I'm not a normal girl. Even your own parents saw that. I'm now the reason why you're not speaking to them. *Your parents, Nick.* At least they are still willing to love you and be in your life, regardless of how fucked up things are with you."

"That's all you've ever tried to do from the beginning, Taylor, is push me away. You're doing it now."

"It's for the best."

"Is that what you *really* want? If it is, I'll leave, but I'm not coming back this time. I'm tired of being pushed away."

My words have rendered her speechless. Good. It's exactly

what I want from her, to think long and hard about her decision.

"No, it's not what I want, but I don't want to be in a relationship where I have to always doubt whether it's worth being in," she proclaims. "You won't even say you love me anymore, Nick!"

"I don't say it because I'm tired of being the only one who says it. Why should I when it's clear you don't feel the same way?"

"How can you say that? Of course I love you," she croaks out.

"You have a funny way of showing it. Or *never* saying it is more like it."

She looks perplexed, her mouth opening and closing as she absorbs my declaration. "I'm sorry," she apologizes with her head dropped down. Walking over to her, I place myself directly in front of her.

She lifts her head up to say, "I hadn't realized I never said the words, but I'm always thinking them. I've been in love with you, probably from the beginning." Her eyes shyly drop down before she continues. "It's why I kept putting up with your stubborn ways."

Taking her into my arms, she wraps her arms around my waist, returning my embrace. "You sure it wasn't because I was so good looking?" I tease.

"No. But it may have been that cocky attitude of yours," she teases in return, making me laugh. Tilting her chin up to look at her face, I notice her expression has grown serious.

"I truly do love you, Nick," she says shyly as I lean down to kiss her. "Will you stay?"

"I didn't plan on leaving," I tell her, hoping I never have to.

TWENTY-FIVE

Second chances

Six months later . . .

Taylor

"TELL ME AGAIN why I agreed to this?" I ask Nick as I struggle to pull up the zipper of my dress. How is it zippers always win in a battle against me?

Nick's hand can be felt at my back, taking over the task. When done, he places a kiss on my shoulder before making his way up to my ear.

"Because you love me." Slightly turning my face to look over my shoulder, I skeptically look at him. "Are you sure?" I tease.

"I'm pretty sure by the way you were moaning the words

in the shower an hour ago you do."

"Sex has nothing to do with love," I express.

"No, it doesn't," he says on a sigh. "We better get going or else we're going to be late," he proclaims, making me feel as if I've just ruined a very special moment.

Turning, I face him and ask, "Are you sure this is a good idea? It didn't end well the last time."

Lifting his hand, he brushes a loose strand behind my ear. "I know, Taylor, but I promise it won't be like last time. They know the rules. Me and you, no matter what they think." Taking a deep breath, I absorb his words. I'm still doubtful, not of Nick, but of the possible outcome of tonight.

"You trust me?" he asks.

Time has gone by faster than I would have expected since the dreadful night when I feared I lost Nick forever, the night I refer to as my *period*. The future is still uncertain when it comes to Nick and I, but with every day that passes, our relationship grows stronger. With his season over, it makes it easier for Nick and I to spend more time together.

In the last six months, Nick and I have done everything possible when it comes to dating. I've visited more places than I would have ever imagined and experienced what it feels like to be in a *true* relationship. We've gone on dates, exchanged gifts on certain holidays, and have taken the final step and moved in together. The delay was all me. I was hesitant, fearful of what would happen. Where would I go if he changed his mind? I had to force myself to cease being afraid and take a chance.

Remembering what Nick asked, I look up to him with a smile.

"Of course."

"Good," he says as he leans down to kiss me. "Just remember you do," he says, slightly frightening me with the statement.

Taking my hand, he's about to lead me out of the room when he looks down at my feet. "Do you plan on wearing shoes?"

"Shit. Sorry. I was looking for my black strappy shoes when you distracted me."

Tilting his head with an amused smirk, he says, "I do seem to do that to you a lot."

"Yes, you do."

"I don't think you've unpacked them. Aren't they in your luggage?"

Scrunching my nose, I'm reminded that I still haven't tackled that task. I've been purposely avoiding the duty, although the memory of our excursion has me beaming inside.

Our trip overseas was a pleasant surprise. I hadn't known exactly where we were traveling when he advised me to request vacation days. Nick's only orders were I pack for two and a half weeks and have my passport ready to go. It began in Italy. From there we headed to Paris, ending our trip in London. As a child my mind would wander off to a foreign country of my own imagination when I wanted to shut my harsh surroundings out. So to see a fragment of my vision come to life was beyond what any words can describe.

Nick exits the closet with the shoes dangling from his hand and a mischievous smile upon his face. "If I recall, these shoes are the cause of the scars on my ass."

I can't help but laugh at the way he's now sneering down at the shoes. I reach out to take them, but he holds them from my grasp, ordering me with his eyes to sit on the bed. Kneeling down, he begins the task of putting the heels on my feet, finishing with a kiss on my inner thigh.

"That kiss right there is what got you those scars," I remind him, palming his head still at my knees. Unable to resist, I lean down and fervently kiss him. As expected, I'm now on my back as he leans over me on the bed. His bright blue eyes are passionately looking down at me.

"I love you," I say up to him, my entire body feeling as if it's floating on clouds because of the smile he is giving me. He kisses me once more, this time with much more determination. We're both hungrily looking at each other when I have to remind him, "Nick, don't we have to go," I strain to say as he kisses down my neck.

He abruptly stops, groaning into the crook of my neck. If it were my choice, we would stay and continue what we started, but I know it wouldn't be the right decision. Lifting himself off me, he reaches down for my hand and helps me up from the bed. My heart is still rapidly beating, but as we exit the apartment and step into the elevator, my nervousness is also increasing.

When Nick informed me his parents would be visiting Chicago this week and requested to have dinner with us, my first thought was to refuse. The despair in his eyes begged me to reconsider. I knew to refuse their request would be impolite.

I had to take into consideration how their relationship with Nick has improved. It began with regular phone calls, which eventually turned into visits with his father. Over the last several months, Nick began to bring me along. His visit with his mother, on the other hand, occurred out of convenience. He happened to be in New York for one of his games and she had come along with his father while they met for lunch. It was then she had insisted we all meet for dinner when they came to town this week, and Nick had agreed.

Nick had warned me dinner would be taking place in the same restaurant as the last occurrence. He's even gone as far as reassuring me that if at any time I no longer felt comfortable, we would leave. No questions asked. Only this time I had to agree we'd cordially make the exit. He refused to allow me to show them any more weakness, and disappearing without a word proved they had won that first night.

The drive to the restaurant is made in a blur, my mind distracted with every possible scenario that can go wrong. When we arrive, Nick rushes to my side to help me out of his car, tucking me securely at his side as we walk into the building.

Same as the first occasion, his parents are already seated and waiting for us. Unlike the previous time, there are no bitter scowls upon their faces. This time, his father is beaming with cheerfulness, far from the previous manner in which his mother greeted us with.

"Nick, Taylor, it's so nice to see you both again," Nick's father greets, reaching out to give Nick and I a hug when we reach the table. Pulling myself from his arms, I see Nick gently placing a kiss on his mother's cheek, a small smile on the corner of her lips as her eyes stay focused on me. Forcing a smile onto my face, I take my seat next to Nick and take his hand in my own. He gives me a reassuring squeeze for comfort.

The waiter takes our drink order, and when he disappears Nick's father immediately begins a conversation. "How was the trip?"

"Wonderful," Nick answers for the both of us. "Can't wait for our trip to the Bahamas next," he says, referring to yet another trip Nick is planning after the winter holidays.

"Wonderful." His father looks directly at me with a smile. "Nick informs me you're living together now." I mentally prepared for this line of questioning, but didn't expect it so soon into the conversation.

Giving his father a pleasant smile, I say, "Yes, it's true. His apartment is closer to my work, making the commute much easier."

"Plus, having our own place gives us more privacy," Nick comments, lifting our entwined hands up to kiss the back of my palm.

Regina's brow arches high and I brace myself for her retort. "You're still working?"

"Yes. I love my job very much."

"What is it you do again?"

"I'm a physical therapist, specializing in sports injuries. I help injured athletes recover so they can return to doing what they love most."

"Was Nick one of your patients?" I know from the manner in which she asked, she wants to know if I had been sleeping with him during his therapy.

Nick looks like he's about to answer, but I quickly cut him off, feeling the need to answer myself. "Yes, he began as one of my patients. However, he refused to oblige to my guidelines during the first few visits so I had him transferred to another therapist by the second week. I refused to allow him to waste my time."

Nick's mother looks surprised by my response as she turns to look at Nick for confirmation.

"She did," he laughs out. "It only made me chase after her. We started dating a month later," he explains.

The conversation comes to an end as the waiter arrives to take our dinner order. The rest of the evening is spent discussing our trip and all the different places we should visit next. The smile on my face is one full of nervousness. Here they are discussing situations which should take place years from now, yet I have no clue as to what will happen tomorrow. Nick and I are still trying to adjust to sharing a roof.

Dinner ends and I'm so distracted in my thoughts that I'm faintly startled when Nick's father pats my hand. "I'm glad to see the both of you so happy," he comments. "Can I be hopeful we will be hearing wedding bells in the near future? Regina and I are not getting any younger and would love some grandchildren to spoil."

The question has my heart halting then erratically beating back to life. Since the pregnancy scare, I've been meticulous about taking my pill every morning. As much as I would have welcomed a child had there been one conceived that night, it is clear it wasn't meant to be. I thus returned to my original plan, adamant I would *never* become my mother. But to ensure that would mean I would *never* have children.

The discussion of marriage has only been brought up once, when Nick and I were in Italy and watched a couple walking the streets after their ceremony. He'd seen a future with me being a housewife with half a dozen children running around. My vision was the opposite: a relationship we would continue to build without any children. Just Nick and I. Always. The conversation escalated into an argument, leaving us silent for the remainder of the afternoon. I have been cautiously avoiding the subject since then. It's too soon to be discussing *forever* just yet.

"We haven't actually discussed the subject," Nick lies to his father. The resentment is clear in his eyes as he briefly glances at me after answering. I can already feel the guilty tears welling in my eyes. The familiar dread of discussing the subject is arising.

"Soon, maybe?" his father questions, sounding hopeful.

His question makes me feel trapped, as if the room is closing in around me.

"If you'll please excuse me." Nick's eyes go wide with worry as he stands with me. "I'm not leaving. I promise. I just need some air, Nick," I reassure him. He gives me a nod of understanding before I walk away from the table, making my way towards the back of the room where I have spotted a set of French doors. Once outside, the brisk cool air surrounds me, allowing me to breathe as I wrap myself in my arms.

My mind is racing with visions of my mother. Screaming at me, berating me. Always drinking to shut out the world. My nightmare. I envision my children's frightened faces as I scream in the middle of the night. I see myself failing to keep Nick happy, and at some point leaving for someone who isn't damaged or broken. These are the reasons why I choose to not surrender.

My mind is completely distracted by my wayward thoughts that I'm unaware there is someone at my side.

"You have every reason to be frightened." Regina's voice startles me back to reality. Turning to face her, she stares directly in front of her, out into the lights of the city. "Marriage is a serious commitment. It shouldn't be taken lightly."

"I know."

"Do you think you're ready for it?" Her expression is blank as she asks the question, slightly terrifying me.

"No," I truthfully answer. "I never plan on marrying. I tried telling Nick so he wouldn't waste his time on me, but he refuses to listen."

"It doesn't surprise me."

She continues to look out onto the city in silence for the next few minutes, my eyes following her direction.

"The first night we met, I was expecting the typical imbecile who wanted nothing more than publicity from my son. However, you proved me wrong. I believe that is why I like you so much, Taylor. It's a quality I value in you." I'm surprised by the admission. "You could care less about what he has, but care more about who he is. I didn't quite see it in your eyes that evening, but it's clear tonight. You love him."

"I do."

"But you're scared?"

I keep silent, somehow fearful to admit she's correct.

"I do have to apologize for that evening. My actions were uncalled for, but I don't regret them." In my mind, I'm painting her as the cruel and evil bitch she once proved herself to be, until she continues to explain. "They showed me how much Nick truly cares for you. You had already captivated his heart by that evening, which is why I ask you don't let your fears make your decisions. Everyone deserves happiness. Including you."

Those are her last words before she steps forward to surprise me once more when she hugs me. She releases me and turns to reenter the restaurant, leaving me alone on the balcony with my thoughts. Minutes pass and I'm soon following her same steps to return to our table where I find Nick looking anxious to know the reason why I had disappeared.

"Are you alright?" he apprehensively asks.

I kiss him to take the worry from his mind. "I'm fine," I say then give him a reassuring smile.

As we say our goodbyes to his parents, his mother hugs me and comments into my ear, "Listen to your heart."

Nick assures his parents he will keep in touch before we depart for the evening. The drive to his apartment is made in silence, but it allows me the time I need to compose the speech I plan on delivering. The ping of the elevator I've become familiar with over the last four months announces I have mere minutes to gather my wits.

Stepping inside his apartment, Nick goes straight to the living room, seating himself on his couch and tossing his head back. He lets out a large sigh. I recognize the frustration I may have caused by leaving the table earlier tonight. Taking the leaded steps over to his sitting form, I reach down and remove my shoes before I straddle his lap so I'm face to face with him.

Gabbie S. Duran

Placing my hands on his shoulders, he lifts his head up; his bright blue eyes stare back at me, searching for what to say.

Instead, it is I who speaks.

"I haven't seen my mother since the day I left her. I haven't thought much about her, and to be honest, I still resent her for everything she did." His head slightly jerks back, stunned by my declaration. "I know you've told me your mother can be cruel sometimes, but regardless of her actions, she has never done anything so cruel to make you believe she doesn't love you."

Nodding his head in agreement, he says, "True."

"You know how I sometimes still get nightmares?" He nods his head, but keeps silent. Taking his face between my palms, I continue. "When I said I never wanted to have kids, it wasn't because I'm too selfish to be a mother. I just don't want my children to have to endure what you do when you pull me from my dreams. My nightmares now consist of me becoming my mother."

"Taylor, that would never happen," he grimly replies.

Feeling the pain in his words, I try to reassure him. "I want to believe it, but until I know for certain, I want to wait. I may not want kids today, or maybe tomorrow. However, maybe in time I will. Right now I just want to enjoy *us.*" Leaning down, I follow my words with a kiss.

We end our kiss by leaning our foreheads against each other's. Nick's hands grip my waist. I can feel his internal struggle as he says, "I love you so much, Taylor. So damn much I would do anything for you. But sometimes you make me feel like it's not enough." His declaration has my heart shattering in pieces inside my chest.

"Without you, I would still be the girl riddled with nightmares, refusing to trust anyone. I never knew what it was to love until I met you. Every day that passes is another day my love for you grows deeper. Stronger. To a point where I can't imagine a day without it."

"Enough to spend the rest of your life with me?" His question stuns me into silence. Would this be considered a proposal? "I'm not asking you to marry me, because I know you'd just say no, but I am asking you to spend the rest of your life with me. I love you, and I can't imagine spending another day without you."

"I can't either," I confess. I truly can't. He makes me . . . *feel.* He's done it from the beginning. He's the clarity I've been searching for to guide me to the light. Until now, my life never felt complete.

Nick lets out a reassured breath.

"But—" I pause as I choose my next words carefully. "What if *I* wanted to marry you?"

He grins, tugging me forward so our faces are mere inches apart. "I'd be an idiot to tell you no," he declares before closing the gap between our lips.

EPILOGUE

Taylor

"HAPPY ANNIVERSARY," NICK'S sleep filled voice murmurs into my ear. Moaning my satisfaction in return, I snuggle deeper into the covers to savor the last minutes we'll have before we truly have to rise. The warmth of his arms and body has always been my sleep advocate, which makes it harder every day to get up.

"I'm surprised you remembered," I mumble into his chest.

He stiffens, and when I lift my chin up to look into his eyes, he looks shocked. It makes me giggle. Of course he remembers. In the last ten years he's never forgotten. After all, it was he that suggested we wed in the Bahamas exactly one year from the day we met at his very first appointment.

The ceremony was simple and intimate, merely a handful

were in presence. Katie stood as my maid of honor, his brother was his best man, and his parents were witnesses.

Nick stood across from me as we declared our love to one another and became man and wife. It was perfect in my eyes. I still ask the stars above how I got so lucky.

Rolling our bodies, my legs willingly fall open as he hovers above me. I can already feel what will most likely be my first anniversary present of the day. He nuzzles the stubble of his five o'clock shadow against my neck, slowly torturing my senses.

"How can I ever forget the day you left me chasing after you for the first time?" he asks, laughing as I remember that very same day. "I don't think anything has changed since then," he adds.

The comment dampers my mood as I recall my only defense when we disagree. I do still walk away to avoid any confrontation with Nick, leaving the argument without a resolution and forcing Nick to chase me in order to come to a resolution. Bad habits don't die easily and this one is still living strong.

"But I do love the result when I've caught you," he continues.

My smile returns, along with all the memories of those results. Makeup sex with Nick has and will *most likely* always be worth fighting for. Our relationship still hits bumps in the road every now and then, but finding mutual ground has made our love for one another stronger. There isn't a day that passes he doesn't give me a reason to love him more.

The grinding of his hips lets me know just how happy he is to have me in his life, and sparking the desire I feel for him on a daily basis. His lips trailing kisses down my neck further ignites those desires. Wrapping my leg around his waist, I pull him harder to me, earning me a moan which vibrates against the nipple now in Nick's mouth. We've only just begun our teasing and I'm already pulsating from head to toe. Reaching between our bodies, my hands are struggling to push Nick's boxers down when I hear the stomping of little footsteps. Seconds later, our door is thrown open and a burst of giggles is heard.

"How is it possible they wake up so damn early?" he groans into my neck.

My giggle echoes those that were heard only moments ago.

"Daddy is kissing Mommy again!" is shouted right before I answer Nick. "It's because they have *your* energy," I laugh out before gently shoving Nick off and adjusting my tank top Nick had managed to pull down to get to his prize. The boys have already climbed up into the bed and are shoving themselves between the two of us.

"Why do you guys always have to be in the middle? Daddy wants to be next to Mommy sometimes," he whines, sounding like his sons when they don't get their way.

"No!" one stubbornly shouts, while the other responds with, "She's our mommy!"

"She was mine first," he argues, adding a wink as I laugh at his response. "What time is their nap?" Nick asks from the other end of the bed, now wagging his brows.

"No naps! No naps!" they chant, making us both groan. Nap times can sometimes be a struggle in our home.

"Nobody ever said having twins was going to be fun," I sarcastically reply.

The boys will be six soon and from the moment they arrived, they've been a handful, but Nick has been there from the moment that little stick turned blue. I don't regret one day that I agreed to Nick's request to have a baby. We were just surprised we were blessed with two. The day of our first ultrasound, when they'd delivered the news, I knew then my life would never be the same again. And from this day forward, it would only get more hectic as I present Nick with his anniversary present.

From my side, I watch as the boys both climb onto Nick, playfully wrestling with him, producing a bout of giggles to boom throughout the room. Every morning I look forward to this, regardless of how exhausted I feel when I open my eyes lately. Minutes later, all three are in a tangle in the middle of the bed, leaving me practically pushed to the edge. Nick's eyes are looking in my direction, desperately pleading for help.

"Emmitt, Ethan, I think Daddy has had enough. You win." They both throw their arms high into the air in triumph as Nick tosses himself back onto the bed, arms spread wide as his chest rises and falls as he pants for breath.

The boys look every bit still full of energy when they turn to me. "Mommy, are Grandma and Grandpa still coming today?"

"Of course," I happily answer. "But not until much later this afternoon," I inform them, earning me two little pouts.

At their suggestion, Nick's parents will be taking the twins so he and I can have the evening alone. "Now run along and go wash up and meet Julia for breakfast."

With little protest, they do as ordered. Nick follows closely behind them to help the boys with their task. The ping of a text message alerts itself on my phone, as it does every morning. I've come to depend on those alerts from Nick.

I love you.—Nick

Normally I would reply with something as simple as *I love you more,* but today I decided to change it up.

I'm pregnant.—Taylor

With a wide grin, I push send on my phone. Nick's familiar footsteps can be heard making their way back into our bedroom, as I'd expected. The click of the door is heard and I turn to face his wide eyes. With a grin, he crawls back onto the bed and hovers above me.

"Really?" His voice cracks from disbelief and joy. I nod my head. The shock lingers on his face for a couple more seconds before he widely smiles down at me.

"I believe we have some unfinished business, Mrs. Hunter," Nick seductively growls into my ear, making me laugh. The sound of being called the same name I'd taunted him with from the beginning always makes me smile.

"Nick, the boys," I remind him.

"They'll be fine with Julia." The husky tone he uses sends shivers down my spine.

"I thought you were too exhausted from wrestling this morning," I tease, tilting my head so he can trail more kisses along my neck.

"I'm never too exhausted to wrestle with *you*."

His hands are already working their magic and disrobing us both. Once we are both naked, his lips return to kissing their way down my stomach. He stops at my abdomen, his eyes intensely studying it. My fingers reach up to run through his hair as he lifts his head to look up to me.

"Are you sure?" he asks again, as if still unable to believe my news. We've only been trying for a little over a month. Because it took months to conceive the boys, we thought it would take just as long this time. I nod my head in answer. "I've got some strong little swimmers," he brags.

"I hope your strong little swimmers give me a girl this time so we can be done," I laugh out.

His eye grow serious before he looks back down to my stomach and places a kiss against my skin. "Boy or girl, I'm happy you're in there." His words melt my heart.

"Our life is about to get a little crazier."

"But you trust me, right?" he asks with his usual wicked grin.

I've come to learn that nothing in life comes as expected. You have to believe in trust, but most of all, you have to believe in the ones you love.

"Of course," I happily reply, believing with every ounce inside of me that Nick will not fail to be by my side every step of the way. From the very first moment he asked me to trust him, I have, and without a doubt will continue doing so until my very last breath.

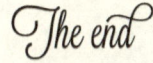

The end

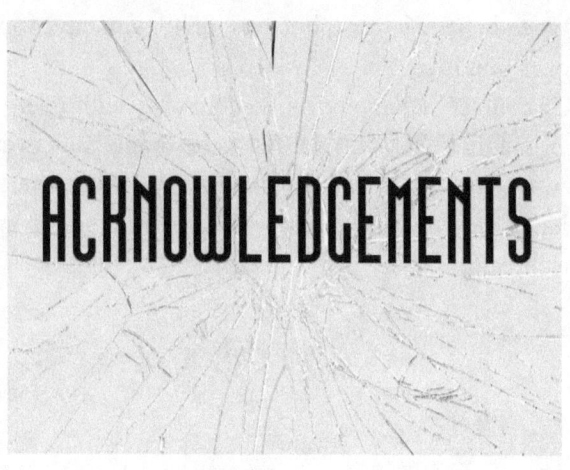

ACKNOWLEDGEMENTS

As always, to my wonderful husband and children, who manage to always be patient with every book I write. Thank you.

To Taylor, for always having an open ear to ramble my frustrations to. You never judged, always listened, and always believed that I'd push through.

To Skye Turner, Barbara Ronevich, Missy Stegman, and my daughter Stephanie. Thank you for all the texts messages that make me spit out my coffee, those are the best. You ladies keep me from going insane.

Chelsea Camaron, for all the advice. You have me see reason at the end of every phone call.

To my all star team, the beta team, my editor Edee M. Fallon, my cover designer Sarah Hansen, my graphic designer Rebecca Marie, Stacey Blake my formatter, my promotional crew Jennifer Greef and Ena Burnette, ending with my street team, who are too many to list. All you ladies are the core of my career and without you I wouldn't be as strong as I am.

My wonderful beta team: Missy Stegman, Barbara Ronevich, Rebeka Perales, and Melissa Martin.

To the ladies who took the time to be my second pair of eyes: Missy Stegman, Janett Gomez, and Barbara Ronevich.

Last, but not least, to all the readers, and bloggers who took the time to read the Clarity. Without you I wouldn't have a reason to write. Thank you from the bottom of my heart.

Author page: http://gabbiesduran.com/
Facebook: www.facebook.com/authorgabbiesduran
Tsu: https://www.tsu.co/gabbiesduran
Twitter: @gabbiesduran
Goodreads: https://www.goodreads.com/author/show/7093957.
Gabbie_S_Duran

ABOUT THE AUTHOR

Gabbie is a Southern California native, who lives with her wonderful husband, two amazing kids and a senior citizen kitty. When she's not writing you can find her reading or sneaking off for a run. Some might say it's a crazy life, but she wouldn't change anything about it.

And now, check out these excerpts from authors
Briana Gaitan and Casey Harvell.

THE ONE THING
by Briana Gaitan

The One Thing
By Briana Gaitan

www.bookswithbree.com
www.facebook.com/booksbybree
Copyright © 2014 by Briana Gaitan
Lyrics from "Ginger" used with permission by Josh O'Brien.
First Edition, 2014
This is a work of fiction.
All characters appearing in this book are fictitious. Any resemblance to real persons living or dead are purely coincidental.

CHAPTER ONE

The raindrops mix with the tears streaming down my face. Each drop of water cools my burning skin and for the briefest moment, I stop and lift my head to the sky. As the water washes away my thick layers of makeup, it feels as if I can finally breathe for the first time in over two years.

"Wait!"

The voice calling out pulls me back to reality, and I take off running again through the parking lot. When I reach my car, I pull the keys from my purse. Before I can press unlock, the keys slip from my wet grasp and slide behind one of the front wheels.

"Shit!" I yell above the rumbling thunder. Yesterday, my life was perfect. Yesterday, I'd have settled for the wool being pulled over my eyes. Today though, I have to deal with the sting of life. I bend down. Ignoring the mud that now stains the front of my priceless designer dress, I feel around with my fingers. I can't see a thing, but dammit, I will not give up this easily. I need to get out of here.

"Ginger! Please!"

I ignore Barrett's voice and fumble around on the dirty pavement quicker. My fingers encase my prized Fendi keychain. *Gotcha!* I run my fingers down the filthy matted down fur. I take a brief second to mourn my favorite, and at the lovely price of three thousand dollars, most expensive accessory.

"Ginger! I told you to stop." Strong arms wrap around my

waist and pull me up from the ground. I brace myself, not sure what to expect. Is he going to push me around? Taunt me? In the two years we've been together, he's never laid a hand on me, but still, do I even know him? After everything that's happened tonight, *did I ever know him?*

"Don't leave like this," he begs. He pushes me up against the car and presses his cheek to mine. He breathes heavily against my chest, struggling to catch his breath. Normally, I crave the drama, the fights, and the make-up sex. This time, I'm unresponsive to his tactics.

I've felt this hurt before, and each time it's gotten a little bit easier to bear. We're just two selfish people going through the motions of another breakup.

"Barrett—I—I can't deal with this right now." I fight to push him off me, but he only clutches me tighter.

"I love you, Babe."

"Ha!" I push my soaking wet hair out of my face and shake my head. The red tendrils slap my cheeks; each as a reminder of how easily he has said this before and how foolishly I had believed him. "Do you even know what love is? Love isn't hurting me over and over again. You expect me to keep on forgiving you, but I'm sick of it! I'm not gonna do *this* anymore. It's over!"

"I'm sorry, okay? I admit it, this is entirely my fault. I adore you, Babe. There's no one else like you. Please don't make a scene. Come back inside, and finish dinner."

"Really?" I gesture toward the dirt that covers my entire dress. It's a five star restaurant; do the math.

"You can dry off in the bathroom."

His voice is gentle, and if I didn't know better, I might believe him. Yet, the whole world will be watching as this scandal falls down around us.

They'll be expecting me to either stand by his side or kick his sorry ass to the curb. Our producers, our agents, they want me to stand by his side to help his image, to help our show's ratings. It's one of the reasons why I've stayed with him for so long. I suppose some would say I chose my reputation over my happiness. I raise my fists and beat against his shoulders until he backs away from me. *Ah, that felt good.*

"You sent a picture of your penis to some stranger. What were you thinking? You slept with some eighteen-year-old slut and expected her not to share her story with the world? You're disgusting!" I speak slowly, enunciating each word like I'm talking to a three-year-old.

He wraps his hands around my waist and buries his face in the crook of my neck. "I wasn't thinking, baby."

"You've fucked us both!" I use my remaining strength to, once again, push him off me, and watch him fall to his knees. This makes too many times. Too many girls. Too many broken promises.

"And what's worse, you let me walk in there tonight like some gullible fool. Your agent and the producers already knew what was going on. Everyone was thinking 'poor pathetic Ginger' while I was oblivious to it all."

"I'm sorry. I shouldn't have picked a public restaurant to break the news."

"In private!" I poke him in the chest with one of my long, fake nails, wishing I could cut through his skin and impale him straight through the heart. "You should've told me alone and in private."

"Stop being so dramatic. You'll get over it. You *always* get over it."

"No! I've put up with the rumors and gossip but I've never gotten over it. I can't feel like this anymore. I want someone to love me. Someone to take care of me. It's what I've wanted since I was a little girl. That was my fuckin' dream, Barrett! And you've destroyed both it and me! Why couldn't you have just loved me? All I wanted was for you to love me. Just love me!"

My teeth chatter as I wrap my arms around my body, craving warmth. Hell, here I am screaming, outside in the pouring rain, like a maniac. I dig deep inside to find the strength to walk away. For good this time. No more taking his bullshit just because I hope he'll change one day. I've waited long enough for his love.

"I won't settle." I pull the enormous pink diamond from my finger, the one he gave me just days ago. The nerve, asking me to marry him while he's sleeping around. The rock represented everything I wanted from this life. The fame, the huge wedding, the money. I don't want that anymore. Not at the price of being one of those women. The women who put up with their husband's infidelity because they want the nice things in life. I'm better than that.

"Take it." I hold it out, but Barrett doesn't move.

"No, you'll change your mind. You always do. This is what we do, Ginger. We break up then we get back together."

Unable to argue any longer, I slip it safely on my right hand. On that hand, it's just some useless decoration.

"Goodbye, Barrett." I climb into my black Range Rover and start it. I'm shivering, cold, and wet with chattering teeth and a runny nose. The heater should warm me up in a minute. I use an old sweater in the backseat to dry my face. I just broke up with my fiancé, I should be heartbroken. Instead, I am numb, but when that ends . . . how will I feel then? I have my own rituals for dealing with pain and disappointment. That's why I need to get home.

"Go away!" I yell, when Barrett begins knocking on my window. The tapping doesn't stop so I put the engine in drive and speed away leaving my troubles in my rearview mirror.

My house is located smack dab on the top of the Hollywood Hills. I bought it last year after seeing the view of the city lights below from the back porch; I knew I had to have it. If there was ever an earthquake, I would surely die, but I would do it in style. My cousin, Quinn, lived with me for about six months, but now I live alone. Good thing I never took the plunge and moved in with Barrett. Maybe a part of me always knew it would end this way.

When I get home, I stumble across the darkness toward the kitchen. The burning in my throat, the ache in my head, I know exactly what I need. It's what I do at the end of a shitty day. Don't hold it against me. I'm sure all twenty-two year old girls love to drink. Inside the cabinet, next to my fridge, is a brand new bottle of cupcake vodka. My favorite. I hold the opening of the bottle up to my lips like a hello kiss, and let the liquid flow straight down my throat.

Hello, sweetie. I've missed you.

In ten minutes, I won't feel a thing. In twenty minutes, I won't remember a thing. *What to do, what to do.* I tap the marble counter with the tips of my fingernails and try to think of something to pull me out of this mood. *I need to have some fun.*

There's only one friend of mine that's even remotely fun these days. Jo Gillian. Jo is an old co-star, turned reality TV star. If anyone knows how to have a good time, she does. I scroll to her number in my contacts and press send.

"It's me," I say when she answers. "Come get me. We're going out tonight."

She's already out at a party, and there's music and yelling in the background.

"What? I can hardly hear you!" she says.

"Just come get me."

I set the phone down on the counter and slip my ruined cocktail dress down over my slender hips before waltzing up the stairs into my changing room.

"Barrett is going to regret ever letting me go!" I yell as I stagger through the room looking for the sluttiest thing I own. I'll show him exactly what he's missing. I give a villainous laugh as I pull on a tight red dress. And then the world becomes a blur . . .

****

A pain in the right side of my head radiates down through my neck and body. *Where am I? What happened?* I crack one eye open slightly and immediately shut it. *Ugh, the pain.*

"I'm gonna be sick," I mumble as I roll over to puke on the floor. My Italian silk sheets are worth a hefty one grand, and even though that's mere pennies to my bank account, I won't ruin them. They were my first big splurge after I bought this house.

"Here." I recognize Quinn's voice and am thankful as a bucket appears at my bedside. My stomach empties into it, and I roll back, quite certain that most of it missed the bucket. Whatever, the maid will get it tomorrow. I wrack my brain for memories of the night before. Absolutely nothing. I remember breaking up with Barrett then going home and drinking an entire bottle of Vodka.

"Oh dear God, what happened?" I ask, wiping my mouth with the back of my hand. I have the worst taste in my mouth which makes me gag.

"Let's see, you got wasted last night, and we had to come over to make sure you didn't hurt yourself." I can tell from the tone of her voice that she's not happy. She has every right to be mad. She should be at home resting and getting ready for the new baby, not taking care of me. I sit up sluggishly and lean against my headboard. She's an awesome cousin.

"I'm sorry." I reach out to rub her huge stomach. I miss and end up patting the air instead. I laugh; I'm possibly a little drunk still.

"You should be," her boyfriend and baby daddy, Chase, says. He appears in my doorway with an unhappy scowl drawn across his face. "I can't believe you—"

"Chase, let me handle this, please." Quinn's voice takes on a firm motherly tone. She holds one hand out to hush him.

Chase shuts his mouth, but continues to glare at me from his spot with his hands crossed in front of his body. I glare back. I love him. He's done so much for Quinn, but we still have our tense moments.

"Can you both just . . . shhhh . . . it down a bit." I hold out my hand to shut them up and smack my numb lips together. Yep, I'm tipsy all right.

"Ginger, I feel terrible. I should have seen this from the beginning. I mean, from the instant I moved in, it was apparent you loved to drink. But this." She gestures toward me while tugging at her long brown hair. "This is becoming too much of a regular thing. You need help. I—_we_ think you may have a problem."

"Yeah, I got a problem all right. My fiancé is a sex addict, and he can't keep his dick in his pants."

"Not that type of problem, a drinking problem."

I give out a dry laugh. "Ha, ha. An alcoholic? You think _I'm_ an alcoholic?" Deep inside, I already know I have a problem, but if I admit it, that means I'll have to quit. Drinking helps me; it's a medicine that I'm not ready to give up just yet. Is this

286

an intervention? Seriously? Next thing I know they're going to be asking me to go to celebrity rehab.

"I think it's a disease that runs in the family," she says. There's a tense moment as we glare at each other. She can't talk about that with Chase in the room. I don't want people to find out about my family history. "I think you know what an alcoholic is and does. I think you're behaving recklessly. So yes, I do believe you are an alcoholic or on the fast track to becoming one."

"If I didn't have such a killer headache, I would roll my eyes at you."

"I don't think it's gotten that bad yet, but you can stop this. You can do it, Ginger. You're better than this. You really scared me last night."

I let out a long dramatic sigh. I'll agree with her, if only to calm her down. For the record, I don't have a drinking problem.

"Fine . . . no more drinking. Besides, I just woke up; do we *have* to do this now? Can't the intervention wait for a more convenient time?"

"No better time than when you are feeling the wrath of your actions," Chase shoots from the doorway. He's leaning against the wood with a smug look on his face.

"Oh shut up, Chase. You drink all the time too. How many nights have you spent at the club getting wasted with Barrett?" I wrinkle my nose at him and stick out my tongue which is followed by a burning sensation shooting up through my sinuses.

"What the—" I reach up to my sore nose and feel a small stud on the top of my right nostril.

"Oh yeah . . ." Quinn says. "Apparently you and Jo got a bit wild last night."

I delicately move my fingers around the small stud. Body jewelry? I would never do that! It's so tacky. Another feeling of dread washes over me. "Were the cameras with her?"

"I think so," Chase tells me. "But it's okay. I bet your publicist can get the footage destroyed or something."

"Thank God." I breathe out slowly and feel around on my body. I've been on Jo's show more times than I can count, and each time it stirs up some sort of controversy in the media. What else happened last night? All my body parts are still intact. I don't feel violated in all my intimate areas. Thank God!

"You changed a few other things as well . . ." Quinn grabs a lock of my hair and covers a smirk with her hand.

I grab a handheld mirror off my nightstand and hold it up to my face. Besides the diamond stud in my nose, my naturally copper hair is now a fire engine red.

"Oh shit. My beautiful hair!" I cry out as I twist the tendrils around my finger. At least it doesn't make me look that bad, then again, nothing could.

"I like it," Quinn says, putting a hand on my shoulder to calm me. "It's different, bolder. "

"I look like a circus freak! Can you fix it?" Quinn went to beauty school, maybe she can lighten it back up.

"Your hair is already red, this is just a . . . new you."

"Did I get any tattoos?" I begin to examine the most obvious places. My shoulders and lower back.

"Thank you, Jesus!" I cry out while lifting my face to the sky. No tramp stamps here. I immediately regret raising my voice and press on my head to dull the ache.

Quinn stands up and walks over to Chase. She gives him a quick peck on the cheek. "I'm gonna go get Ginger some aspirin."

He watches her walk away and as soon as Quinn is out of ear shot, his face spins back towards mine. Chase is a looker, the perfect catch for Quinn. He gets his Hispanic good looks from his mom's side of the family, along with an intense family loyalty.

"A little privacy?" I demand as I swing my legs over the side of the bed and hold my blanket over my chest. Chase is a friend, we even work together on a soap opera called *Timelines,* but I still don't want him to see me in my pajamas.

"Oh come on, my dear, I practically saw you naked last night." He moves closer with a playful look in his eyes and offers to help me up. He isn't flirting with me. Chase is too far gone with Quinn and their soon to be child to care about me. He's just trying to be nice. He feels sorry for me which is worse.

"Quinn was super stressed out last night. You can't do this again. She needs to be focusing on herself, not worrying about you."

I swallow hard, still unable to recall any memories from the night before. I'm being selfish, I know this. But ask any old reporter. Ginger Teague is an obnoxious bitch who doesn't care about anyone except herself. But I never wanted to be that way. "What happened? Did I do something. . . . bad? You know, besides mutilate my perfect body?"

"No, you didn't harm anyone if that's what you mean."

"Thank God," I practically exhaled the words. I've been singing an awful lot of praise this morning.

"But . . . Barrett called me. Apparently, you showed up at his house at one in the morning. The camera was there with Jo. There were words exchanged, things got physical . . . fortunately we got you before the cops showed up."

A flash. Something tugs at my memory, but I can't tell if it's real or something I made up inside my head. Barrett. Yelling. I hit him.

I hold up my right hand, sure enough my knuckles are red and hurt like a bitch.

"I broke my nails." I turn over my hand to examine a few of the broken acrylics.

"The press is having a field day with this. You were at the club drunk, and let's just say your actions were . . . less than admirable. Barrett is downstairs, by the way. He wants to talk to you."

Without knowledge of last night, I don't want to see him. Who knows what happened. What I said to him and everyone else. I'm beyond mortified.

"Send him home."

"I let him in. You both need to put your differences behind you, for the sake of the show. I know Barrett can be a prick at times, but he's not that bad of a guy."

"Not that bad? He made me look bad in front of the entire country. I can't believe you're taking his side!"

"Who's taking sides? You're the one who got drunk and out of control last night. If anything the world feels sorry for you."

Yeah, that's just what I need. Sympathy. I'd like to stay off the front page for once. "Uh, uh. No way, everyone can go home." I chuck a pillow at Chase, pull the blankets up over my head, and lay back down.

"Trust me; he isn't going home until he speaks with you. Just talk to him. Just for a moment. We can't have tension like this on set."

Chase pulls my blanket from the bed and holds a hand out to me. After hesitating, I take it and let him pull me up. For the show. My career means the world to me. Without it, I'm a failure. I'm not a genius or street savvy. I can't do anything else except pretend and look pretty. I wrap my robe around me and follow him downstairs. The same thunderstorm from last night still pours outside, which is great because the dimly lit house helps keep my headache at bay. As I make it to the last step, my eyes center in on him. Barrett.

His blond hair falls in a mess around one swollen black eye, and he's dressed in board shorts and a t-shirt. I'm still a little uncertain as to why he's here so I move closer with caution.

"Barrett." My voice is cold.

"Ginger, baby."

I wince, but not only from his words of endearment. My splitting headache has gotten worse at the sound of his voice. My body must know that he's the one that drives me to drink.

Chase grabs Quinn by the hand and drags her into the kitchen. "Let's give them some privacy."

"But—" She looks at me as she's dragged away and gives me this death glare. We both know she hates Barrett, and if I take him back, she won't be happy. In fact, she'll hate me.

"Move the hell over," I demand as I cautiously sit next to him on the couch. "Fuck, I feel like crap."

All I want to do is sleep. The cushions move as Barrett scoots closer to me and slips my feet in his lap.

"Ginger. About last night."

"Whatever happened, I don't wanna know."

"But—."

"I said no."

"Okay . . . then on a happier note. Do you remember our first date?"

Now that is a moment I haven't thought about in years. "Barely, it was almost three years ago. I really don't wanna think about that right now. Why are you bringing this up?"

"You were an extra on Timelines. Even from far away, I knew there was something special about you. You were so fuckin' beautiful. Eighteen, all bright eyed and innocent . . ." He reaches out to stroke my hair. I let him, not having the strength to push him away. Then I remember what he did to me. His betrayal. I quickly cower away from his touch and bring my legs up close to my chest.

He keeps speaking. "I love you. I have since that moment. I guess I always will."

Oh no, here come the water works.

"Why wasn't I enough? What's wrong with me?"

"Baby, nothing is wrong with you. Everything is wrong with me. I just—I don't know how to be the man you deserve. I'm self-centered, and I bring everyone down with me."

He isn't even fighting for me, and though I don't want to be with him, I want him to try. I want him to want me, and feel all the pain I have felt for the past two years. I swallow all the words I want to say and let go instead. I'm in far too much pain to argue.

"Aren't you going to tell me how you got that black eye?"

He chuckles. "Let's just say . . . you put me in my place."

"I would say I'm sorry, but I don't believe I am."

"I deserved it."

"Yeah, you kinda did . . ."

And there's that awkward silence.

"Well—"

"But—"

The tension is relieved as we both begin to laugh.

"You first," I say.

"Your drinking . . ."

"Ugh! I know. Don't you get on me, too."

"Fine, fine. I guess I don't have much room to talk."

"You sure don't. You party just as hard and just as much as me and all of our friends."

"I'm just worried about you. You used to hate the stuff, and now it's every weekend. I know my limits. I don't think you're aware of yours. "

He's right. I used to hate the stuff, that is, until I realized how much fun it was. That's all I'm doing. I'm having fun. There's nothing wrong with that. I'm not gonna die. I'm not gonna kill anyone. I don't drink and drive. I sure as hell don't sleep around.

"If I had a drinking problem, would I do this?" I stand up a little too fast, but use the couch for support before I stomp in to the kitchen and throw open my liquor cabinet. Without thinking, I unscrew the cap and pour three bottles of vodka, two bottles of whiskey, and a half-empty jar of moonshine down the drain. Quinn and Chase are sitting a few feet away eating a sandwich. Quinn stops mid chew and raises an eyebrow at me. Chase gives me an encouraging nod which I return with a pretentious scowl. I have a few racks of wine in the pantry, but decide not to mention it.

"No more drinking. Shouldn't be too hard." I swallow the panic that billows inside my chest. No more drinking. No more drinking? Can I handle this? After all, drinking is only a habit. A glass of wine with dinner. A martini with the girls. It isn't a disease. Not to me. For some people, maybe, but I don't have a problem.

"That's great." Barrett walks into the room with me and grabs my hand. "If you're serious about it being over, I deserve it, but as I suggested last night, let's wait a few weeks to make a public statement. Let's just pretend that everything is fine. Please, let this whole affair die down. We work together, Ginger. We have to be grownups about this."

At the mention of his betrayal, my humiliation to the world, I pull my hand from his grasp.

"I don't want to wait. I want to move on from you. We both know how fake relationships turn out!" I point to Quinn and

Chase across the room. Chase let the whole world believe he had a pretend relationship with a co-star to promote their movie, but Chloe James turned out to be a psychotic freak. When she found out that Quinn was pregnant, she sold the story to the tabloids and made it seem like Chase had cheated on her. It had almost torn Quinn and Chase apart.

"Hey, leave us out of this." Quinn pipes in as she slides a bottle of aspirin across the table.

"Too late!" I shoot back. I slip the bottle in the front pocket of my robe and turn back toward Barrett, who pushes his hair off his face and sighs.

"This is different. Are you planning on dating anyone else in the next few weeks?"

"No."

"Then what's the problem? We issue a public statement *after* this whole affair thing dies down. Please? My career is already being pissed on by the media. I'm trying to do theater."

I throw my hands into the air. "You really expect me to give a damn about your career? What about mine? I'm trying to move on from network television."

"Please?"

I consider his request for another moment. "Is this you or your publicist talking?"

His eyes roll upwards. "My publicist."

"And remind me again why we listen to them?"

"Because they keep the rumors at bay . . . when needed."

"Ugh! Fine. We'll do this your way, but don't expect any more favors from me. Now if you guys don't mind, I have a flight to Nashville in about six hours, and I need to get ready." I stomp from the room with every intention to start packing, but I stop and listen to them from the hallway.

"You better not fuck this up again," Chase demands.

"I said I was sorry. I'm trying to help her. Why don't you believe me?" Barrett says, a bit louder. For a moment, I'm embarrassed, listening in on their conversation, but who the hell cares? This is my home.

"Because I have watched you play with her heart for months!" Quinn shouts out. I can imagine her sticking her finger in his chest as she speaks.

"I want to help her."

"If you want to help her, stay away from her."

"Calm down," Chase tells Quinn. "I think Barrett has learned his lesson."

"What? Cause everyone has seen his tiny dick?"

"Hey, I don't have a tiny—"

"Enough! Both of you!" Chase interjects. "This affects more than just us. This is about Ginger and making sure she doesn't keep drinking. She could ruin her career."

"That includes letting her move on with her life," Quinn says.

I've heard enough. I turn around and climb the stairs back to my room. Is it possible I just screwed myself on this one? Whatever the tabloids are saying about me, I hope it's good.

CHAPTER TWO

I pull off one of my green high heels before rubbing the back of my ankle. There is definitely going to be a blister there tomorrow. Wincing slightly, I put the shoe back on my foot and continue to walk uphill toward my destination. The chilly wind engulfs my small body, and I can only imagine how cold I would be in this tiny dress if I hadn't already worked up a sweat. I forgot how cold it gets in Tennessee. *Ten more blocks. I only have ten more blocks to go.* I trudge on, putting one foot in front of the other, careful not to trip on the old, cracked sidewalk. *Almost there, Ginger.* The thought alone inspires me to keep marching forward. I'm late, but I've walked too far to turn back now. I was supposed to meet with the casting director, but my stupid GPS gave me the wrong directions. After paying over thirty dollars to park, and asking the parking attendant if I was in the right place, I soon figured out that I wasn't anywhere near my intended destination. Not even close.

With my purse in hand, I hurry through the dirty streets, one eye on the lookout for muggers. I don't have any more cash to park anywhere else, and I'll be damned if I'll walk past that parking attendant again. It's embarrassing enough that I had to ask for directions. Stupid pride. It's the story of my life though. When people see me, they automatically assume I'm a ditz. People continuously try to take advantage of me, and most of the time they succeed. But not today. After having the worst week of my life, I'm determined to make today much better.

A bus speeds past me with curious faces peering out of the window. I am tempted to hop on, but who knows what type of infectious diseases I might catch. Better to be safe than sorry. After another block or so, I stop and pull a hair tie out of my Gucci bag. I twist my long hair up into a high bun. After spending hours washing and rewashing, the bright color has finally faded. My makeup is beginning to melt off, and my short dress has inched dangerously high, but I keep my head up and my eyes locked forward. Who am I kidding? They won't hire me anyway. After two years in show business, I haven't gotten anything more than low-budget commercials and a supporting role on a primetime soap opera. I drop my head and bite my lip so that I can suck back a sob. I lean back against a brick wall to catch my breath and regain my composure. I slide down against the brick until my I can lean my face into my knees and take a few deep breaths.

"What's a pretty young thing like you doing wandering the streets all alone?" a voice says from beside me. Looking up, I blink against the bright sun to try and find the source. I stand up.

"Over here."

I follow the sound of the voice and spin around to see a lanky guy, a little older than me, sitting on the stoop of an old brick auditorium. My eyes graze his shaggy, dirty blond hair that falls in his eyes and his strong, square jaw. When he smiles, there's a cute dimple in his left cheek. His eyes are kind, clear blue engulfed with dark lashes. My eyes move downward against his lean chest and tight skinny jeans. As if by instinct, I flash him a flirty grin. *Man, this guy is beautiful . . . in a grungy skateboarder kinda way.*

"Just taking a leisurely stroll," I comment. I examine the cigarette in his hand and wrinkle my nose a bit. He notices my displeasure and quickly smashes the butt under his old Converse. *Converse? No, no, no.* I quickly talk myself down. He takes a swig of water from a plastic bottle and sets it down on the ground. This guy isn't cute, he's shabby. He's an emo. He's—and I'm—he isn't my style at all. Oh, gross. How could I have stooped so low as to even for the briefest moment consider him attractive? I tend to go for more classic, metro-sexual men. Armani suits, expensive cars, slicked back hair and Rolex watches. That's what turns me on; not smokers with tattoos. Though from what I can see of his, they look quite impressive. A flash of something large on his right bicep, but I can't make it out. Not wanting to get caught staring, I look up at the bright sky instead. The urge to walk away consumes me, but I need another moment to catch my breath and rest my aching feet. He stands up and walks closer, making my heart pound against my chest. *Oh, shit.* I stare straight ahead at his old gray tee shirt and black jeans that hug his lean body. He stops right in front of me and rests an arm on the wall behind me to support himself.

"You look really lost. Need some help?"

God, that sexy voice. Heat begins to pool between my legs. No, this isn't a safe position. He's a stranger! I straighten up and look into his face, that beautiful face. *Focus, Ginger!*

"I'm not lost. Would you kindly back off?" I snap.

Men don't randomly offer to help women. They always have ulterior motives. They always expect something in return. He backs up with his hands out in front of him in surrender. His face is sincere, honest. *Like I even know what that looks like.*

"Hey, I didn't mean to scare you. I'm only trying to offer you some local hospitality."

I sigh in exasperation and pull my phone out to check the time.

"Thanks, but no thanks. I'm late for an audition, like it even matters now. I won't get the job anyway, and your little distraction . . ." I dangle my fingers in the air at him. "It isn't helping either."

"Their loss." He shrugs while giving me a wide smirk that makes my body tingle.

He has perfectly straight white teeth. It's amazing. He has the kind of teeth that only dentist's kids have. I lean in to get a closer look at his mouth. *Stop that! Just look at him. He will use you and throw you away with a broken heart. He isn't a safe choice.*

"Are you okay?"

I realize I'm scowling at him, and staring at his teeth like a gawking monkey. I'm tempted to smile, but refuse to. Attraction or no attraction, I'm not about to let him know how affected I am by his presence.

"I'm fine, thanks for asking. You can go back to . . . whatever it was you were doing." I wave my hand as if he's a minion out to do my bidding.

He laughs, but doesn't take the hint. "I'm just taking a smoke break between sets. We're doing a sound check for a show tonight. Hey, you should come check us out." He motions toward the building beside us, an ancient looking place. Great, he's a musician. They're even worse than actors. I raise an uninterested slim brow at him, but don't say a word.

"Doesn't like music, duly noted." He laughs again. *It's so intoxicating.* He articulates all of his syllables, but I can't pinpoint the accent. His voice isn't suave or deep. He definitely sings with a wide range, kind of like Ben Gibbard. That's right; I like music. In fact, I love music and Death Cab for Cutie is one of my favorite bands. I just don't like the reputation that precedes musicians. I open my mouth to protest, but stop. I don't need to explain myself to this guy.

"Thanks for the neighborly concern." I roll my eyes and

wait for him to go back inside, but instead we both anxiously stand there daring the other to walk away first. With a crooked grin plastered upon his devilishly handsome face, he digs into his back pocket to pull out another cigarette. He lights up, but blows the smoke away from me. My nostrils flare, and I have to keep from kneeing him in the balls. How dare he trap me in a corner while he puffs on those death sticks. Such a disgusting habit, if you ask me. After a minute, I give up, push myself off from the wall, and turn my back to him.

"Have a good one!" he calls out from behind me. "Fuck you," I mumble to myself as I strut away. I throw my purse over my shoulder and curse myself when a smile appears on my lips. He was an interesting character. It's not every day I get to meet someone who isn't a stuck up social climber.

My feet scream in agony with each step, but I refuse to turn around. Well, that is until I make it about two blocks down the road. Only then do I allow myself to stop and peek over my shoulder at him. He's still standing in the same spot on the sidewalk. His eyes are locked on me, I think. From far away, his hair appears darker, making him seem more mysterious. When he raises his hand to wave, I quickly turn around. My pale skin heats in excitement. I haven't been this worked up over a man in a long time, not since I first began dating Barrett. I should feel bad for getting so turned on by another guy when I just broke up with my fiancé, but I'm not. Barrett screwed it up. Ergo, I don't care.

The crosswalk flashes green for me to go, but before I step across the street, I take one last look behind me. Disappointment fills me as I gaze at the empty sidewalk. He must have gone inside. Nashville is a big city, and I'm only visiting for a few more days before I return to LA. It's unlikely that I'll ever see him again.

The One Thing (Hollywood Timelines series) is now available:

Reach out to Briana Gaitan
www.bookswithbree.com
www.facebook.com/booksbybree
www.twitter.com/bookswithbree

THE WRONG WAY
by Casey Harvell

Edited by Fancy Pants Formatting
Cover by Fancy Pants Formatting
Interior Design and Formatting by Fancy Pants Formatting
Featuring Poetry by Julie Mishler

Dedication . . .

This book is dedicated to my friend Jordan Bault because anyone with that much passion for books deserves a story all her own ♡

Prologue . . .

Jordan

I'm always in the background. I fade away into it, a mute obscure nothing in the huge world around me. In life there are certain moments when the world around you sparks or dims. Everything brightens or dulls. My world has been grey for so very long now. There's not even the faintest glimmer.

There's this hope that maybe—just maybe—everything will be okay . . . that *I* will be okay. Yet somehow that hope scares me more than anything. To try and to fail is expected—but to hope and to fail is just downright soul-crushing. Whether they want it or not, everyone needs to be saved sometimes . . .

Chapter One . . .

Jordan

Anyone who walks through this place on a Friday night that I don't know is just passing through. Believe me—I know *everyone* in this town. I have lived here almost all my life. So when something like *that* walks through the crappy bar doors, I notice. Hell, every damn woman here notices.

What's the difference between me and the rest of the women that now swoon over Mr. Hottie-pants who leans casually against the bar? I know damn well that I don't have a chance in hell. Girls like me? We're meant for the background. Meant to fade into it and go without notice.

I continue on with my job like any other night—a night where some Adonis doesn't ooze sex appeal that wafts around like a pheromone-filled cologne. I sneak a peek at him while I bring the zillionth tray to my disorderly customers and he catches me. Shit he's hot.

I grab the final glass to fill the small drink tray in my hand (again). My table is a rowdy bunch of college morons and to say they're drunk is a gross understatement. They're so drunk that they begin to worry me. After this round I'll have to send Danny over to cut them off. I don't get paid enough to do that shit.

"Hey—" a slurred voice says as an audible slap sounds. He. Did. Not. Yep—he did! This guy seriously just grabs my ass. "Put the pitcher here." He laughs at his own drunken rudeness.

I know that I shouldn't do anything, but I can't really stop myself. "I'm sorry." I say sweetly. "Where do you want this pitcher?" The fucker points to the table in front of him with a smile on his face . . . a smile that quickly changes to a look of shock when I proceed to pour the entire contents of the pitcher over his head.

"You bitch!" The guy screams and flips the table as he stands with more speed than someone as drunk as him should. I flinch and back away slowly.

Uh-oh. See—*this* is why I'm not supposed to do this. Danny (aka my boss/bar owner/bouncer) is busy across the bar. The drunken beer-covered fool in front of me is hella-pissed and towers over me. Whoops!

You think that's enough to give me pause, make me back down or shut the fuck up? Nope, not me. See, that makes sense and I'm not a fan of that at all. "I'm sorry!" I say brashly. "I assumed when you grabbed my ass you wanted to wear your beer."

The man raises his hand high above him and I know what comes next. I don't flinch again though—instead I stand my ground. His group of friends behind him splits as half of them try to calm him while the other half eggs him on. Maybe a second before the drunken asshole's fist crashes into me an even larger more impressive hand shoots out from behind me. I expect to see Danny behind me so I'm quite speechless when I see the gorgeous piece of man from the bar instead.

"I'm not sure how things work around here," God, even his damn voice is sexy as hell. "But where I come from we don't raise our hand to a lady."

This gives the drunken asshole pause. Mr. Sexy-pants is a whole lot of man and I doubt the asshole can take him on sober much less in his current inebriated state. "Whatever." The douchebag says as he throws some cash on the table. "She's not fucking worth it anyway."

His group of friends follows suit. A few give me apologetic glances as they pass. Some glare instead. Next week they can be sure to sit in Holly's section or go to the next town to act like assholes. When the last one leaves through the door I breathe a small sigh of relief . . . until I realize I actually have to talk to the sexy fuck that still stands behind me.

"Um, thanks." I manage. It's a good thing I say this before I face him because when I do something in my brain fries and any hope of articulation flies right out the window.

"Not a problem." He rumbles—actually rumbles. Fuck me six ways 'til Tuesday.

I stand and gape at him like an idiot for a second when an arm wraps around him from behind.

"Don't mind Jordan here." A voice purrs. Ugh. Great. Marilyn's here. "She's not important enough to worry about. Why don't you come back over here with me? I can use another drink." Marilyn tugs on his arm, but he doesn't budge.

My head drops and I examine my shoes closely. I know way better than to bother arguing with Marilyn. She's always been hot shit to my complete nothingness—thus my complete shock to the sex God's reply.

"The bar looks to be in working order to me. If you're thirsty then go get yourself a drink."

My jaw drops again as my gaze meets his. Marilyn's no longer touches him. Did he seriously just blow off the hottest girl in town? From the look on Marilyn's face, I'd say he did.

"What?" She sputters. "You *can't* be serious. You're going to choose this piece of shit over me?" I feel my cheeks warm because I know she's right. I'm not fit to be the dirt on her boot.

"Listen Miss, I'm not sure how y'all treat people around

here, but it doesn't seem very pleasant." Something about the calm way he says this makes me look up to see Marilyn blush and actually look at him in embarrassment. That's definitely a new look for her.

The man's green eyes bore into mine now. Not once does he look back to Marilyn as she huffs away. My spine tingles under his gaze. This is just a little too awkward for my taste.

"Um, like I said—thanks. I need to get back to work." I say quickly in a voice that's two octaves too high. I even manage to stumble when I spin around. Smooth Jordan, really smooth.

The remainder of the night is much more uneventful—with the exception of my savior who parks his fine ass back at the bar and stays there. He does something no one else in this shit town does. He watches me. He *notices* me. What the fuck's going on?

I use my time to act like I ignore him, but I feel his gaze follow me. I sneak glances to see how his chocolate brown hair falls messily across his forehead . . . or how taut his navy blue shirt pulls across his muscular chest and clings to his biceps. He has a sinewy look about him, a lean lengthiness that makes me begin to imagine just what lies under those clothes . . .

Bam! That's the mental slap I have to give myself. I'm not one of *those* girls. No way, I'm a ridiculous twenty-three year old virgin who never gets noticed by anyone—much less someone like *this*. All that road can lead down is a world of hurt. I may not have any experience, but I'm not stupid. A man like that is trouble with a capital T. No. Thank. You.

My shift ends at one in the morning. I take my time in the back before I return to the bar to cash out the remainder of my orders and notice my hero isn't there anymore. A mix of relief and disappointment washes over me. I try to remind myself that it's better this way.

I pull my 1994 Plymouth Colt down the bumpy road that leads past all of the other shitty trailers to my shitty trailer. Well, not mine—my step-mom's. Since my Dad went away it's just been us. She's no fun to live with, but I don't exactly have a lot of options. I cut the engine and can hear the music blast inside. It almost makes me turn the car back on and look for a nice parking lot to sleep in for the night. Loud music at this hour means only one thing: Shirley's drunk . . . again.

This can go one of two ways. Either Shirley will be a happy drunk or a mean one. Happy Shirley will mean lots of dancing about while mean Shirley will throw shit at me and belittle me. I can't even really say that one is more fun than the other.

It's inevitable that I'll find out as I shut the door and move towards the rotting plywood porch. The bottom of it has some time left, but the top leaks. A hole gapes precariously and I always wonder whether it'll be me or Shirley who catches it when it finally caves.

It appears I'm in luck tonight. The music blasts, but Shirley lays on the couch—down for the count. A wave of relief washes over me. I check to be sure she's alive (she is) and turn the music down most of the way.

When I make it to my broom closet of a room I notice just how lucky I am that Shirley ran out of steam. Often when she goes into a rage my room is her first target. Tonight's no different. I scoop up some clothes and jam them in the washer. It takes almost an hour before I'm finally able to go to bed.

It doesn't bother me that Shirley hates me so much because nobody can possibly ever hate me more than I hate myself.

I manage to wake up before Shirley which rocks because the less time we spend together the better. I take a shower and begin to put my clean clothes away (again) when I hear movement. Shit. This won't be good. Cranky hung-over Shirley is almost worse than drunken Shirley . . . *almost*.

"Jordan! Why didn't you make any damn coffee?" Shirley screeches. "Shit, why didn't you buy any coffee?"

I know I better get out of here quick and jam the rest of the clothes into the drawer. Chances are I'll just have to put them away or wash them again later anyhow. I throw a few things into my ancient fraying messenger bag and shut off my light before I carefully slip into the hallway and out the back door of the trailer. I feel like an idiot while I crouch down and run around to the front, but I make it to my car without further incident.

Two dollars and change buys me a medium coffee and a bagel at the gas station. I sit in the car and eat before I turn the engine over. Almost every day I sit here and contemplate driving my car as far as it will take me before it dies. The only thing that holds me back is that there's no way to run from my past. I know I deserve this life so why bother?

I don't have to work until four so I have a few hours to kill. The options for entertainment are few and far between in this town. I drive down to a local trail and grab my latest library paperback and a blanket I keep for times like these. It doesn't take long to park and to hike down my favorite trail. It's chilly—fall begins to take hold of our Northeast town, but I have faith in the warm sun overhead so I plop down on the blanket rather than wrap myself in it. It doesn't take long for the sun to come through and burn off the last of the fog. After a while the sun hangs high above me and I finish the paperback. It's warmer now so I tie my hoodie around my waist for the walk back to the car. At least I can hit the library and grab a quick bite before work.

I park in town and take my time as I walk to the library. It doesn't take long to swap out my books for new ones. The billboard catches my eye on my way out the door. I see an ad for a part-time cleaning person during the day. It's not like I can't use the extra money or the distraction so I grab the little tab with the phone number and tear it off.

After a quick lunch I pull out my flip phone and dial the number. I leave a brief message and wonder what the hell I should do for the next hour and a half. I just settle into my driver's seat with the intention to read until work when I hear my phone go off.

"Hello?" I answer.

"Hi, I'm looking for Jordan?" A male voice responds. "I'm returning a call about her interest in a cleaning position."

"Yes, hi—I'm Jordan." I answer quickly.

"Hi. I guess the first step is to ask your experience." The man sounds unsure.

"Well, when it comes to cleaning I only have domestic experience, but I do cleanup at my night job as a server too." I explain.

"Hmmm. Are you sure you're able to work more than one job?" The man asks me.

"I'm sure." I quickly assure him. "Both would be part-time and manageable."

"Alright. I suppose we should set up an interview. When are you available?"

"I could come now," I say after a quick glance at the time.

"Or any time before four during the week."

"Now could work." The man says and rattles off an address.

"Great. I'll see you in about ten minutes." I tell him and disconnect.

It's a short drive to the other side of town. The address leads to an older Victorian house—one that appears to be in the process of restoration. An older man sits on the porch and stands as I approach.

"Jordan?" He calls out.

"Yes, sir." I answer with a smile. It's odd because he seems familiar, but I know I've never seen him in town before. He's definitely a new resident.

"Welcome. I'm Jesse. Thanks for coming by so quickly."

I shake the hand he offers before I answer. "Not a problem." My eyes inadvertently move to the house behind him. Through the window I see box after box. The idea of cleaning that overwhelms me slightly.

Jesse must notice this because he glances behind him and laughs. "Don't worry, that's my mess to worry about, not yours. We just moved in three days ago. I'll have some sense of order in place before you start." He holds open the front door. "Please, come in—take a look around."

I follow him through the door. "Is it just you?" I ask in an attempt to make conversation. It's an awful large house for one person.

"It's me and my son. You'll see him here and there but he mostly does his own thing." Jesse laughs. "He's not too happy with me for moving him up here, but he came with just the same."

"He'll like it here—the schools are really great." I comment.

"Oh, no! He's way beyond school aged. He's old enough to go off on his own, but he decided to help out his old man instead." Jesse says proudly.

"That's nice." I say and take in the big space. Even underneath all of the boxes its size impresses me.

"Okay, down to business." Jesse says. "I need someone to handle the basic domestic stuff around here. See me and Binx, we're not all that tidy. We can gussy the place up—sure, but keeping it that way not so much. Kitchen, bathroom, dusting, vacuuming . . . maybe some light laundry and cooking . . ."

Nothing he says sounds like anything I can't handle. "I draw the line at windows and gutters." I smile when I say it. I like Jesse already.

"Of course not!" Jesse laughs. "We can handle that. We just need—well, we need a feminine touch around here—someone to knock some of the manliness off of the place."

"Okay," I agree tentatively.

"Pay's fifteen an hour—on the books. I imagine it'll be a few hours each weekday. If you're interested you can start on Monday." Jesse offers.

I smile broadly as I answer. "Deal."

"Great!" Jesse says happily. "It'll give me the push I need to finish unpacking." He holds out his hand again. "Thanks a lot, Jordan. I'll see you on Monday."

I give his hand one last firm shake before I go out the front door. "Take care."

I pause for a second in the front yard and glance back at the house behind me. This is all kind of perfect for me actually. No more boredom and some extra cash. A funny feeling washes over me and I shake it off. This *will* work out. It just has to.

Work is about as uneventful as a Friday night can be at a bar until a little after nine. That's when the hottie strolls in again. He saunters up to the bar and orders a burger and a beer. I try not to notice, but his presence is sort of impossible to ignore. I keep myself busy and am overly attentive to my section (blessedly the furthest section from the bar). I manage to avoid the sex-god all night, but again can feel his eyes bore into me the entire time. It's a relief to get into the back and get my apron off. I do menial tasks—like polishing silverware for tomorrow—in hopes that he'll leave and I can cash out in peace.

I sneak a peek out the small window of the door that leads back out to the bar and see that it's empty. I ignore my utter disappointment and remind myself it's relief that I should feel instead.

It doesn't take me long to tally the tickets and enter the appropriate cash into the register. My tips aren't half bad tonight (yay Friday!) and the register drawer closes with a ping. I recount my tips and jump when a voice says my name—not just any voice either—that deep rumbly voice that causes my spine to electrify.

"Jordan, right?"

Holy. Shit. It takes a second before my mouth begins to work again. "Yeah . . . hi." I say cautiously. Why does his close proximity have such an effect on me?

"You're here late." He says in an obvious attempt at small talk.

"It kind of comes with the territory." I answer. At least my brain is back to normal . . . even if my body is frozen in place.

"I guess it does." He chuckles. "You need a ride home or

anything?"

"Um, no thanks. I'm good." What the hell was that? "I should get going actually." *If* I can get my legs to work.

"Oh," Does he look disappointed? No. Fucking. Way. I need to get over myself. He continues. "Well, have a good-night."

"You, too." I watch him leave before I find the ability to move myself.

It's always tough for me during the day. I don't have any real friends left here—the few acquaintances I do have leave for college after high school. We lose touch and now they're just a distant memory. Any time I spend with Shirley is derogatory to my well-being so that's out. It just makes me feel out of place—everywhere.

This Saturday morning I do something that I *never* do. I stay in bed. I sleep in for me, but then I just lay there. It lasts for a little bit before I remember why I don't let my mind wander if I can help it. Idle thoughts always come with the price of memories.

I get up reluctantly and shower. I focus hard on soap and shampoo until I can push the memories back where they belong. I do it, but not before the fluid that runs down my face are more tears than water. Then I do what I do best when this happens. I throw on clothes and rush out the door before Shirley can say a word.

Is it Monday yet? At least I'll have the distraction of cleaning. Today will be much more difficult to fill. I check my wallet and see a few bills in it. What the hell? I drive to the movie theater and spend the rest of the time until work in an attempt to lose myself in the silver screen.

It doesn't surprise me when the sexy hunk of man meat is a no show at work tonight. A guy that hot probably always has Saturday night plans. He's probably out with Marilyn right now. Why that thought feels like a strong punch to my stomach, I don't know.

Alright, maybe I know a little. The attraction I have towards the handsome stranger is undeniable at this point. My body may betray me at every turn, but at least my mind holds strong. No hot guy for me.

It's definitely below freezing when I make my way to my car. A cold front must be on its way. It makes me all the more grateful to have something to occupy my weekdays. My blanket-reading weather seems to have run out early this year.

Last year I read in my car with the blanket over me instead of under me. I'll put the heat on intermittently if I resort to that (which I inevitably will at least once in the next weeks) and let the car warm before I shut it down again. Hopefully my second job will prevent too much of that.

When I pull into the small dirt patch which represents our driveway I notice something's off right away. It's silent. Even when the music isn't blaring there's always some type of noise that travels through the paper thin walls. Yet there's nothing but silence.

I don't know what I'll find inside and my overactive imagination sure doesn't help things. I picture Shirley as she finally succumbs to the years of abuse she's put herself through. I shudder at the idea of finding her dead. What if someone else is in there? What if she needs my help?

I take a large swallow and build my courage. I don't even lock the car in case I need to make a fast getaway. My hands fumble with the crappy doorknob lock because I shake from the combination of cold and fear. Finally I get it to open and step inside.

It takes a moment for me to realize that we haven't been burglarized (mostly because all of our stuff is crap) and that Shirley is just on a super rampage. I hear her towards the back of the trailer and she's still at it.

The door to the bathroom is shut and I can hear things inside of it shatter. I slip into my room and push the dresser in front of the door. Most of the time I can handle Shirley, but this extreme fit I can do without.

I keep the light off and stay very quiet on my bed. Before long I hear the bathroom door open and the door to Shirley's room slam shut. The tiny hallway is no buffer for the things that break while she screams. I have to cover my ears at her words. *'Damn you, John! Why'd you have to leave me?'*

It makes me get up quietly and add a bit more to my barrier. I know why. It's because of me.

Soon the door opens again and I try not to jump when Shirley begins to bang over and over on my door. My tears fall silently as her words cut deep.

"You little bitch!" She screams hoarsely and her words slur together. "This is your fault. You know what, princess? You can get the fuck out! You hear me? You're not fucking welcome here anymore!"

I don't know if she'll remember this in the morning, but even more so—I don't know if I want to be here to find out.

As much as it goes against my nature I take the coward's

way out. After Shirley runs out of steam and I'm sure she passes out I gather my clothes, toiletries and few keepsakes into a couple of garbage bags and put them in my car. I sneak back in and grab my sheets, blankets and pillows. I look around the small room I have spent so much of my life in. It's so easy to empty. One life that shows so little . . .

I don't bother to pick up the mess Shirley leaves. I know I cause this pain she feels, but maybe if she has to clean herself up it will be therapeutic. I accept my guilt . . . I just think she's better off without me. She's only my step-mom after all.

I lock the door and pull it shut behind me. Too bad I can't leave my past behind me with it.

As crappy as my life is at times, this is a first. Thankfully my shitty car is in my name because it's the only shelter I have. I don't even have work the next two nights to warm up in. I debate my next move as I pull over to count the bills in my wallet. At least my tips last night are good. At least I'm not penniless to boot.

I stop at the gas station, but only grab a coffee despite the grumble my stomach gives off. I go up to the counter to pay and see Jeremy from school is behind the register.

"Hi, Jeremy—do you guys have a phone book I can look at quickly?" I ask.

"Sure, here." He plops the book on the side of the counter.

"Thanks." I say and flip through the pages until I find what I'm looking for. I grab a lotto card and the pen besides it to write down a couple of phone numbers before I return the book and pen to Jeremy.

"Bye, Jordan." Jeremy says before he helps his next customer.

I wave and go back outside.

The numbers I have are for a few local roach hotels. Some advertise everything from hourly (shudder) to weekly and monthly rates. I grab my phone and try to find a room I have a chance of affording.

It boils down to two options. The most logical choice lies about twenty minutes away in a small country city. It's not really a nice city, but definitely in my price range. One hotel here in town is affordable—but just barely. If I want to eat and drive (and I don't know—buy tampons) I need to go to the shitty-city and suck it up.

I don't really know what's in store, but I reluctantly call back the city hotel and reserve a room. I reserve it for one week in hopes that job two may bump me up to afford the room here in town next week.

With the final swig of my coffee I begin my journey into country-urban hell. God help me.

About the Author . . .

Amazon Bestselling and USA Today Recommended Author Casey Harvell resides in the great Hudson River Valley of NY with her husband and their two sons. Casey is slightly zombie obsessed. She uses the word 'boom' and attaches 'pants' on the end of words frequently. You can find all of Casey's books on her website http://caseyharvell.com

Website: http://www.caseyharvell.com
Find Casey on Facebook: https://www.facebook.com/pages/
Casey-Harvell/238364846204319
Find Casey on Twitter: http://www.Twitter.com/CaseyA-
Harvell
Find Casey on Goodreads: https://www.goodreads.com/au-
thor/show/4996856.Casey_Harvell
Wattpadd: http://www.wattpad.com/user/CaseyHarvell
Youtube Channel: https://www.youtube.com/channel/
UClSV6GMN7phkU04GLpQAtcg

Other Books by Casey Harvell:

**Links can be found to all eBooks and paperbacks at
caseyharvell.com**

The Decisions Series:
Righteous Decisions (Decisions Series Book One) eBook always free!
Harsh Decisions (Decisions Series Book Two)
The Electric Series—USA Today Must-Read Romance Series!
Charged ~Reboot~ (Electric Series Book One) eBook always free!
Shocked (Electric Series Book Two)

Stand Alone:
Doesn't Play Well With Others (18+)
Lingering . . . (18+)
Aliens, Death & Zombies: A Compilation of Short Stories

Coming Soon (2014–2015):
Soul Decisions (Decisions Series Book Three) *Final Series Book
Wired (Electric Series Book Three) *Final Series Book
Eclipsed Agony
Don't You Cry
Proceed With Caution